About the Author

Adam Dickson is a novelist and screenwriter. His first novel, *The Butterfly Collector*, was published in 2012. His second novel, *Drowning by Numbers*, was published in 2014. He has also co-written three non-fiction books in the sports genre, and a book on mental health, *Surfing the Edge: a survivor's guide to bipolar disorder.*

His screenplays include adaptations of both novels, and a pilot for TV. In February 2020, he appeared as an expert in the CBS Reality crime series *Murder by the Sea.* The episode titled *Neville Heath, the Lady Killer* documents the real-life case of ex-RAF pilot Neville Heath, who was hanged at Pentonville Prison in 1946.

www.adamdickson.co.uk

Billy Riley

a novel

by
Adam Dickson

Castra publishing

Billy Riley - a novel
Copyright ©2020 Adam Dickson

A special thanks to Alex Dickson for cover design and illustration

ISBN 978-0-9934776-5-2

1

Homecoming

The gate slammed shut and there he was, back in the world. Green trees, blue skies and birdsong. Behind him, the high red-brick wall topped with razor wire, keeping all the bad boys in and the civilians out. And him one of them now. No longer a number, having it daily on the 'ones and twos'. Let loose in a crumpled suit and shoes that pinched his feet, all his goods in a plastic bag.

He called Eileen from a phone box on the main road.

'Hey, doll. Guess who's up and running?'

An old woman crossed the road, dragging a shopping trolley. She took her time, holding up the traffic, back bent to the toil. He admired her struggle through the phone box window, wondering at the odds against her getting even this far.

'You coming straight home?' Eileen said.

'Sure. Where else would I be going?'

A fella came out of the bank on the corner and tucked a wallet into his back bin, before striding away. Civilians everywhere, going about their daily lives in a trance. Shamefully, he wanted to look like them, blending in, no bother to no one. But even in a suit, he looked different, felt different. The tattoos on his hands gave him away. The look on his face that marked him out as a foreigner, a deregulated, rubber stamped nobody in his own back yard.

The train rolled in on time. He took a window seat and looked out at the scenery. Slate rooftops and television aerials. Terraced houses with cars parked outside. A fella reading a newspaper on the far platform, briefcase at his feet. Everywhere, the illusion of normality, ordinariness.

A whistle blew. Doors slammed shut. For a second he was back on the wing, key-chains jangling, feet shuffling out on the landing. Then they were moving. Every second taking him closer to home, away from the blarney hole with all its attendant ills.

'Tickets, please!'

The guard strolled along the aisle, dispensing machine at his hip. Hands reached out offering ticket stubs for inspection; two yapping businesswomen further along, who barely paused their conversation to look up.

'Tickets, please!'

'Parkway Central, fella.'

'Single or return?'

'Single. I ain't coming back this way too soon, that's for sure.'

The machine coughed a ticket. He rooted in his jacket pocket and found a crisp twenty pound note, courtesy of Her Majesty's repatriation scheme. Forty-six quid for five years faithful service. Living like a monk on three meals a day. Bulking up in the gym and making full use of all the amenities. Knocking one out under a thin grey blanket to relieve the tension, the stultifying, mind-eroding boredom that festered behind the door.

Stations came and went. Ploughed fields and green meadows, the odd farmstead thrown in. Soon, he'd be back in the fold, swallowed up in the hectic day-to-day. Thoughts and energies beset with the need to make a living, catch up with folk he hadn't seen in a long while. He should have felt more up for it, more excitement at the thought of all the things waiting on the out. Nerves kicked-in instead. All the bods he knew who owed him favours, money. Some of them would have forgotten he even existed, so he'd have to remind 'em a bit quick. Billy Riley was back on the manor. All wrongs would have to be righted. All debts paid.

The next station loomed, and the yapping businesswomen got up to leave. He watched them go, missing their laughter, the reassuring chatter of female company. More civilians got on, taking the empty seats further up the aisle. Opposite him, a fella who'd been asleep the whole way, his head resting against the window.

Time passed in a dreamscape, a lullaby of carriage wheels over the tracks. Thoughts of Eileen, waiting for him. The kids, the dog. Somewhere back of it all a memory, framed like a picture inside his head. The one that kept him going in the blarney hole when the grey brick walls closed in and it all came on top. A life waiting for him on the other side. So close now he could reach out and touch it.

'The station you are now approaching is Parkway Central.'

The train slowed.

Brushing the creases from his suit, he joined the exodus for the door. A cyclist in a high-viz jacket stared out the window, a mud-splattered mountain bike by his side. A young bird sucked on an unlit cigarette, a glazed-over disdain for the outside world. Civilians everywhere. Businessmen in suits. Porters pushing trolleys loaded with boxes. And high up in the vaulted roof, rows and rows of pigeons jostling for position. He could almost hear the sweet refrain. Welcome home, Billy-boy. Fill your boots, son!

Dazzled by the vastness of the station, he stepped down onto the platform. Commuters rushed for the exit, the next train, glancing at watches, the clock on the wall. All of them gripped by an urgency he couldn't fathom. Watching them race by he felt clueless, lost, like a reject on the dance floor when the lights come on.

There she was, waiting for him by the cafeteria. A solitary figure in dark jeans and red puffa jacket, hair tied back and gold earrings in. He almost missed her in the crowd, thought she was someone else. But no mistaking that proud stance and inbuilt aggression. No mistaking it at all.

Strolling over, he felt the quickening of his heart-rate, the nerves of a first date. Would they have anything in common – anything to talk about, or would she blank him completely?

'Hey, doll,' he said. 'Is this it – the welcoming committee?'

'What did you expect, a brass band?'

They embraced stiffly, human traffic racing by. He drank in the scent of her, the freshness of her hair and the coldness of her cheek. The first time they'd been alone together in five years without a screw looking on.

She led him out to the car park and took out a set of keys.

'What you driving?' he said.

'Nothing special. Shifty sold it me a couple of weeks ago.'

'Seriously?'

'Don't start that. It gets me from A to B, OK?'

They came to a blue Ford with beaded seat covers and a hole where the stereo should have been. He opened the passenger door and looked it over, shaking his head.

'Jesus. The fella saw you coming, didn't he?'

She glared at him over the roof. 'D'you wanna lift home, or not?'

Into the sprawl of Parkway Central; grimy, red brick buildings and faded shop fronts loomed ahead. Pendik Kebab and Beds R Us. The Labour Club on the corner where his old fella used to drink. Memories attached to every brick and every turn in the road. Places he'd been over and over in his mind during the long stretch upriver.

'What happened to the Portman?' he said.

'They turned it into flats. Everything's changing round here.' She focused on the road ahead, solemn as a magistrate. Now she'd have to get used to him being back. All the changes to her daily routine. No more lying there in the big double bed, taking up all the room.

He kicked off his shoes and massaged his toes. 'Can't wait to stick on a pair of trainers. These fuckin things are killing me.'

She looked over with a smirk. 'You look like a second-hand car dealer in that suit.'

'Thanks … How's me little girl?'

'Getting bigger every day. If she goes much longer they might have to induce.'

'Bless. Good of her to wait for me to get out, weren't it?'

'Story of our lives, that. Sitting round waiting for you to get out.'

He squeezed her thigh, almost expecting a knock back – a bolshie screw in the visiting hall telling him to keep his hands on the table. She let him carry on, her eyes on the road. All that soft flesh beneath his fingers, denied him for so long, the thought of it intoxicating, taking away his ability to think straight.

'Have you missed me?' he said.

'Oh, sure. Couldn't wait for you to get back and start eating me out of house and home.'

More surprises on the north side. The Three Cherries was now the Starlight Club. Twenty odd years since he'd worked the doors, ejecting leery youngsters and underage girls who screamed abuse and puked all over the pavement. Bang 'em down Billy, making his mark on the town. And all that time passing in-between. Turning forty up the factory. Being ghosted up north when the riots kicked-off. Coming back home was baffling, like sensory overload.

'What's your plans?' she said.

'Couple of fellas to see. Pick up some cash I'm owed.'

'Put some of it my way then, can't you. I've got bills to pay.'

'What happened to the money I sent you over?'

'It's gone.'

'What, all of it?'

'Fuck sake, Billy. I had the car to pay out on and food to buy.' She crashed the gears at the lights and swore, irritated by his good-natured ribbing. He couldn't stop looking at her. Like a stranger to him, exotic and alluring. His Irish princess. The most desirable woman he'd ever seen.

'I'll talk to Gary,' he said. 'Get you summat decent to drive.'

'Don't start having a go at me.'

'I'm not having a go at you, I'm just saying.'

'Well don't. It's been hard enough as it is without you putting your oar in.'

She had to have the last word. He hadn't been around. She had to get by on handouts, and lifts from Pauline when the car broke down. He half-listened, accepted her accusations without buying into them. He had been away a while, it was true. Now he'd have to make up for it. Bring in the moolar. Give her something to smile about as she served up his scran.

They passed a field filled with caravans; washing lines strung between vehicles, and clothes jigging in the breeze. He made a joke about her family coming over, thieves, rogues and tarmaccers from across the water. A whole tribe of them who'd fled the coop and settled somewhere else. His own roots over there too, going way back. The infamous O'Reillys from County Cavan, who came over to work on the docks and never went back. Hard drinking, fighting men who set the style for the generations to come.

Dim orange lights lit the underpass as they headed into the tunnel. The same route he'd travelled in a sweatbox five years before, heading upriver after sentencing. A profound sense of loss with each passing mile. Everything he held dear taken away. Family and friends. Love and laughter. All traded in for a set of plastic cutlery and drab prison greys.

Out from the tunnel and into the financial sector; the white walls of the Prudential Insurance building up ahead. Money flowing ceaselessly to the company directors and merchant bankers in their big offices overlooking the city. He envied their lifestyles, the cars they drove and the houses they lived in. Once you'd had a taste of it you wanted more. Fancy restaurants and Five-Star hotels, ordering up girls and Dom Perignon at three-hundred quid a bottle. In his younger days he'd been invincible, didn't think about consequences. Now it was all that much harder to come by. The risks were greater. You could end up going away for a long time.

As the streets went by, Eileen opened up a bit. People they knew. Latest developments on the Parkway. He listened with envy, like a kid who'd missed out on a treat and had to swallow all the details.

'Sonia had a run-in with a journalist fella. Threw a drink in his face, apparently.'

'What for?'

'She was having lunch in town and the fella walked in asking questions.'

'What kinda questions?'

'Someone said they were making a documentary.'

'About what?'

'Leonard, I suppose.'

Someone had shown him the headline up the factory. 'Crime

Boss Dies Mowing the Lawn'. The Big Fella, mourned by those who knew him and some who didn't. Poor folk, touched by his generosity and the money he'd poured into various charities. Local gangsters who'd benefited from his connections and knew how profitable it was to be seen in his company. Somehow, Leonard had beaten the odds and made it to folklore status, bowing out from a heart attack in his own back garden.

Somehow, none of that mattered with her sat beside him.

'How about you?' he said. 'Been out much?'

She flashed him a look. 'Oh yeah, all the friggin time.'

'How's Pauline?'

'She's OK.'

'Not divorced the other fella yet then?'

'Not yet, but it's on the cards the way those two carry on.' She told him about Gizmo, putting all his money through the fruit machines, and how Pauline was a mug to put up with it. Soon he'd know what half the estate had been up to, and they in turn would know all about him. Billy Riley, back from a stint upriver to stake his claim.

'Get up the club much?' he said.

'Coupla times with Gemma and Luke.'

'Get a smooch in with old Sammy before last orders, did you?'

'Huh – I keep well away from that fella, don't you worry about that.'

He pictured the dance floor, the coloured tiles. Shady alcoves of beered-up men leering all over her.

Glancing over, she read his look. 'Don't you be starting that nonsense with me, you hear? I've enough to be thinking about.'

Turning into the Crescent from the lights inspired a mild nostalgia. He remembered the old joke they used to tell on the streets and in the ale houses 'Warning – you are now entering bandit country. Please do not leave your vehicles unattended.' Past the common and the leaning goalposts, graffiti-splashed walls by the Co-op. The remnants of a dream he'd turned up in by mistake.

A kid on a BMX shot into the road and raced alongside the car, cutting in behind. Then a second kid, from nowhere, the two of them like motorcycle outriders.

Eileen shook her head. 'Little fuckers. They get worse every week.'

'Beats a police escort, that's for sure.'

He could sense the curtains twitching, the gleeful whispers. The neighbours all lined up along the street to witness his return. Billy Riley – last seen swearing at the judge in Courtroom Number One. Proud and unrepentant with his polished bald head and crumpled suit, muscles ripped and ready to roll.

Home.

A waft of lemon-scented air freshener as Eileen opened the door. Good and bad memories mixed into one. Dragged out by the armed response one morning and bundled into the back of a waiting van. Tried and convicted and sent on his way. Shipped from one airless dungeon to another at the first sign of trouble.

A dark shape nudged its way past Eileen, tail wagging, tongue hanging out. He grabbed the dog's head, playfully, and kneaded its flanks, the once powerful body less agile with age. 'Hello, son! Who's this come to see you then, eh? Who's this!' Sorrowful black eyes looked up into his, paws resting on his knees. The best welcome he'd had since he'd set foot on the platform at Parkway Central.

'You wanna bath?' Eileen called from the kitchen. 'There's plenty of hot water.'

'I will in a bit, doll. Stick the kettle on and make us a brew!'

Photo portraits lined the dresser in the front room. Connor, Tommy and Gemma, the absent welcoming committee. He hadn't wanted a fuss. No surprise parties and people leaping out with silly hats on. But this was an anti-climax, a feeling he'd been let down in some way.

The view from the armchair felt surreal. Flat screen TV in the corner. Marble fireplace and hearth dotted with brass ornaments. All those missing years like a weight around his neck. Memories of good times when he'd been out and grafting, earning good money. Sunday league football and roast dinners to come home to. Muddy boots kicked off in the hall. A houseful of noise and raucous laughter. Never a dull moment with the Riley clan.

Welcome home, Billy-boy.

Five years locked away was like five years on the moon. He'd have to learn to acclimatise. Breathe the oxygen again.

2
Walking the Dog

Light filtered through the curtains. Strange shapes took form in the room. For a moment he wondered where he was; a clean bed in the prison hospital wing; the same dream he was yet to wake up from. Next to him, Eileen's warm body under the duvet, barely breathing. He thought about waking her up and riding her bones again, but the old anxiety kicked-in. Now he was back he could take his time, make a better job of it. Not do his gravy in under three-seconds.

The clock said 5.35. He scratched, yawned and got up, bedsprings groaning. In the top drawer of the dresser he found a pair of boxers and slipped them on, enjoying the strange sense of freedom. From a six-by-nine prison cell to this – a luxury pad with double bed and en-suite facilities, even if they were along the hall.

Creeping to the window, he peered out. The road was deserted, lit by the streetlights. A ghostly white layer of frost clung to the line of parked cars. The view made no sense at all, confusing to senses dulled from sleep. An alien landscape, a foreign country. But this was home, the place he'd imagined night after night, laid up on his kip.

The dog came out to greet him, tail-wagging. He ruffled the broad head, whispering words of affection. 'Take you over the common soon, eh? Chase some pigeons. Would you like that?'

Kettle on and two bits of bread in the toaster, he searched cupboards rammed with food: peanut butter, breadsticks and pasta, tins of baked beans and Bolognese. He marvelled at the abundance. Like a cellar stocked for famine or nuclear war.

Gazing out at the garden, he drank in the view. Nothing much changed in five years. The same old rickety shed at the end of the path. Dew-covered lawn. The stone gnomes Eileen had bought just before he'd been lifted.

A magpie landed on the grass. He watched, mesmerised, as it hopped around the garden, all fat white breast and shiny black wings. 'Where's your mate?' he said out loud, and scanned the rooftops looking for more. Seeing two was supposed to cancel out the bad luck of seeing the first one. Like stroking a black cat, or touching wood, all of it dumb superstition, but once it was in your head it was hard to get rid of.

Eileen shuffled in in dressing gown and slippers, an unlit cigarette in her mouth.

'What you looking at?' she said.

'Fuckin magpie. Can you believe that?'

The bird flew off and perched on a neighbouring garage roof. He watched until it took off again, muttering to himself at the audacity. Him just out the factory and already the first signs of unrest.

Eileen opened the patio door and sparked the cigarette, sucking in a lungful of nicotine and cold air. 'Ma's coming over this morning. Will you be here?'

'Not if I can help it. She might put the scuss on me like that fuckin bird.'

Eileen leant against the wall, puffing away. The smoking annoyed him, almost as much as the magpie, but he couldn't say too much in case she copped the spur. Five years away was a long time. He couldn't expect to walk in and change all her bad habits overnight.

'You want breakfast?' she said.

'What you got?'

'Bacon and sausage, fresh from the back of Dai Lewellyn's van.'

'That greasy-haired Elvis lookalike been round here, has he?'

She stared at him. 'D'you want the friggin breakfast, or not?'

He sat at the table, awaiting his scran like a mug in a roadside café. She moved around him, opening cupboard doors and rattling hardware; cracking eggs in a pan sizzling with pig fat. How good it was to be back. Even his performance between the sheets didn't seem too bad now he thought about it. What did she expect? All those years behind the door, having one off the wrist in the early hours of the morning. He'd have to work on it. Get his confidence back.

Flipping through the Echo, he looked for anyone he might know in the crime section. Bored with this, he kept turning the pages. Adverts for department stores and garden furniture. Weekend breaks at bargain prices.

'Fancy Benidorm?' he said. 'Says here we could fly out for seventy-nine quid.'

'You've only been out five-minutes, now you want a friggin holiday?'

'Why not? Bit of sunshine. Do us good, wouldn't it?'

'Good for you maybe. I've got things to do around here.'

'Like what?'

'Like look after a daughter who's about to have a friggin baby, or had you forgotten about that?' She stacked a plate noisily on the drainer, the suds glistening. Soon the bacon was cooking, the sausages browning in the pan. He felt like the lodger in his own home. The real owner might come back at any time and serve him an eviction notice.

Back up the factory he'd have been lying on his kip, thinking about the gym and who he might run into on association. The sights and sounds of ordinary domestic life were alien to him. He didn't know what to say next, where to put his hands.

'You want something to do later, the shed door needs fixing,' she said.

'What am I – the fuckin handyman?'

'Wouldn't take five-minutes.'

'Neither would a quick jump, stick that on the list, too.'

She flashed him a look. I forgot you were a comedian too, pal. Now he was back she'd take advantage. Find chores for him to do and things to fix. For that reason alone he planned on spending plenty of time out of the house.

Fried breakfast followed, liberally splashed with a real bottle of HP sauce. He tucked in like the king in his castle, back from a long crusade.

'Boss scran, luv, you've done me proud there.'

'Yeah, well don't be thinking I'll be waiting on you hand and foot.'

'Why not – that's what you're here for, isn't it?'

She sloped off to the kitchen with a breeze of attitude. Sometimes he wished he'd married someone with less lip. Life would have been easier. He'd have spent less time dodging saucepans and bits of crockery whenever she went on one. But the banter felt good. Like they were feeling their way back in, getting used to a difficult situation.

Showered and dressed, he felt revitalised; the smooth feel of a crisp white shirt against his skin; the sting of aftershave on his cheeks and neck. All his jewellery stored in a Quality Street tin, waiting for the day he came home. Gold sovereign rings and thick necklaces, a bracelet worth at least two grand. Taking them out one at a time, he gloated over them like a miser. Gold conferred status on a man, changed his whole demeanour. The hallmarks of victory over the system and all the petty rules and regulations imposed inside. When he stepped outside the front door he'd be someone. A man deserving of respect and admiration, instead of the faceless shadow prison had tried to turn him into.

Grabbing his hat from the peg, he looked along the hall.

'I'm off out, luv …'

No answer. The dog looked up at his feet, tongue out, tail wagging. Man and his faithful companion, reunited after a long sojourn.

Caught between a wave of anxiety and the need to project a certain image, he stepped outside. The curtain-twitchers would line the route, eager to relay information to the neighbourhood gossip committee. Billy Riley, out and about in his sheepskin coat and black leather gloves, flat cap pulled low over his eyes. Word would soon go round. He was back. Transported from a time warp and dumped in a place he used to know. And while he'd been away things had changed without him giving his permission.

Walking the dog. All he had to do was follow the squat rear-end from one bush to another, pausing for the mutt to sniff the scent and cock its back leg every few seconds. He unclipped the lead and let it roam, amused at the bow legs and muscular back, the ceaseless foraging. They had a perfect understanding, him and the old mutt. He was the master. The dog did what it was told. Most of the time.

A gang of youths loitered outside Co-op, smoking cigarettes and trying to look mean. Hitching the dog to the rail, he made his way up the ramp, conscious of them watching.

'Nice dog, mate,' one said. 'Does he bite?'

'Only when he's hungry.'

He grabbed an Echo and joined the queue, struck with the novelty of the situation. Yesterday, mooching about on 'the ones', waiting for the word to ship out. Today a free man, waiting in line with a bunch of civilians.

The bird behind the counter stared at him with a look of terminal boredom. He put the Echo on the counter and raked his pocket for change, overcome by another attack of anxiety. Everyone watching him. The whole store, waiting for him to make a mistake so they could rip the piss out of him.

'Anything else?' the bird said.

'Give us a scratchcard, luv.'

'Which one?'

'The winning one. We'll go halves, eh?'

He counted the money into her outstretched hand, and headed for the exit. Like a test he'd just about scraped through to prove he belonged, intimidated by the punters inside, heartless civilians who had no concept of the hardship he'd been through.

Watched by the gang of lads outside, he scratched off the numbers on the card. He sensed their boredom. All that testosterone with no outlet.

'Win anything, mate?' one said.

'Not this time, fella.'

They watched him go, unsmiling and quietly aggressive. The jail was full of them. Pocketbook gangsters and playground militants, cocky and arrogant when they first came in. They soon had it knocked out of them one way or another.

Strolling back with the dog he felt better, less geared-up for trouble, and slightly more comfortable with the garb he had on. Up ahead, an old fella leaned on a gate; a young bird pushed a kid in a buggy. Familiar streets and houses, a broad patchwork sky. Five years dreaming about coming back, visualising the mundane like it was a special panacea. Couldn't wait to see the wife and kids, the new grandchild. Sup a pint of ale in the Grafton and hear the ring of the cash register, the crack of the pool table. The reality was different. Not quite what he'd expected.

He called Gary on the mobile Eileen had given him.

'It's me. Billy. Can you talk? …'

The dog cocked its leg and sprayed another bush. The young mother pushed the buggie towards the Crescent. The same time-bound scenario he'd experienced inside, except out here there were no boundaries, only wide open spaces waiting to be explored.

Gary wasn't happy. Kids had broken in to the office at the car lot and trashed the place, leaving a turd on the desk as a calling card. 'Scumbags,' Gary said. 'I catch 'em I'll break their fuckin legs.' But now wasn't the time for petty grievances. What about the man of the moment, Billy Riley? How did it feel to be on the out after so long?

'I'm cracking on with it, fella,' he said. 'Had me fried breakfast and a quick jump. Now I'm walking the dog round the common, just like old times …' He said how much he was enjoying his first taste of freedom. Spending the night in a double bed with clean sheets and two pillows. Waking up to birds singing outside the window instead of cons shouting abuse along the landing.

There were a few things in the offing, Gary said – all legal and above board; nothing that would violate his parole conditions, which could be taken care of soon enough. An outstanding debt for a haulage company: some fella who'd run up credit by the thousands then gone into hiding. Couple of missing persons he might be able to track down.

'Drop by the office, I'll give you the details. Need anything else?'

'Decent set of wheels might come in handy.'

No problem, mate. I'll sort you something out asap.'

Gary talked about the four-bed semi he'd moved into near the Heights. Listening to the pride in the fella's voice, he couldn't help a touch of envy. Gary had gone up in the world and done alright for himself. Managed to stay out of jail long enough to focus on the moolar to the exclusion of all else.

'Anyway, enough about me. How's Eileen?'

'Same as ever. Gotta list o' jobs for me to do long as your fuckin arm.'

'That's women for you, mate. Say hello to her for me, won't you.'

Laid out on the recliner back home, he reviewed the morning's work. Walking the dog had been harder than he'd anticipated. Normal bods did stuff like that every day without thinking. But they hadn't spent five years behind the door, having every move processed and categorised by the system. It made him nervous thinking about it. Not good for the image he wanted to project. The look people expected of him.

Eileen came back. She stood in the doorway looking down at him.

'What you doing?'

'Resting – what's it look like?'

She unbuttoned her coat, eyeing him suspiciously.

'Where you been?'

'Walking the dog. What's for dinner?'

'Faggots, chips, and peas. That alright?'

'Fine.'

She frowned. 'What's up with you?'

'Nothing.'

'Try telling your face.'

She left him to brood, surrounded by all the brass and the porcelain, the portraits of his kids on the wall. Nothing had prepared him for this. Upriver, he had his own space – even if it was the small and cramped confines of a prison cell. The noises filtering in all had their own meaning, a kind of Morse code he could listen out for and decipher. You could tell the whereabouts of the screws by the jangle of key chains and the squeak of rubber-soled feet, the barking of some meaningless order across the landing. The days could be broken into manageable sections, everything worked out on a daily rota. At any given time of day or night you knew where you were and where you were supposed to be. Out here in the wilderness everything was random. Nothing made sense, a complicated system he hadn't worked out yet.

'Gemma and Luke are coming over tomorrow,' Eileen called from the kitchen. 'Will you be here?'

'I might be.'

'What kind of an answer's that? Either you will or you won't?'

'I said I might be. Don't keep on!'

For some reason the thought disturbed him. His own daughter. He should have been mad keen on seeing her, but he wasn't. Sometimes it all seemed too much; other people's expectations of him to fulfil a certain role. Billy Riley, proud father of three kids, the youngest of whom was about to drop at any minute. The other two couldn't have been more different. Connor, away at college, like a seasoned academic. Tommy, set to follow his old fella's example, in and out of jail for the rest of his adult life.

Eileen served dinner. He tucked in heartily, the taste like no other. Prison food defied a description; some of the most bland and unpalatable concoctions ever prepared by human hand. This was top-notch, five-star stuff in comparison, almost worth waiting for.

'What's the crack with that fella you told me about?' he said.

'What fella?'

'The one Sonia threw a drink at.'

'Oh, him. He's lucky he didn't end up in the canal.'

'Hang around here long enough he still might do. What's his angle?'

'I told you, he's making a documentary about Leonard.'

'Says who?'

'Pauline.'

'That figures.'

'What's that supposed to mean?'

'Never mind that. How did she find out?'

'Gizmo had a drink with him in the Grafton. The fella's been getting in there every afternoon, apparently.'

He tried to picture Gizmo – a man of limited means and less-than dazzling intellect – entertaining the journalist fella at the bar.

'Maybe I'll go see Sonia,' he said. 'Find out what the score is.'

'Don't bother. Nothing but trouble, the pair of them. They keep snooping around like that they'll both end up in the canal.'

'Have a heart, luv, Gizmo can't swim.'

'I'm not talking about Gizmo. I'm talking about the journalist fella and the woman he hangs round with. Pauline reckons she's all done up to the nines. Looks like something out of a Freemans catalogue.'

The funeral must have been something. Photographs in the papers showed the cortege turning into Latimer Road from the junction to Five-ways. Crowds of people lining the pavements. The dibble out in force. The Big Fella himself, weighing in at a bloated twenty-one stone, carried through the streets in a horse-drawn carriage.

She took the bowls away. Pleasant, domestic sounds filtered in from the kitchen. Water running in the sink. Her feet on the lino. A weakness on his part to get too comfortable, too settled in. But for now it felt good, safer inside than out.

She came in buttoning up her coat.

'Where you going?' he said.

'Gemma's.'

'What for?'

'Give her some clothes for the baby.'

'How long you gonna be?'

'Jesus – do I have to keep reporting to you every five minutes?'

Alone in the house, he thought of all the things freedom had bestowed upon him. The opportunity to soak in a hot bath. Watch the box with his feet up. The luxury of being able to knock one out in private with no one watching through the Judas hole. But things weren't right. Even the dog looked at him funny sometimes. And if he had to be honest with himself he'd have said it was a struggle. His youth had come and gone. Now he had to look for new ways to stay on top.

Maybe the journalist fella was the answer. New possibilities.

3
Reclamation

The lift was broken. He took the stairs, two at a time, avoiding the greasy wooden banister for fear of contamination. On the third floor, a long, dingy corridor smelling of must and stale piss. Tatty blue doors with spy-holes so the occupants could suss out cold callers or the dibble and take immediate evasive action. Along the hall he went, ears tuned for signs of movement. Life on Mars. Snippets of muted conversation from the aliens inside. The odd shout from a child, or the blare of a radio. And there he was at the centre of it all. Billy Riley, striding down the gangway like the cyborg in *Terminator 2*.

He stopped outside 107 and rang the bell.

The door opened a few inches, snagged by a chain. A feral-looking woman peered out, lank hair over a thin, Medieval face. Behind her, a subterranean passageway, gloomily-lit and reeking of stale chip oil.

'Your man Dennis there, luv?' he said.

'No, he's not.

'Any idea when he'll be back?'

'No, I haven't.'

He thought about kicking the door in and pushing past her, searching every room for the miserable twat. He handed her a card instead.

'When he comes in, tell him to give this number a ring.'

She took the card without looking at it. 'You're wasting your time. He don't live here no more.'

'That's not the information I've been given.'

'Well the information you got's wrong then, innit.'

She slammed the door, leaving him alone in the dank hall. He grinned to himself at the radical change in routine. Some way to earn a living. Better off selling phonecards up the nick. But the likes of Dennis could wait. There were more cerebral issues to deal with.

He walked the few blocks to St Anthony's and sat on a worn pew at the back. Candles burned in the vestry, scores of flickering yellow lights illuminating the gloom. Looking up, he admired the vaulted ceiling with its interconnecting dark wood struts. Several rows in front, a woman knelt, head bowed in prayer. To his right, a man lay curled on a pew in the shadows, his body covered with an old coat – a homeless drug addict or alkie, sleeping off a bender. The church welcomed them all, regardless of age, colour or gender.

A shadowy figure slipped in beside him and made the sign of the cross. They sat for a moment in silence, each alone with his thoughts.

'How are you, Billy?'

'I'm good, thanks, Father.'

'And the family?'

'They're good, too.'

He felt the father's eyes upon him, searching. The fella looked older, his thin beard flecked with grey, but the eyes were bright and full of humour.

'Eileen said you were coming out,' the father said. 'It's great to see you. You're looking well.'

'Must be the home cooking.'

'Aye, it could be that, Billy. So what're you up to? Do you have anything planned?'

He mentioned the work he was doing for Gary, emphasising that it was all legit. Chasing debts for various businesses that would get him started. The more lucrative jobs would come later, once he'd settled in.

The goodly father nodded his encouragement. 'That's good, Billy. And I hear Connor won a scholarship to Newhaven. You must be very proud.'

'The kid done good, as they say. Better'n I was doing at his age, that's for sure.'

The inevitable question about Tommy never came. Instead, the goodly father sat there with a faint smile, eyes glinting in the dim light. He knew the family history and all its quirks and shenanigans. Eileen's brief stint upriver for theft and assault on a police officer a few years back. Tommy's wayward behaviour and constant re-offending since he left school. Not to mention his own chequered form over the years, in and out the factory since the age of fourteen. Connor had escaped all that by getting himself an education and excelling at sport. If he kept on doing what he was doing, the lad would never see the inside of a police cell, or get lifted by the dibble on a Saturday night. Of course they were proud. Who wouldn't be?

A figure stirred in one of the pews in front of them. The man sat up and scratched his head before lying back down.

'Poor fella looks a bit confused,' he said.

The father sighed. 'With all the wealth in the world there will always be poor in the city. I feel for the kids growing up here, I really do.'

'Amen to that, Father.'

Childhood seemed a long way off, full of memories good and bad. Lazy days fishing down by the canal. The truant officer coming round and hassling his old ma, who tried to keep it a secret from the old fella, who'd beat the crap out of him if he found out. No matter what they did – the old fella, the teachers, the juvenile courts – he always rebelled. Refused to listen. Now Tommy was set to go the same way and there was nothing anyone could do to change it.

The goodly father coughed, discreetly, mindful of his sleeping congregation. The coughing went on for a time, hollow in his chest like a death rattle.

'Don't sound too good, that, Father?'

'I've a mind to take a holiday,' the father said, wiping his eyes. 'Somewhere hot, preferably. This northern climate doesn't suit me, gets right in the bones.'

'I'm thinking of taking Eileen away somewhere. Give her a

break from it all.'

'That'd be nice, Billy.'

'She deserves it, don't you think – putting up with me all them years?'

The father chuckled. 'Well, you've been together a long time. There's something to be said for that.' The tone was soft, almost comforting in the airy confines of the church. The place instilled a peacefulness inside him, a way of seeing his problems in a different light. But still those nagging thoughts at the back of his mind that he couldn't get rid of. Things that had consumed him night and day up the factory.

'I expect Eileen's looking forward to the baby,' the father said.

'Oh, she is, Father. Every spare minute she's over our Gemma's, helping with the pregnancy an' all.'

'Has Gemma long to go?'

'Anytime now, apparently. House is like a friggin nursery – pardon the language.'

The father nodded. 'Well, Eileen's got you home now, hasn't she. It'll be good for her. Good for the both of yous.'

He pondered all the things he couldn't say. All the fears and worries that had stacked up in the jail, making it harder to think rationally about the whole thing. Seeing Eileen on visits and questioning her about her whereabouts, who she'd been spending her time with. The arguments this had caused between them, threats from her that she'd up and leave him if he didn't get a grip of himself. Maybe she'd forgotten the times he'd looked out for her – the night he battered some fella in the Grafton for making derogatory comments about her accent, insinuating she was in the IRA. Getting Gary to send money over regular while he was away upriver. Always doing his best to make sure she was looked after, that she didn't want for anything. But somehow it was never enough. She'd made her own life on the out, and he was never a part of it, locked away in some grim mausoleum to reflect.

The father avoided the subject, unable to betray a confidence because of his vows. All those guilty whispers he must have heard in the confessional. The sins of the community weighing heavily upon his back.

'Ever come across the Big Fella, Leonard Simms, Father?'

'Not to speak to. I heard a lot about him, though. Was he a friend of yours?'

'I used to work for him, back a while.'

'I heard they closed off a whole section of Latimer Road on the day of the funeral. Must've been quite a sight.'

The homeless fella stirred on the pew in front. He thought of Leonard, carried through the streets in a horse-drawn carriage. Everyone meeting the same end, whatever the journey it took to get there.

'Word is, some journalist fella wants to make a documentary about him. Been hanging around the estate asking questions.'

'Really?' the father said. 'And what're your feelings about that?'

He shrugged. 'None of my business really. I've got enough problems.'

'Well, you've certainly walked the long hard road, Billy. Maybe you could put some of that experience to good use.'

'How d'you mean?'

The father gave him an odd quizzical look, the hint of a smile. 'I'm involved with a scheme on the south side, helping young offenders. You'd be just the man to come along and talk to them.'

'Me? ... What could I say?'

'They'd listen to you because you've been there yourself. Trodden the same path, so to speak.'

'Hardly a shining example, though, am I, Father?'

'But you've a message all the same. And if you could prevent one of those young lads from going the same way ... Think about it, Billy.'

Looking at his tattooed hands and gold sovereign rings he felt awkward. The father had a genuine passion for the work, that was obvious. But he, Billy Riley, was different. He had no real interest in reforming anyone, least of all himself. The father was like the counsellors and social workers who came into the jails, full of ideas and schemes about cleaning up the system. They couldn't see the tide they were swimming against. Besides, it was too deep-rooted in him. He'd made an enemy of authority all his life.

The father saw him out. The two of them stood in the passage on the dust-flecked mezzanine floor, the sanctity of the church comforting around them.

'So long, Billy. Give my regards to Eileen, won't you.'

'I will do, Father.'

'And be sure to think about what I said.'

He told Eileen about it when he got back. The thought of him, Billy Riley, giving a talk to young offenders about the perils of crime. She found it as daft as he did, unable to help a righteous smirk. 'What's the matter with the fella? Has he gone soft in the head all of a sudden?'

'You don't think I could make a go of it, then?'

'Huh – I feel sorry for anyone gets you as a careers advisor!'

He went upstairs, and stopped in the bedroom doorway. Laid out over the bed in plastic wrappers, were men's shirts in a variety of colours. He picked one up and felt the smooth, shiny surface. Expensive-looking material with neat blue stripes and button-down collars. The kind of thing he might wear himself on a Saturday night.

He took the shirt downstairs and tossed it on the kitchen table.

'What's this?'

'It's a shirt, isn't it?'

'Don't get clever with me. Where'd it come from?'

'Pauline. She thought you might like one as a coming home present.'

'That all of 'em up there, is it?'

'Yeah?'

'Got any more coming in?'

'No?'

'Get rid of 'em.'

'What?'

'You heard me. Put 'em in the boot of the car and take 'em back round Pauline's, or I'll bin the fuckin lot!'

She fumed quietly, giving him the leery eye.

'Don't look at me like that,' he said. 'The dibble come knocking and find that lot round here, I'll be back upriver before you can think.'

She grabbed the shirt and marched off along the hall. He watched her go, brimming with self-righteous anger. Selfish cunt. Risking his freedom for the sake of a few knock-off shirts – even if they were brand names. Things had to be done proper, or he'd kick-off and make his feelings known that way. Send a clear message round to all the people she knew. Stamp out rebellion like the Roman legions he'd read about up the factory.

The dog came in and gave him the sad eye. Watching it from the armchair he felt a measure of guilt. 'Don't you start, pal. It's bad enough with her on me case.' The dog wandered off, and curled up on the sofa, muzzle flattened on a cushion. He loved it beyond words. The simple devotion it showed him, never questioning his authority or trying to do him a wrong turn. And him being away up yonder all that time and the old mutt still remembering him. Fair touched his heart to think of it.

A car door slammed in the drive. The engine fired and the car pulled away. He pictured Eileen, all red-faced and angry, muttering curse words about him as she drove off down the road. When she came back he'd have a quiet word. Restore the equilibrium.

With nothing on the telly but adverts and irritating people, he put on a DVD instead. Ali vs Frazier, 1972. Two former giants of the ring, unleashing raw power in the hundred and twenty-degree heat. No matter how many times he watched it, there was always something he'd missed.

He dialled the number Gary had given him.

'Gordon Smith?'

'Who's this?'

'I'm calling on behalf of Longfleet Haulage Company. There's a little matter of twenty-five grand still outstanding.'

Ali danced around Frazier in the middle of the ring, flicking out jabs and staying out of range. He marvelled at the each man's ability to soak up punishment and keep coming back.

The Smith fella must have had a degree in evasion tactics. He let the waffle go on a bit longer until he'd heard enough. 'Lemme stop you there, pal. Basically, there's two ways we can do this. The easy way or the hard way. Which one d'you want?'

Frazier countered with a body shot, forcing Ali on the ropes.

Ali covered up in the time-honoured way, elbows tucked in, gloves protecting the face.

The Smith fella still wasn't listening, determined to dig the hole a bit deeper. But there was fear in his voice too.

'Listen, pal – you've had enough warnings, right? I've taken the debt on now, so you owe me. D'you understand what I'm saying?' He kept his tone even, conversational, but the fella kept trying to cut in. 'Listen to me now … I said listen… Tell you what we're gonna do …'

He hung up with a feeling of certainty. The fella's resistance would mellow. He'd have time to reflect upon his wrongdoing and change his mind. They could discuss the repayments in a civilised manner, but always with the understanding that any further lapses would incur penalties, even the prospect of hospital food. This was business pure and simple.

When Eileen came back he felt better disposed towards her. The call to Gordon Smith would net a few grand when the fella paid up. Dennis Swales was a more personal target going back a long way, but even closure there would give a sense of satisfaction. At last she would see he was bringing the moolar in and paying his way.

'Stick your glad-rags on,' he said, 'we're going out.'

'I've just walked in the friggin door.'

'So? Be the first time you've been out with me in five fuckin years. Give the neighbours summat to talk about, won't it?'

4

Out on the Town

They strolled through the Archway, past the rundown buildings and boarded up shop fronts towards the old town. Eileen's heels beat out a rhythm beside him, echoing in the street like a regimental horse on parade. He kept stealing a look at her as if she was someone else's wife, entranced by her makeup and jewellery, the slim black leggings cut high on the ankle. The sight of her reduced him in some way, did something to him he wasn't able to fathom. Her womanhood, all sleek and glamorous and beguiling. Deep inside him, a fear of the power she had. The effect it might have on other men.

A queue formed outside Paradisio. Young lads in designer gear and girls in skimpy dresses, hugging themselves with the cold. Two bouncers stood outside, immaculate in dark suits and bow-ties, an advert for extra muscle.

'Don't think I'm going in there,' she said. 'Look at the queue.'

'How about Gulliver's?'

'That closed down ages ago.' She mocked him gently with a sidelong look. Do you not remember, Billy? Have you been away that long?

The Neptune Bars was still there. One night he fought two gypsies outside, weighing one in with a pint pot and head-butting the other, until the dibble arrived to break it up. And him a mere pup of eighteen at the time, fit from the gym and hodding bricks up a ladder. Proud moments like these infused in the memory circuits, knowing he'd never backed down, never given in without a fight. Bragging about it to the lads on the site the next day, rolling up his shirt and showing off the purple bruises on his ribs where he'd taken a kicking. The lads all clapping him on the back and praising him up, well impressed by his raw machismo.

'Fancy one in here?' he said.

'Only if you promise to behave.'

'I'm on me best behaviour, doll. Scout's honour.'

Hemmed in by noisy youngsters, he stood behind Eileen as she waved a ten-spot at the flustered bar staff. Years ago, working the doors, he'd have thrived in such a place, on the lookout for dickheads selling drugs and the odd psycho intent on causing trouble. Now it felt different, intimidating in a strange way. The music was louder and more aggressive. The kids' faces were leery, distorted from the booze they'd supped and the chemicals they'd taken. He felt old and outdated, the grizzled veteran from a bygone era.

Eileen leaned over to order the drinks. A strange feeling came over him like it was all about to come on top. Panic rose. His heart-rate shot up, every fibre in his body sensing danger. The more he tried to control it the worse it got.

She found him outside, gasping lungfuls of air.

'Fuck you playing at – walking out on me like that!'

'It's rammed in there, doll. I had to get out.'

'Oh, so you just leave me standing there like a fuckin idiot!' She marched off, coat tails flying. He took off after her, past the steak houses and the kebab shops, a rancid mix of foreign food and stale beer in the air.

She slowed enough for him to walk alongside her. Shame and embarrassment jarred him. Walking out on her when they were supposed to be together. Letting the fear get to him instead of facing it like a man.

'Are you talking to me now, or what?' he said.

'Why should I? Leaving me in that place on me friggin own.'

'Gimme a break, luv – I've just come out the factory.'

They took a table at the Working Men's Club, with a view of the dance floor. Couples bopped and gyrated to the sweet sounds of the Fifties. Supping his pint, he watched from the shadows, one arm over the velvet backrest behind Eileen's head. The terrible fear that had taken hold of him earlier faded, in its place a warm and comfortable feeling of nostalgia. This was more his kind of place, his kind of people.

Eileen looked up. 'Happy now?'

'I'm good.'

She shook her head, more amenable now they were settled in. 'Getting old, that's your problem.'

'See about that when we hit the dance floor, sweetheart.'

Sid wandered over, burdened with arthritis and emphysema. Shame what time and the drink did to some people. Twenty years ago a force in his own right, now a kind of joke among the locals, a harmless buffoon who slopped drink over his trousers and harped on about the good old days.

The old fella clapped a bony hand on his shoulder and leaned in close. 'Good to see you, Billy. Always good to have one of our own back in the fold.' He tapped his nose artfully. 'Took care of your missus while you was away. That right, Eileen?'

'Giving all our secrets away now, are you, Sid?'

'Oh, don't worry – your secret's safe with me, girl.'

Eileen waved him fondly away. 'Get on with you, Sid. And remember to put your teeth back in before you hit the dance floor, you'll frighten the kids!'

As the night wore on he got steadily creamed, firing back the whisky sent over by well-wishers at the bar. Billy Riley, celebrating his homecoming back among his own. But still the fear lingered from the incident in the Neptune Bars. The loss of control. Showing weakness in front of his woman.

She left him to mingle with the punters – a star in her own right, laughing and joking with the old folk and flirting with the youngsters. He saw glimpses of her as a stranger, beyond his reach; the old jailhouse worries eating away at his mood, spoiling any real enjoyment he might have had.

Watching her move among the rank and file with her bangles and jewellery he felt the same impotence. All the Friday nights that had gone before, with him away up yonder, knowing she'd be all dressed up and weaving among the menfolk like a polecat on heat. The leery bastards all loosened up by the drink, baiting her with the spiel and the blarney, knowing her old fella wouldn't be there to defend his patch.

The DJ announced a birthday, and cheers went up on the other side. Eileen came back and sat beside him, supping half a lager.

'Who bought you that?' he said.

'Jason.'

'Who?'

'Pauline's cousin.' She stared at him. 'Don't you be starting that nonsense, you hear? The fella just bought me a drink.' She had the skewed and slightly dangerous look he remembered from their nights touring the pubs and clubs together. The semi-humorous glint in her eye that could quickly turn at some minor provocation. He chose to ignore the slight, but it rankled. These people were seasoned liberty-takers. Let one thing go and they'd be queuing up to rip the piss out of him.

The DJ played a medley of Fifties classics – Gene Vincent, Eddie Cochran, and Elvis Presley. Couples jived on the dance floor, linking arms and moving gracefully. Even old Sid, giving it his all with a lanky two-step. Eileen supped the drink the Jason fella had brought her, while the music played on.

He stood, gazing down at her.

'You want another one?'

'I'm fine.'

He lingered, undecided. Something about the look on her face he didn't like. 'Send Jason over to keep you company, shall I?'

'Keep on like that I'll get a friggin taxi home.' She held his gaze, unperturbed. This was how it was and he'd better get used to it.

On his way to the bar, an old crone reached out and grabbed his wrist, muttering his name in a toothless gibber. Shaking her off, he went on his way – the portals of heaven and hell opened up by too much alcohol and a touch of paranoia. He'd sworn off the hooch and the drugs in the jail for the same reason. Stuck with the gym and the exercise instead. Fifty push-ups with an arm behind his back, switching to the other arm and counting again. Running laps of the exercise yard in all weathers when the screws would permit it. The body both a weapon and a statement, a declaration of intent.

Inside, he was someone, had an identity, a place; gave respect and earned respect without compromising his integrity. Outside, it was different, a meat market with no boundaries, no rules to follow. People jostled you in the street without thinking. Cut you up in their shiny new cars. Bought your missus a drink on the sly and expected to get away with it.

A fella in a white shirt and black trousers stopped beside him at the bar.

'How's it going, Billy?'

'Fuck off and mind your own!'

'Steady on, mate, I'm on your side.'

Watching the tables under the monochrome lights, he tried to relax. Eileen had moved on to join another group, her spangled black jacket reflecting the lights.

'Drink?' the fella said.

'Red label with ice – if you're buying.'

The fella signalled the barman, swaying lightly back and forth on his heels, as if he'd supped more than a few ales himself. The barman fetched the drinks. The fella held up his glass and rattled the ice; a silent toast to events past and present.

'Good health,' the fella said.

'Aye.'

They supped together, him and the bod in the white shirt and black trousers, whose name he couldn't recall.

'Shame about Leonard.' the fella said.

'Tragic.'

'Heart attack, wasn't it?'

'So they say.'

He sipped the whisky, aware of his volatile state and the need to remain vigilant at all times. The fella's face loomed on his nearside, a flicker from the distant past that started to bother him.

'Do I know you, pal?'

The fella laughed. 'I worked the doors with you about ten year ago. Twilight Club and the Grosvenor Hotel.'

He clocked the face and felt a vague recollection. The fella seemed alright, pleasantly skimmed and not out to cause trouble. Working the doors gave them a common ground, something to talk about. Comrades-in-arms, sharing tales of derring-do on the frontline.

The fella knew all the names, men he'd worked with in the clubs and the bars on the north side all those years ago when he was an up and coming youngster. The rivalry between Leonard's firm and the bunch of outsiders who tried to take over the waterfront. 'Remember the night they firebombed Maxine's?' the fella said. 'That was it for me. I mean, you expect the odd slap now and again, it's all part of the job. But blowing people up? Fuck that. Might as well have gone to the Falklands like me brother.'

'What you up to now?'

The fella handed him a glossy red card with fancy gold lettering. 'I run me own business. You ever want a job, give us a call.'

He clocked the card under the bar lights. John Pullen. Electronic surveillance and installation. Tucking the card into his pocket, he gave a nod of approval, mildly impressed by the fella's ingenuity.

'What's the money like?'

'Pretty good. I've got a contract with a big firm on the north side, fitting out office blocks and warehouse units.'

'Work away?'

'Sometimes. I'm not married, got no kids. It's ideal, really.'

Last orders came. Couples rose from their tables like ghouls from a crypt, joining the swell on the dance floor for the traditional smooch. The Pullen fella supped his drink, ready for the off.

'Good to see you, Billy. Take it easy, man'

'And you, pal. I might give you a call one day – install a home cinema for me!'

Watching the fella go, he decided he liked his style. Not one of these flash cunts, bragging about what he'd done and trying to impress folk. And electronics was the future. You could spy on people and find out what they'd been up to.

Taking Eileen by the wrist, he tugged her gently towards the dance floor. 'Come on – shift your Irish ass, it's time for the smooch.'

They danced to Phyllis Nelson's 'Move Closer', the coloured

tiles lit up beneath their feet. The music soothed and caressed, a hypnotic pulse to melt away the darkness. Billy Riley, happy and sad in equal measure, seduced by the mournful tones of the singer, locked in an embrace with the woman he loved and wanted to be with forever.

The record ended too soon, and with it the warm, sensual feeling of being held in her arms, protected and cared for. Garish lights came on, a carnage of empty glasses and discarded crisp bags, punters in varying states of inebriation. He sobered quickly, snatched from one unreality to the next. Paranoia returned, stalking him on the outskirts like a winged demon.

'Let's go,' he said.

'What's the hurry?'

'I need some air. Can't fuckin breathe in this place.'

Eileen sauntered ahead of him, saying goodbye to the regulars, relaxed and at ease. They passed an alcove table where a group of lads sat drinking. Eileen nodded briefly to them, and a thickset lad with a wedge of spiky hair nodded back. A flash of eye contact that might have gone unnoticed beneath the lights.

Stopping at the table, he grinned. Billy Riley, just a regular bod exchanging pleasantries.

'What's your name, son?'

The lad looked up, warily.

'Jason.'

'Nice to meet you, Jason.' He stuck out his hand in a gesture of friendship; the lad took it, forced to make eye contact. 'Had a good night, have you?'

'Been alright, yeah.'

'That's good. I like to see the youngsters enjoying themselves – know what I'm saying?' He squeezed the proffered hand and tightened his grip. The lad's eyes registered shock, then pain. He squeezed harder still, crushing the lad's fingers in a makeshift vice.

'Fuck you doing!' Eileen grabbed him and tried to pull him off. 'Leave him alone!'

He let go and stepped back, pleased with the result. The lad pulled back his injured hand, mouth open in disbelief. Eileen was already away, marching off towards the exit in a show of disgust.

Neon lights flashed in the taxi windscreen as they sped home; a blur of pubs and shopfronts, young dollies tottering home on their high heels. He replayed the incident in the club. Couldn't get the Jason fella out of his head. An image of the two of them together, the lad beating one into Eileen in some darkened recess while he was away upriver.

He put a hand on her thigh, and slid his fingers between her legs.

'Don't!' she said.

'What's up?'

'I saw what you did in there. Embarrassing me like that in front of everyone.'

'I shook the fella's hand, that's all. What's up with you?'

The lights turned green at the Crescent. He calculated the distance remaining, a few short minutes before they pulled up outside. Leaning across, he whispered in her ear, all the things he was going to do to her in graphic detail when they got to the bedroom. All fired up by the whisky, the tribal song and dance. Five long years locked away from it all like a caged animal. Coming home to this. Disrespect and liberty-taking in all its treacherous forms.

5

McGuinn

The dog watered the bushes as they wandered the green. Just the two of them, man and beast, his most steadfast and loyal companion. Three kids played football by the bent goalpost. One of them miss-timed a kick and the ball came his way. He trapped it, deftly, and kicked it back, half-hoping they'd notice his natural ability. He'd been good at that age, too. Anything physical. Football. Boxing. Cross-country running. Without the injury to his ankle, things might have been different. He could have been up there with the Alan Shearers and the Roy Keanes of the world, instead of being farmed out to Her Majesty's hell-holes for the best part of twenty-six years.

Watching the kids caused him a moment's regret, a glimpse of what might have been had he taken a different turning. The young offenders the father was trying to help had it all to come. You could see them popping up all over the estate like clones with their hoodies and trainers on. Some might have had talent, too – just like he had at that age. But the Parkway had other ideas. Gang fights and jail sentences. Drug deals and shootings. Guns hadn't been around when he'd been growing up. All that came later, when the world took another turn.

Incorrigible, the judge called him. No option but to impose a custodial, given the persistent nature of the offending. Fourteen years old and up the M1 in a prison van with a bunch of other kids, all sniggering and cracking jokes. No idea what was coming. Miles of country lanes and green fields later, there it was – a two storey, red-brick building with white metal windows. And waiting outside to greet them, the meanest-looking bunch of screws ever assembled on one production line.

He clipped the dog's lead on as they neared the road. Shouts from the kids on the green blended in, a sense of the past and present in a kind of symphony.

A car approached from behind, slowing alongside him. A distinctive nasal voice called out a greeting. 'Afternoon, Billy. They let you out in the end, then?'

He kept walking, eyes on the dog's muscular rump.

The car crawled alongside, the voice goading, needling. 'I was just saying to my colleague how quiet it's been round here lately. Nothing to do with you being away, would it?'

The dog stopped to sniff a clump of weeds. He stood by, the lead wrapped around his fist. The car engine ticked over in the background.

'Need a lift anywhere – we're going your way?' McGuinn's eager face baited him from the driver's side. Next to McGuinn, a younger one he'd never seen before, clearly enjoying the show.

'Big man in that car, incha?' he said. 'Come on over that bit of common, see how much chirp you got then.'

McGuinn laughed heartily. 'Nice to see you've still got a sense of humour, Billy. We'll have to pop round one morning, have a little chat.'

'You come round mine I'll set the fuckin dog on you.'

'Nice talking to you, son. Say hello to Eileen for me, won't you.'

The car turned a bend up ahead. He pictured it engulfed in a fireball, McGuinn and his leery oppo burning to death in the road.

He tugged on the lead and they moved on, the ambience of the day ruined. The quiet of the neighbourhood filled in. Beside him, the dog, irrigating another set of weeds.

Eileen came back laden down with bags of shopping. The sight of him lounging in the armchair caused her added grief. 'You coulda helped,' she said. 'You saw me struggling.'

'I'm thinking.'

'Well think yourself outta that chair and give me a hand!'

He heard her out in the kitchen, rustling carrier bags and

banging cupboard doors. All he could see was the car pulling alongside, McGuinn's grinning face in the window.

She set a mug of tea down in front of him, lingering.

'What's up with you?' she said.

'McGuinn turned up while I was walking the dog. Only been out five-minutes, cunt's hassling me already.' He went to the window, and parted the net curtains, scanning the road. Strange how quickly the mood could change. The likelihood he was under surveillance from one police department or the other. Still a potential target wherever he went, whatever he did. 'Make sure there's nothing dodgy in this house,' he said. 'I don't wanna give them cunts the chance to nick me.'

'There's nothing here. I got rid of it all – remember?' She looked him over from the doorway. 'What d'you want for tea?'

'McGuinn's head in a basket.'

'I was thinking more along the lines of cod 'n' chips, actually.'

'That'll do for starters.'

She came back with fish and chips on a tray. He relaxed, tearing off strips of succulent cod with his fingers and cramming them in his mouth. Two more boxing legends slugged it out on the TV, providing the entertainment. Just how the ancient Romans would have liked it, laid out on couches while the slaves brought in the main courses.

'What's this?' she said.

'Thomas Hearns and Marvin Hagler.'

'Great – can't we watch summat else while we're eating?'

'Sure, luv – what d'you want? Ali, Foreman? Tyson, Holyfield?'

She talked through the action on the screen, a sacrilege he couldn't understand. This was as good as it got. Flakes of cod melting on his tongue. The most formidable collection of prize-fighters ever assembled in one room. All it needed was the dancing girls and a barrel of pale ale and the evening would be complete.

'You know what we need,' he said.

'Not while I'm eating, please.'

'CCTV, like they've got in town. McGuinn starts sniffing round here I wanna know about it.'

'You're just being paranoid. Fella's winding you up.'

He mused on the options. 'I met a fella in the club the other night, does electronic installations. Got all the latest kit, he has.'

'You're not putting cameras in here and that's the end of it.' She sat with that pious look of the self-righteous, guaranteed to put his back up. But he had to admit that a part of him liked it. Back in the cosy domestic lull, sharing the banter over the evening meal. Even with the likes of McGuinn on his case, he had it good.

When she'd taken the plates out, he made the call.

'Gordon?'

'Yeah?

'We had a little chat yesterday about your outstanding debt to Longfleet Haulage. What you got to say to me, pal?'

Silence.

'How about I take you through the repayment options? Get it all sorted, then you can go back to your egg and chips.'

Punters came in two standard sizes: the remorseful type, willing to capitulate and make up for their wrongdoing at the nearest opportunity, and the bolshy ones, who'd do anything to avoid paying, even at the risk of a serious hiding. Gordon Smith was of the former type, willing to do whatever he could to account for his wrongdoing.

He ended the call with a feeling of satisfaction. Closure and a decent pay check up ahead, without having to put much effort in.

Eileen came in with his mug of tea.

'Who was that?'

'Work.'

'Oh yeah? Satisfy your parole conditions, does it?'

He chose to ignore her smug comment. Soon he'd have to chase down some serious moolar. The debt collecting was a stopgap, a means to pay the bills until something better came along. And that something would come along soon. He'd spent five years preparing himself for it.

6
The Landlord

As public houses went, the Swan was a relic, faded red-brick and stone mullions set back from the main road. A convoy of flatbeds and 4 x 4s were parked outside. Two fellas and a coarse-featured woman supped ale at a bench. They broke off their conversation to watch his approach, a look of collective suspicion reserved for strangers. Squaring his shoulders, he sauntered past, the dog lead coiled tight around his fist, the mutt straining to get ahead. The barman put his pint on the mat and waited nervously. He took his time, easing his leather gloves off one by one. The dog sat at his feet, black eyes gazing up with eager anticipation.

'Anything else?' the barman said.

'Bag of pork scratchings for the dog, pal.'

The barman leaned over the counter, saw the mutt and frowned. 'Sorry, no dogs allowed inside.'

'You hear that?' he said to the mutt. 'Fella here says you ain't allowed in.'

The dog panted eagerly, flecks of saliva on his pink tongue.

He beckoned the barman closer. 'Listen – I've had a quick word with him and he promises not to play up. So fetch the scratchings and stop fuckin about.'

The barman fetched the bag and laid it next to the pint, on his face a look of strained acquiescence.

He took a sip, savouring the taste.

'Landlord about?'

'Er – he should be in around one, I think.'

He nodded, his mood enhanced by the surroundings, the old ale house seduction he knew so well. The dog lapped up the scratchings on the flagstones, shards of hardened pork breaking off between his teeth. The landlord was an unknown quantity, one of the new breed drafted in from out of town by the brewery to prop up failing concerns. Gary reckoned the fella had fingers in other pies too and was worth checking out. There might be an angle to exploit.

More punters came in from the cold. He didn't recognise any of them, as if the five-years he'd been away had culled all the regulars. Images of raucous Saturday nights from the past played back like a cine film in his head. Scrapping in the car park with some marine who got him in a headlock and wouldn't let go. Gary running over and smashing the twat over the head with a pool cue while some mad bird attacked him from behind with one of her stilettos. The place had changed since then, adding Sky TV and posh food to the menu, a major refurbishment in the main bar. The new landlord had tried to make a name for himself, barring known troublemakers and putting bouncers on the door at weekends. But the place would always be beyond all that. A real drinkers pub, not open to change from outsiders.

The landlord turned up around midday – a big old lump with heavy jowls and dark, slicked-back hair. He loitered by the optics with a pad and pen.

'When you're ready, mate?'

The landlord jumped, dropped the pad and pen, and hurried over to pour his pint, whistling inanely. The fella had a vague, shell-shocked look about him, as if he'd wandered into the place by accident and couldn't quite work it out.

'How you finding it?'

The landlord looked up. 'Sorry?'

'The pub. Just took it over, incha?'

The story came out in a fashion, how the fella had been running a pub on the north side, but had moved down when his wife had died. He hadn't intended on taking another tenancy, but the brewery had suggested the Swan and reluctantly he'd agreed. 'So here I am. Not quite the retirement I had in mind, but there you go.'

'What happened to your wife – if you don't mind me asking?'

'Cancer. It was all very sudden. She was diagnosed in July. Three months later she was gone.'

'Sorry to hear it, fella.' And he was sorry, too, picturing the poor woman fading away on some hospital bed, and the landlord's grief at the prospect of living without her. Hard to imagine his own life without Eileen. Somehow, the idea didn't compute.

'Are you local?' the landlord said.

'I am indeed. Just got back from a long stint working away.'

'What do you do?'

'I'm a sorta troubleshooter for a big haulage company. They bring me in to tie up all the loose ends, chase debts and the like.'

They chatted like old friends, united by a hankering for the past and a mistrust of the unwritten future. The landlord's concerns were many and varied. Bar staff who were late, or didn't turn up at all. The leak in the pub roof that had turned into a major job costing thousands. Then there was the young lads from the estate, who came in at weekends and caused trouble.

He listened politely, having spent countless hours up the factory listening to men whose whole lives were driven by a similar sense of injustice. Everyone wanted revenge in one form or another.

'Oh, well,' the landlord said. 'Doesn't do to complain, does it. Anything else I can get you?'

'Anything on the menu you might recommend?'

'Well, the chef does a very good hotpot, by all accounts.'

'Sounds good to me, fella.'

The landlord went away with his order. Five minutes later he was back, wearing a look of consternation. 'I'm really sorry, but I can't serve you because of the dog.'

The poor mutt looked up with its soulful black eyes and frothy pink jaw. As the owner, he, Billy Riley, felt the injustice, the discrimination.

Elbow on the bar, he drew the landlord in for further discussion. 'I fully understand what you're saying, fella. But he's a special dog, see? You can trace his ancestors back to the First World War. They used 'em in the trenches – bit of encouragement for the lads before they went over the top. Imagine how he feels now, nothing to do but chase pigeons all day.'

The hotpot came, steam rising from the ceramic dish. Tucking in with relish, he savoured the taste, the delicious aroma of the meat and the crusty pastry. A king's faire compared to the slop he'd been used to upriver. Consolation for the shit he'd put up with over the years. The beatings and the humiliation. Forced to exist like a second-rate citizen.

'Everything alright?' the landlord said.

'Certainly hit the spot, fella.' He fished out his wallet to pay, but the landlord raised a hand.

'On the house, that one.'

'Seriously?'

'Well, I'm sure you'll tell your friends about the good food, won't you?'

'I will indeed, fella. I will indeed.' He wiped his mouth with a serviette, enjoying the newfound hospitality. 'You ever need a bit of help at weekends give us a shout. I might be able to sort something out. I know a few people.'

The landlord gave a token nod. 'Thanks, I'll bear that in mind.'

About to depart, he stopped, recalling something the fella had said earlier.'

'You mentioned you had a yacht?'

'Yes, that's right. She's not in the water at the moment, but I hope to rectify that later in the year. It's the only thing that keeps me sane.'

Strolling across the forecourt, black gloves on, and the dog straining at the lead, a wave of optimism came over him. Admittedly, the work he was involved in was on a small scale, but that could change at any minute. When you had the entrepreneurial spirit, opportunities came along, you just had to look out for them.

He called Gary to discuss Gordon Smith, and the recalcitrant debtor Dennis Swales. Gary seemed to think Swales was still holed-up on the Warren, where his ex-wife and kids lived. They discussed the possibility of banging on a few doors to flush him out. But Swales could wait, being way down the list of priorities.

Gary was more interested in the landlord and the potential of his yacht.

'What's he like?'

'Bit of a whinger. Wife died of cancer a while back.'

'Any debts, loans, that sort of thing?'

'He's in over his head trying to run that pub. Scallies off the estate coming in at weekends playing him up. I offered him some extra help to sort it out.'

'That's good, yeah. Next time you go in, sound him out about that yacht. Just say a mate of yours is looking for charters.'

He hung up, vexed in some way. Now, as well as chasing bad debts he'd become Gary's errand boy, buttering up the landlord for future use. But old bonds of loyalty were hard to break. Him and Gary went back a long way. And Gary knew some serious people.

7
Fish

Drawing up at the Viewpoint, he turned off the ignition. Beneath the wooded slope, the city lay like a shroud. Further out, beyond the docks, a grey expanse of sea, merging with the clouds. Years ago he used to bring Eileen and pester her for sex, frustrated by the knockback she gave him and the feistiness she always displayed whenever they were together. Then later, married with kids, he'd come here to think, put his life into some kind of context without interruptions from other people.

A light brown Sherpa van pulled in and parked along the way. The driver wound down the window and sparked a tab – a vision in paint-splattered overalls. Apart from the few stationary vehicles between them they were alone. A moment to savour, after stewing it over in a prison cell for so long.

Easing himself out, he turned up his collar and tugged his cap down low over his eyes, coming up behind the Sherpa on the driver's blind side.

'Well, look at this,' he said. 'Fancy meeting you here, Dennis.'

A waft of stale tobacco and alcohol drifted from the open window. The fella's eyes registered shock, a sudden vision of his own mortality.

'Billy.'

'That's right, pal. Me in the flesh. Come to collect me dues like the Grim Reaper.'

The fella couldn't seem to find his voice; all that came out was a strangled gurgle. In legal parlance he was caught bang to rights. There'd be no serving of writs or court-appointed brief to help him, but he would have the right of appeal – a formality granted all wayward debtors before they got what was coming.

'I left a card with that bat-eared mother of yours. Did you not get the message?'

'I was gonna come and see you, Billy, honest I was. Gizmo told me you was out and – '

'Never mind that. How we gonna resolve this issue without you losing teeth?'

'I was hoping you might gimme a bit longer. I've just had some cash-flow problems lately, that's all.'

'You know your problem, Dennis? You've told so many fuckin lies you wouldn't know the truth if it jumped up and down on your head.'

Some people deserved a good slap. You could take great pleasure in watching them squirm, knowing what the final outcome would be when they'd run out of excuses. But Dennis had survived thus far – not through stealth or cunning, but by his own insignificance. You simply couldn't look at the fella without feeling sorry for him in some way.

'What you got round your place?'

'Huh?'

'The debt's long overdue, Dennis. I need summat you can put up as collateral.'

A gander in the back of the van revealed no great Aladdin's Cave – a few paint tins, mini generator and a rolled up carpet.

'How about a fish tank?'

'A what?'

'I keep tropical fish at home. Tetras, Barbs, that sorta thing.'

'How much's it worth?'

'Dunno. Couple hundred, I s'pose.'

He thought of all the wasted time, running around after the likes of Swales when the debt was so small it was hardly worth bothering with. But there was a principle at stake, a reputation to uphold.

'You're lucky I'm in a good mood, fella – know what I'm saying?'

'Yeah, yeah.'

'But if there's one thing in this world I know fuck all about, it's fish.'

'Oh, there's nothing to it, Billy. The pump and filter keep the water clean. And feeding's cheap, just a few flakes out the tub and some other stuff.'

Down in the valley, the houses were lit up like embers on the hillside. Parkway South – the Devil's workshop. A real collection of chancers and undesirables, all gathered together in the ale-houses and the working men's clubs that no law on earth could hope to contain. Random scenes flashed up from memory – kicking doors in and beating fellas in front of their wives and children; the aura of fear he created whenever he stepped onto the street. There had to be something else out there, a better way of employing his skills and expertise.

Looking at Dennis, he almost felt pity, like you would for some hopelessly inadequate life form trying to stay afloat. But the fella did have talents in other areas that might be put to good use.

'Still drink up the club do you, Dennis?'

'Sometimes.'

'What about that Jason fella, Pauline's cousin, know him do you?'

Dennis shook his head, the willingness to comply defeated for the moment.

'Well you find out anything about him – anything at all, you let me know, alright?'

'Yeah, sure, Billy.'

'Right, let's have a look at that fish tank.'

8

The Birdman of Alcatraz

'What's that?' Eileen said.

'The latest in home entertainment, doll.'

'What the fuck's it doing in here?'

He told her about his little run-in up at the Viewpoint. How the Swales fella had donated the fish tank as an act of goodwill. She didn't seem too pleased with the explanation.

'Who's gonna clean it?'

'That's the beauty of it. It don't need cleaning. That's what the pump and filter's for.'

She watched the fish swimming and shook her head. He'd hoped the soothing gurgle from the tank might have induced the same tranquillity in her as it did in him, but it didn't seem to be the case.

'What about feeding 'em?' she said. 'I'm not doing it.'

'It's just a few flakes from the tub, that's all. The fella showed me.' He pointed out the glass and the coloured stones, the Siamese Fighting Fish with its impressive red and blue fan. 'I mean, look at it, doll. Think of the pleasure you'll get of an evening.'

'Pleasure you'll get, you mean!'

He felt a strange empathy with the fish, the feeling he could watch them for hours and not get bored. He'd been a prisoner, too, and knew what it took to acclimatise to long periods of confinement. Maybe the fish couldn't tell the difference between the glass cage they were in and the tropical paradise they'd originated from. Most likely they'd been bred in captivity anyway, so it wouldn't make much difference. The trick was to blank it out in your mind, something he'd learned in solitary. Even in a prison cell it was possible to transport yourself over the wall and a million miles away where the screws couldn't get at you. Hours spent revisiting the past – sitting by the canal bank with a fishing rod and a tub of sandwiches, or bunking-in the Gaumont Cinema with a gang of mates. The mind had doors, too. You just had to learn how to open them.

Eileen brought tea in his favourite Man United mug. He gave her arse a playful slap as she walked away, but she didn't seem too happy with that either. Here he was, ensconced in his castle, the ordinary domestic setting lulling him into a false sense of security. The two of them bickering as always – this time over a fish tank, of all things! Fresh out the factory and already he was getting soft. The daily regime of weights and push-ups he'd kept up in the jail, sacrificed for bacon sarnies and the occasional walk with the dog. A definite weakness in him he had to overcome.

He heard her yapping on the phone in the front room. Strange, this need she had to talk to someone she'd already seen that morning. If he called Gary up with the same regularity the fella would think there was something wrong with him.

She came in and took his empty mug away.

'Who was that?' he said.

'Pauline.'

'What the two of you cooking up now?'

'Nothing, we were just talking.'

'What's wrong with talking to me for a change?'

'I would if I could get any sense out of you.'

The fish looked happy enough, darting about in the tank, multi-coloured fantails catching the light. Perhaps if he fed them every day and talked to them like people talked to plants they'd develop a bond with him. He could study them and become an expert like the Birdman of Alcatraz. Instead of sparrows and finches, his specialist subject would be tetras and Siamese Fighting Fish. He could write books and go on TV.

Eileen sat in the armchair, and drummed her fingers on the armrest. She switched her attention from the fish tank to him, a look he recognised as a prelude to something serious.

'What's up?' he said.

She stopped the drumming and sniffed.

'I'm going up to see Tommy on Friday.'

He processed the news without reacting.

'I just wanted you to know so you don't get funny about it later.'

He shrugged. 'Do what you want. I got nothing to say to him.'

The photo of Tommy caught his eye, something he'd deliberately blanked out since he'd come out the factory. The kid's face seemed to mock him, eyes narrowed and full of spite. He'd done all he could to treat the kid fairly – only beating him when he deserved it. But in the end it was the only thing the kid seemed to understand.

'I don't want him bad-mouthing me while you're up there,' he said.

'Why does it always have to be about you? Can't you think of someone else for a change?'

The fantail switched direction in the tank; in the background the pleasant hum of the filter. He pictured Tommy as a little kid, pedalling his trike up and down the drive like a mad thing. The adult version was an altogether different proposition, hard and aggressive without any saving graces. Something had happened in the transitional stage that couldn't be recovered.

He pictured St Anthony's with its hand-worn pews and soft lighting, the dim confessional.

'Talk about me when you see the father, do you?' he said.

'I've better things to talk about than you.'

'Like what – all the fellas you been dancing with up the club on a Saturday night?'

'Oh, put a cork in it, for fuck sake.'

'Put a cork in you in a minute, sweetheart.'

He'd read somewhere that women were better at hiding things than men. They could keep an affair going and run the house without causing undue suspicion. And with a husband locked up for several years, who's only source of information was the prison grapevine, she had the distinct advantage. Who was going to tell him his missus was shagging someone else? He'd seen fellas lose it in a matter of minutes once they'd heard the news, smashing their cells up and taking it out on their pad mate.

Eileen stood. 'I'm away over to Gemma's. Anything you want bringing back?'

'Don't be too long, I might want me cocoa a bit early tonight.'

'Make it yourself then, can't you.'

He took hold of her hand as she walked past, gazed up at her.

'Are we all right, doll – me and thee?'

'We will be if you stop keeping on all the time.'

The front door clicked shut and she was gone.

On a whim, he went upstairs and started rooting through the drawers and wardrobes in the bedroom. Maybe he'd find something incriminating, a link to all the devious behaviour she'd been engaging in lately. All he found were boxes filled with old makeup cases and shoes, a stack of women's magazines and old birthday cards from Siobhan and the kids – even one from him going back years, with a cryptic message written in his spidery, almost illegible handwriting.

Searching the room gave him a strange, almost sexual thrill. Justifiable to a point, but where did you draw the line? People who indulged in that kind of behaviour belonged to a class he despised.

Years ago when they were kids, him and Jimmy Tibbs came across an old fella in the park, pulling his meat. 'Touch it,' the old fella said, and Jimmy went over, getting right up close before losing his bottle and running away. They came back with Jimmy's older brother, armed with sticks and a tyre lever, but the old fella had gone.

Later, he came across them in the jail, the perverts and the kiddie-fiddlers whose crimes sickened everyone. And like all the other cons, he took great pleasure in abusing them at every opportunity. Some came on the wing under false pretences, claiming they were in for driving offences or such like. They were always found out in the end, either exposed by a screw or someone who knew who they really were. Anytime they were stupid enough or unlucky enough to end up in population they could expect the same treatment. The only time they could feel comfortable was on the numbers where they could mix with their own.

Jail – a simplified, stripped-down version of life outside.

Everyone fitted somewhere on the scale – the armed robbers and lifers at the top, grasses, nonces and bent coppers at the bottom. That was the way it was and always would be.

He found a box at the top of the wardrobe and opened the lid. Beneath a thin paper covering, intricate patterns woven into the lace, was Eileen's wedding dress. Seeing it there all folded and neat took him back, a strange feeling of yearning and regret. Things had been different then. They'd been happier. None of that depressing business with Tommy.

Eileen came back to find him laid out on the sofa, weary from his exertions.

'How's Gemma?' he said.

'If you'd come with me you could've asked her yourself.'

'I went the other day, didn't I?'

'You've been once since you got out. How d'you think she feels? Her own father, too lazy to get up off his arse and see her.'

She took off her coat, and blew her nose into a tissue.

'Coming down with summat, luv?'

'Get no sympathy from you if I was, would I?' She sat in the armchair, and warmed her hands by the fire.

He felt a kernel of guilt for his neglect; he had only been round once, it was true. But he hadn't felt comfortable. Sat there with a cup of tea and a slice of lemon cake, listening to Gemma chumming Luke's dad because he'd come round and helped do the place up. Didn't seem right, what with her own father being upriver at the time. What could he do to help?

'Remember our wedding day?' he said.

'Aye – and what a success that was, the police were only called once.'

He pictured the hotel, the bar, the crisp white tablecloths. 'I can just see us all now. Me and you. Your ma and the old fella. Jimmy downing the whisky cause he was terrified of making a speech.'

'Well I'm glad you've got such fond memories of it. I'm going to bed.'

He watched the fish complete their endless circuits back and forth. They looked happy enough, even in such a confined space. Perhaps they were glad to be shot of their previous owner, the hapless fly-by-night Dennis Swales, a man who would gladly sell his own mother. Being coldblooded, fish didn't have emotions. They didn't overreact when someone made a chance remark, or sulk for three days because someone forgot to feed them. Humans were complex creatures by comparison, prone to all kinds of vices and liabilities.

The wedding dress was a link to the past, a place he could never revisit. But the memories were there, seeped into the core of him. All the people he'd ever known who'd ever meant anything to him, some of whom had died, or moved on and were living somewhere else. Thinking about them caused him sadness, like it did when he heard a song on the radio and was transported back. They were gone, but somehow they were still with him. All stored in the top box, the main computer.

9

Road Rage

What a sight to behold, delivered kicking and screaming in the early hours – a tiny, screwed up face, eyes shut tight at the strange new world. The first thing he did was count all her digits to make sure they were all there. Satisfied everything was in place, he could relax a bit more and enjoy the show. And lying there, cradling the little bundle in her arms, exhausted but happy, was his Gemma, the trauma of her recent upheaval conveniently forgotten.

Touching one of the tiny fingers, he felt an overwhelming joy, a genuine love that transcended all else and left him weepy-eyed like the womenfolk. 'Looks like your mam first thing in the morning!' he said, getting a pained laugh from Gemma. Eileen ignored him, beaming down at the precious bundle from the other side of the bed. Grandmother for the third time she was used to it, joining a long line of matriarchs used to taking over while the menfolk were detained elsewhere.

And there by the fruit and the magazines and the well-wishers cards was Luke, the proud father, looking like he'd been through twelve hours of labour instead.

'What's it like to be a daddy, then, son?'

'Dunno, Billy. It ain't sunk in yet.'

'It will do when you're clearing up the mess up at three in the morning, that's for sure.'

'Listen to it.' Eileen rolled her eyes. 'The man who never changed a nappy in his friggin life!'

The nurse came in with a bunch of flowers sent up from

reception. Taking advantage of the distraction, he grabbed Luke's arm and steered him towards the door. Eileen clocked them and fixed him with the evil eye.

'Where d'you think you're going?'

'Taking the lad outside to get some air. He's come over a bit queer with all the excitement.'

They sought refuge in the public bar of the King George. A few codgers in tweed jackets and flat caps sat around drinking stout by the open fire. Faded fleur-de-lis wallpaper hinted at better days, when the pub had been a mecca for pleasure-seeking youngsters. Now they could celebrate proper. The next generation of the Riley clan, born with all limbs and faculties intact. She'd never want for anything, fussed over and adored by countless relatives from both sides of the water.

He raised his glass in a toast. 'To Charlotte-Marie. Health, wealth and happiness all her days!' They drank to the little one, watched by the old boys at the bar. Luke still had the glazed, contented look of fatherhood, not quite reconciled to his new position. And he, Billy Riley, felt a strong bond with the lad, pleased to have him as part of the family.

'I'm happy for you, son,' he said. 'Real happy.'

Luke grinned sheepishly. 'Did you feel like this when Gemma was born?'

'Can't remember, son. I was banged up in Leicester at the time.'

The birth of each of his children had been marred by calamity of some sort. Court cases and jail sentences. Months spent on remand waiting for a hearing. The time he'd gone on the run and ended up in Dublin with Eileen's mad Uncle Pat. But dwelling on the past put a dampener on things, threatened to spoil the lad's day. Hopefully, the new-born would take a different path and never experience a taste of blarney. There were opportunities for the young that hadn't been there in his day. Computer courses and stints at university. A step up the corporate ladder. He might have fancied a crack at it himself back in the day, had he not been busy grafting.

Formalities over, more serious issues had to be addressed. With a friendly arm around the lad's shoulders he began the spiel.

'Listen, son. I'm only gonna say this once and then it's out the way …' In fairness, the lad took it well, swearing on the baby's life that he wouldn't dream of causing grief to Gemma or the newborn, and intended from there on to do everything he could to make them happy. All he'd ever wanted was a family of his own, the lad said, and with such sincerity it fair brought a tear to his own eye. 'You're a good kid,' he said, giving the lad a hug. 'I knew you was alright when our Gemma brought you up the nick to visit me.'

Enthused with whisky and a warm happiness, he allowed himself to relax. This was progress. Fresh out the factory and toasting the birth of a new grandchild. An image of the bab lying in Gemma's arms to remind him of his filial responsibilities. One day they'd build a shrine to him for all his efforts. He, who'd risen from the pit of defeat to overcome setbacks and trials, committed to building a better future for his family. 'The sun always shines on the righteous, son. Remember that and you'll be alright.'

He figured he was doing the lad a favour, schooling him in the ways of the world. Gemma was his daughter and he loved her more than his own life, but where women were concerned you had to draw boundaries or they took advantage. The lad lacked experience, sheltered by his ma and pa for too long like so many other kids his age. The work ethic, bred into them by schoolteachers and careers advisors, who touted the same message: the only way you could find fulfilment in this life was by lining someone else's pockets.

'How much you pulling in on the tarmac?' he said.

'About three-hundred a week.'

'Manage alright on that, do you?'

'Sort of.'

'Good, coz it's your round. Get 'em in, son!'

He thought back to his early days of gainful employment before he went on the rob. Up and down a ladder all day keeping three brickies going, sweat pouring off him like a drain. The ganger said he was the best labourer they'd ever had, and even kept his job open while he did a stint upriver.

The barman brought drinks and a bag of pistachios. Now they

could begin the celebrations proper.

'Good health, son.'

'And you, Billy.'

They touched bottles in the gloomy light. He grabbed a handful of nuts and thought about Eileen. Hard work getting the lad to open up about anything. Maybe he had a reason to stay quiet. Something to hide, perhaps.

'Been up the club lately?' he said.

'Went a few weeks back. Me, Gemma and a couple of friends.'

'Eileen go?'

'No.'

'She get up there much while I was away?'

'Dunno, Billy.'

'What about the casino?'

'We went once on Gemma's birthday. Eileen won twenty-eight quid on the blackjack.'

He saw them out together, laughing and joking, Eileen under the lustful eyes of predatory men.

Forcing the thought from his mind, he finished his pint.

'Come on then,' he said. I'll drop you back at the hospital.'

Driving back through town, he felt better. Sixties classics played on the radio. Beside him, his future son-in-law and drinking partner, the two of them newly acquainted. Nostalgia merged with the breeze, a feeling of optimism that things were going to turn out all right.

A black Ford Escort shot out from the next junction and eased into the traffic, hip-hop music pounding inside.

'Look at that cunt,' he said. 'Total lack of concern for other road users.'

He stayed close to the Ford all the way to the lights. The driver kept touching his brakes, and clocking them in the rear view mirror.

Luke put one hand on the dash, angling his body in anticipation.

'Slow down a bit, Billy.'

He glanced at the lad, mildly disappointed at his lack of enthusiasm.

'I can't have it, son. Let one go, they'll all be queuing up to have a crack – know what I'm saying.'

Pulling up behind the Ford, he clocked the kid through the back window. His brains had obviously been scrambled by the music – gangster rap like some of the cons used to pump out up the factory. The kid stared back through the rear-view mirror and their eyes met. For a second there was a distant connection between them; a link from the streets and the alleyways; generations of brawn and testosterone, recycled and fed back into the system.

The lights changed and the kid pulled away, giving him a brazen middle finger in the mirror. He gave chase, enjoying the rush. The code he lived by demanded it of him. Let no insult be borne without payback. And with his future son-in-law beside him, witness to everything, he couldn't afford to show weakness.

At Bird's Hill lights the Ford was forced to stop, stuck in a long line of traffic.

Unclipping the seatbelt, he opened the door and made to get out. Luke stared at him in disbelief.

'What you doing, Billy?'

'Just wait here.'

Marching over to the Ford, he wrenched open the door, fist drawn back in anticipation. The kid behind the wheel let out a strangled gasp and backed off, hands up in a gesture of surrender.

Way back in the queue, a horn blared.

The lights turned green.

Traffic began to crawl forward.

Adrenalin pumping, he hesitated, caught in a moment's indecision. The kid's eyes locked onto his, a silent plea for mercy.

All anger drained out of him. Stepping back, he pointed a warning finger. 'Watch your fuckin manners, son. Next time you'll be chewing tarmac!'

He dropped Luke back at the hospital, and headed back towards the Parkway. The incident with the Ford played over in his mind, overshadowing the birth of his grandchild. A moment of rashness that could have jeopardised his liberty and had him sent back upriver.

But far worse was the kid's face, his earlier bravado replaced with fear.

No getting away from it. The kid had reminded him of Tommy.

10

Vesuvius

The dog settled into its usual, loping stride, head down, muscular haunches rocking from side to side. The stub of its tail amused him, stuck up from the bluff rear-end like an antenna, guiding the rolling gait and the arch of the bowed legs. A fine-looking mutt by anyone's reckoning, intent on foraging and picking up scent.

A car approached from behind; the sound registered dimly against the backdrop of his thoughts. Then he heard it. The same obnoxious drawl. The unmistakeable vein of sarcasm disguised as friendly chat.

'Morning, Billy. Nice day for it.'

He kept walking, tugging the dog lead. McGuinn's grinning face loomed on his nearside.

'Enjoying your rehabilitation in the community?'

'Up yours.'

The car crawled alongside him, a symbol of everything he found loathsome in the world. A sense of outrage grew. McGuinn, daring to accost him on his own territory, using his position to take liberties.

'Seen the news this morning?' McGuinn said.

'No, I haven't.'

'Nice little number they did on the south side last night. Smashing shop windows and turning cars over. Thought you might've been part of the wrecking crew.'

'You're wasting your time talking to me, pal – tucked-up in bed with me Ovaltine, I was.'

'Course you were. Vandalism's not really your style, is it, Billy?'

The dog stopped to cock its leg against a wall. McGuinn took advantage of the lull to press his attack.

'How's Eileen? Still having rare-ups with traffic wardens, is she?'

'Ask her your fuckin self.'

McGuinn laughed heartily. 'Nice talking to you, son. Next time you're over our way, drop in and see us. The Super'd love to see you.'

The image stayed with him all the way back, coupled with a profound sense of injustice. The dibble, taking liberties with the civilian population, trying cheap intimidation tactics on him when all he was doing was walking his dog.

Eileen noted his grim expression when he got back.

'What's up with you?' she said.

He sank into the armchair and stared at the wall. 'There oughta be a law against it.'

'Against what?'

'McGuinn, hassling me for no good reason. I see him out on his own I'll run the cunt over.' He pictured the car going up in a fireball, destroyed by a grenade or rocket launcher. McGuinn's coffin being lowered into a freshly-dug grave.

'Ignore him,' Eileen said, 'he's just trying to wind you up.'

'Wind him up in a minute. Taking it out on me coz he didn't make chief inspector!'

Giving voice to your fears increased the likelihood of them happening. He'd read that up the factory, and the theory had stuck in his mind. Better to cultivate a good defence than to wallow in thoughts of failure. The best revenge was success – he'd read that up the factory, too – but his previous record made that one a bit harder to swallow. Success, for him, meant staying on the street for as long as possible and avoiding a pull from the dibble. Nothing would frustrate the likes of McGuinn more than to see him strolling around the neighbourhood with his sovvie rings and designer jackets, fresh from a night out on the town. Revenge could also be a subtle thing that, like a good wine, took years to ferment; he'd spent many a long year plotting ways and means of getting back at someone for some perceived slight. In the end it came down to your attitude. And as the Big Fella used to say on numerous occasions, it was 'in the nut', pure and simple.

He took a bath to unwind, soaking in the froth from one of Eileen's many herbal concoctions. Simple pleasures in life that people took for granted. Eating a meal without the clamour of leery men to invade your privacy. Locking your own door at night, instead of being banged-up by some over-zealous toe-rag with personality problems. These things mattered more when you had the time to dwell on them. All that wasted opportunity. All those calendar years spent lying on a prison mattress dreaming of going over the wall.

The dog lay curled by the fire, legs outstretched in a parody of rigor mortis. Eileen rattled around in the kitchen, clearing up the debris. He'd forgotten what a workhorse she was, always on the go like her old ma, washing and tidying, polishing work surfaces. The place was spotless – like a show house for McCarthy's – but somehow it would never be good enough.

Later, she settled down to watch *Coronation Street*, the nightly ritual she rarely missed. He joined her on the new recliner sofa she'd got from a credit card scam. Like sinking into marshmallow – an experience in itself after five years up the factory.

'You didn't tell me you'd been up the casino?' he said.

'What?'

'The lad told me. Said you won twenty-eight quid on the blackjack.'

'That was ages ago.'

'What else you been hiding from me?'

'I'm trying to watch the telly, for fuck sake!'

He put an arm around her and kissed her neck. She pulled back irritably. Ignoring her resistance he slid a hand under her top. She tried to wriggle away, but he pressed on regardless, freeing the button on her jeans and easing down her zip. The struggle intensified. He forced himself upon her, biting her neck and pinning her down with his superior weight. Freeing one arm, she slapped his face and swore at him, heightening his arousal.

Then the dog barked and broke his concentration. Seizing the moment, she cracked him on the head with the remote control and sat back with a look of victory. 'There!' she said. 'Will you leave me the fuck alone now!'

As a means of communion, romping on the sofa had its drawbacks. The damage in this case was minimal but it could have been worse. In previous skirmishes she'd blacked his eye and split his lip; the volatile Irish in her coming to the fore, always ready to defend her honour.

'Is that the way for a grandmother to behave?' he said, rubbing his head.

'That's what you get for being an arsehole.'

Later, in the master bedroom, he managed to rectify his failed attempt on the sofa. They went at it like porn stars beneath the lights. For one sublime moment they were joined in a passionate embrace, her urgency and need matching his own.

Lying back, purged of his demons, he was filled with a sense of peace and harmoniousness instead. Eileen lay beside him, looking up at the ceiling.

'We should do this more often,' he said.

'What – you jumping all over me while I'm trying to watch the telly?'

She got up and strode over to the dresser, parading her naked-ness in front of him without shame. He watched, fascinated, as she fastened her bra. All the times she must have done the same thing before, alone in the house without him.

'Did you perform like that with anyone else while I was away?' he said.

She half-turned to stare at him, the clasp still undone.

'What?'

'Just a thought.'

She fixed her bra, and grabbed her top, pausing to look back at him from the door.

'I can't be done with all this, you know. You need to sort yourself out.'

'I just did, didn't I?'

'Don't be getting clever with me, it's not even funny.'

He dressed and went downstairs. She was on the phone in the kitchen, and changed her tone when he walked in, talking about Gemma and the baby in an unnaturally pleasant voice. Finally, she hung up.

'Who was that?' he said, buttoning the sleeves of his shirt.

'Pauline.'

'You spinning me a line, or what?'

'I'll call her back, shall I – you can ask her your friggin self!'

He sat in the armchair and stared at the TV, his gaze drawn to the photo of Tommy on the dresser. The kid in the Ford had looked just like him – a real shock to the system when he'd wrenched open the door to pan the little fucker.

Eileen came in and sank down onto the sofa, their little interlude now over. She hadn't mentioned Tommy at all, as if it hadn't happened.

'How did the visit go?' he said.

'I thought you didn't want to talk about it?'

'I'm just asking.'

She aimed the remote, and turned on the TV. 'They're moving him, but he's not sure when. Somewhere down south, probably.'

Memories from his teenage years. The pale, Victorian grimness of Portland Borstal rising above the high wall, as him and a handful of lads were transported up the hill in a prison van. His sentence of nine-months to two-years meant more discipline, more punishment from the screws and more contempt for the system that had already labelled him a common criminal.

'Long way to go to visit,' he said. 'Hope he appreciates it.'

'I'm his mother, aren't I? What am I supposed to do, abandon him completely?'

He felt bad for not going, but it was a matter of principle. Ever since Tommy stuck the nut on him in the front garden things had never been the same. Connor was different, a quiet lad with an eye on the future. Tommy had to learn the hard way, just as his father had to all those years ago.

'You want to know what else Pauline said?'

He looked up, intrigued.

'What?'

'That journalist fella's been in the Grafton again. Gizmo thinks you should have a word with him.'

'What for?'

'How should I know? Go and ask him.'

The thought ate away at him. Ever since he'd first heard of the journalist fella, and Sonia throwing a drink in his face. Something hadn't seemed right. With Leonard gone only six months, his family would still be grieving – although Sonia had the consolation of inheriting the house and the bars and clubs he'd owned. The media interest in him had died away, or so it seemed.

But there was another angle that couldn't be ignored. The undeniable glimmer of opportunity. If these filmmaker types had money to throw around, who was he to stop them?

11

The Journalist Fella

He found Gizmo at the fruit machine, feeding coins into the eager slot. All around him, the Saturday afternoon crowd, getting a few ales in before the Three o'clock kick-off. Approaching the fella in this condition was like interrupting an angry bull elephant in mid-charge.

'What's up, Giz – doing the housekeeping money again?'

'I hate this fuckin thing. I'll rip its guts out, I will!'

Face all twisted at the heartless machine, Gizmo gripped the sides and shook it, cursing it as he might a fella. Lights flashed and reels span; glimpses of cherries and apples clicked to a stop behind the glass panel.

'Maybe you should try bingo with Pauline,' he said. 'Be a lot easier on the old blood pressure.'

Gizmo grabbed his pint and marched off towards the bar. Watching the fella go, he found it hard to understand that strange and self-destructive urge that prompts a man to shut himself off from human contact and give his earnings to a machine.

At last the fella calmed down. They talked of other things: the ascendancy of Arsenal in the Premiership, and the dominance of foreign players. The good old days, and trips down south with the Red Army, taking on London's finest. And he, Billy Riley, fresh out the factory, looking to stake his claim.

Gizmo apologised for his earlier rant, now returned to a state of relative humility.

'Good to see you, Billy. It's been quiet round here without you.'

'That's what McGuinn said when I last saw him. But here I am, bold as you like. So what's been happening?'

The city had changed, even in five years, with wine bars and restaurants opening up along the waterfront. Not like it was in Leonard's day when many of these places were off-limits. Most of the old faces had gone; looking round, he recognised the odd die-hard among them – regulars from the terraces and after drinking sessions – but the rest were all new. He missed the buzz, the feeling of belonging. Boarding trains and coaches to cities all over the country, knowing what was waiting for you when you got to the other end.

'Get up the club much while I was away?' he said.

'Not me, Billy. I got barred two years ago, ain't been back since.'

He mentioned Eileen's late night excursion to the casino with Gemma and Luke, the fact they dropped her off at two in the morning.

'What's that all about? She fuckin hates casinos.'

Trust came at a price. You let people in and opened yourself up to all kinds of humiliation. Then you had to do your own digging to get to the truth. His last stint up the factory had affected everything. Coming out and going straight back into domestic life. Eileen, serving him up bacon sarnies and mugs of tea at the kitchen table, the jangle of key chains still fresh in his ears.

'What's the score with Pauline's cousin – this Jason fella?'

'What about him?'

'Bit of a lad, is he? Fancies himself with the women?'

Gizmo looked mystified. 'Don't know much about him, Billy. Why – what's he done?'

The football mob started to leave, checking watches and draining pints, banging the empties down on the bar. He felt the nostalgia keenly. Life had been simpler back then. Working on the buildings by day and the doors at weekends. His short but memorable stint as an honest grafter on the buildings, with a little bit of thieving in-between. Even his relationship with Eileen had seemed simpler. She was less wrapped up in her own world, more dependent on him.

'I feel like a dog chasing its tail,' he said. 'Ever since I come out the factory it's like I'm one step behind every other fucker.'

'I know the feeling, Billy.'

'You try and be nice to people and they take advantage, walk all over you.'

Gizmo nodded, not given to too much introspection. News of their lunchtime meeting would get back to Pauline, who would soon be on the blower to Eileen, slagging him off.

Gizmo nudged his arm, and nodded towards the door.

'There he is.'

A youngish couple made their way over to an alcove table and eased themselves in. The fella had on a worn leather jacket and crumpled cords. The bird had a distinctive bottle-green coat, a leopard print handbag slung over her shoulder. There was an odd defiance about them. By strolling brazenly into the Grafton they were making a statement, testing the locals.

According to Gizmo the fella had been coming in every lunchtime with his female assistant; the two of them sat in the same place, him with a pint of Guinness, her with a glass of white wine. He complimented Gizmo on his detective skills, picturing the odd couple in a place like the Grafton. As strangers they would stand out, but no one would take much notice of them as long as they kept their heads down and didn't play up.

'You talk to him?' he said.

'Couple of times. He bought me a pint once, asked if I knew where he could find accommodation for him and his bird.'

'What did you say?'

'I told him the YMCA was cheap, but the rooms were dingy. Told him he'd be better off looking for something on the waterfront. Anyway, I think he's sorted now.'

'Did he say what he's doing here?'

'Making a documentary, I think.'

'About what exactly?'

'I dunno, Billy. I didn't ask.'

Just then, the journalist fella left his perch and headed for the Gents. The perfect opportunity to get acquainted.

'Get us one in,' he said. 'I'm gonna stroke the weasel.'

The fella was standing at the trough in his faded black leather and crumpled beige cords. Stepping up beside him, he unzipped and heeded nature's call.

'Better out than in,' he said.

The fella laughed. 'All these liquid lunches, I'm afraid. I keep meaning to get some work done.'

Zipping up, he strolled to the sink. The fella came over, and washed his hands; a serious, thinker's face in the mirror, dark fringe hanging over one eye.

'Just visiting?' he said.

'Er – sort of.'

'I couldn't help noticing the accent. You're not from round here.'

'Oh, right.' The fella sounded relieved. 'I'm doing a bit of work here, actually.'

'What line you in?'

'Filmmaking.'

'What – Jurassic Park, that kinda thing?'

'Not quite on that scale, no. More along the lines of public information. We're making a documentary.' The fella had a smooth, easy-going way about him. Not the type to throw chairs through windows to make his point. But beneath the charm front there was something else. The fella knew exactly what he was doing, as if he had it all planned out.

The jet-stream from the dryer finished. The fella looked over, a glimmer of eagerness he tried to conceal. 'I saw you at the bar. Friend of Gordon's, are you?'

'Gordon?' The name threw him for a moment. Then, from the dim reaches of the past, the realisation that this strange moniker had once belonged to Gizmo. 'Oh, yeah – Gordon. I thought you were talking about someone else.'

The fella laughed, unsure of himself.

'You're a local, I take it?'

'Depends how you look at it. I've travelled a bit, had a few post codes over the years.'

He went to the door, and looked back at the journalist fella.

'Little word of advice, pal.'

The fella looked up, a flicker of concern, perhaps.

'I wouldn't have the chicken curry in here, it's diabolical.'

Gizmo was back at the fruit machine, his cheeks redder than the spinning cherries. The football mob had moved on. Like everything else, the game had changed beyond his comprehension. Gone were the days when the terraces were filled with local lads, singing and chanting all the old songs, ready to dive in en mass to defend the colours. Nowadays, CCTV recorded your every move. The place was filled with season ticket holders from out of town, munching prawn sandwiches and spilling lager on their new shoes.

The journalist fella had re-joined his assistant, the two of them waffling over the table. Several options occurred to him. He could go over and introduce himself as the one-time associate of the late Leonard Simms. Would they care for an interview? A detailed account of all the clandestine goings-on over the past three decades. The ground-breaking deal in a pub in Evesham that led to Leonard's implication in one of the biggest drug trials in British history.

Widow Sonia might have had something to say about it. Such a reckless breach of protocol from someone who should know better. Besides, there were things like your ongoing health and wellbeing to think about.

'Let me know what happens,' he said.

'What, with this?' Gizmo slapped the top of the machine. 'I'm down thirty-quid, that's what's happening!'

'I meant the journalist fella. Keep me updated.'

Still, he couldn't get the idea out of his head. The unmistakable scent of moolar drifting along on the breeze. A chance to reel in a couple of mug punters and have some fun doing it.

12
Dance Hall Days

That night, they smooched on the dance floor like they used to.
The DJ played a selection of oldies from the 60s and 70s, a time
he recalled as being the best he'd ever had. The flashing lights
and dim recesses of the club reminded him of the old Town Hall
Disco where they'd first met. Eileen, a shy and illusive four-
teen-year old, just over from Dublin, not knowing anyone outside
her immediate family. Him, fifteen, and fresh from the school
of correction, having recently fallen in with a bunch of gypsy
fellas who specialised in robbing country houses. Life looked
promising; the chance to learn new skills and pull in the denari.
And this beautiful Irish Rose he'd fallen for, with her dark looks
and sleek ponytail, necking with him at a corner table. Even back
then he'd been possessive. She was his queen and no one could
touch her. Anyone so much as looked at her and Bang! down they
went, no messing.

Soaking up the atmosphere from his seat at the back, he looked
out over the rank and file. On the far side, the old crones and their
menfolk, determined to enjoy the night's excess. Eileen went
among them in her spangled turquoise dress that shimmered
under the lights. Coy and vampish, she laughed along to the
things they said, lingering at one table before moving on to the
next. The dim lighting and pulsing music enhanced the fair sex,
any minor imperfections hidden from the watchful eye. They all
came alive for the night – even the older ones with their saggy
tits and wrinkled skin, the cracks daubed over with layers of
cheap make-up. The subterranean glow gave everyone the same

look, a seductive sleaziness to it all that added to the attraction. Later, for the lads who got lucky, it was off down some shadowy alleyway or deserted car park, aided by the twin devils of alcohol and lust. He used to envy them all from his lonely prison cell, the freedom they had that they would never truly appreciate, while he, Billy Riley, was banged up in the other place.

Sammy took to the floor, tall and bony, graceful as a snake. The old fella weaved intricate patterns on the dance floor, cheered on by his nieces, nephews and an assortment of grandchildren.

Watching Sammy, he felt mesmerised, not just by the fella's slick moves on the floor, but the lineage that went before him. All the pub fighters and grafters who swelled the jails and the institutions. Heroic stands made scrapping the dibble and anyone else who fancied a go. Growing up in these places, he, Billy Riley, had served out his apprenticeship on the frontline. But the years rolled on and everything changed. New generations came along to swell the ranks, and the old order crumbled. The club itself was a throwback to another era, when men were staunch and straight down the line. Honour among thieves existed in an unspoken form, and everyone understood the price that had to be paid for betraying a friendship.

Eileen came back and flopped down beside him.

'Any takers?' he said.

'Only Sammy, and I can do without his paws all over me.'

'I thought you liked the attention?'

'Is that what you call it?'

Supping his ale, he noted the men at the bar, small groups huddled in intimate conversation. He looked for John Pullen, the electronics expert whose business card he still had in his wallet, but saw only regulars.

With Eileen by his side he should have felt more relaxed. Instead, he felt side-lined, forced to take a back seat and observe the proceedings. He couldn't work her out. This secret life she had that didn't involve him; the one she'd fashioned for herself while he'd been away upriver. Their courtship had been like it, too, a strange, stop-start affair arranged through intermediaries, because her parents wouldn't let her go out on her own. Progress came slowly. The night outside the chippie in Parkway South when she let him kiss her for the first time. The touch of her skin and the smell of her perfume. The sheer joy of being huddled together in the clinch, as if no one else in the whole world existed.

'Remember the night I pushed you home in a shopping trolley?' he said.

She frowned. 'What made you think of that?'

'You know me, doll. I'm an old romantic at heart.'

'Romantic? You must be joking. The only reason you do anything nice for me is to get your friggin end away!'

The courtship ritual went on. After weeks of him pestering, she finally gave him her phone number and made him swear he'd hang up if her da answered. After that they were inseparable, a proper couple, parted for the first time by his borstal training at the age of seventeen. Over time, she got used to his increasingly frequent trips upriver, even bringing him cakes and sundries her ma had made because the old girl had taken a shine to him. But the time they spent apart put increasing pressure on them and their marriage. Whenever he came out after a stretch inside, they had to start all over again.

Looking out at the menfolk he felt again that stab of doubt. Who among them might be his usurper, challenger to his domain.

'The Jason fella not in tonight?' he said.

'How should I know?'

'I thought he was a regular?'

'Sorry – I left me crystal ball at home.' She stared at him resentfully. 'What you asking me for?'

Supping the ale quietly, his mood slipped down a long, dark tunnel. Something didn't seem right. He didn't quite know what it was but it ate away at him like a bad case of indigestion. Maybe the Jason fella had been warned off; Eileen had made a phone call to Pauline to say they were coming up. Whatever it was it put a cold, hard feeling inside him, the way he always felt as he prepared to go to war and defend his territory.

Soon it was time for the slow numbers. The opening chords sparked an instant rush for the dance floor. Looking over at Eileen, he felt the pain of his loss. She was his wife, his childhood sweetheart, but her thoughts and her loyalty were somewhere else.

The lights came on. Bodies rose from the tables to begin the exodus. Eileen stood, and smoothed out the creases from her dress.

'Come on, then,' she said. 'Let's make a move.'

'I'm finishing me drink.'

'Well don't be too long, I wanna let the dog out in the garden when we get back.'

Tossing back the dregs, he stood. Eileen strolled ahead of him towards the stairs, hips swaying in her glitzy skirt. The group at the bar watched her go by, a glint of desire in their collective expression; a smirk or two barely hidden.

As he passed by, he saw what he had to do. Snatching up a beer bottle from the bar, he smashed it over the nearest fella's head and stepped neatly back out of range, ready for battle.

'Come on, you fuckin useless wankers – who's next!'

The act started a riot; the women shrieked and the menfolk pitched in to assist their wounded comrade. He fought them all under the harsh white lights, seized with a passion reminiscent of the great tear-ups of his youth. With fists and feet, knees and elbows, tables overturned and glass under feet, he put them all to flight, soaring on a wave of drunken vitality.

Eileen stepped in, screaming and beating him with her bony fists. 'Stop, you mad bastard! Stop!' But he couldn't stop, not for her or for anybody. Each futile blow somehow confirmed his victory, that whatever the outcome he'd made his stand and shown them his mettle.

The taxi driver looked on in shock as they fell through the exit, silent witness to the strange goings on between married couples. Eileen ceased her attack, the last of her energy used up in muttered insults and acid glances. The only downside, as he could see it, was the few splashes of blood on his clean white shirt that kind of spoiled the evening.

'Where to, mate?' the driver said.

'Parkway South. The Crescent.'

Eileen simmered beside him, still flashing him the odd hateful look. He felt pleased with himself, vindicated. Turning forty up the factory had been a real blow to his confidence, something he felt he might not recover from. But tonight's performance proved he still had it in him. The old spark had been there all along.

'Did you like that?' he said cheerfully.

She shook her head. 'Mad bastard.'

'Plenty more where that came from, doll, don't you worry about that.'

The taxi sped on past the Exchange. Shame the Jason fella hadn't been there, he'd have copped for some as well. But at least the tussle had cleared the air. And whatever else happened, there was always the next time. Tonight's performance sent out a message, loud and clear. Mess with the Man and you could expect the same.

13

Business as Usual

The landlord looked a bit pasty, all fleshy jowls and bags under the eyes from lack of sleep. Hard to imagine any youthful vigour in that crumpled mug. No genuine exuberance or lust for life. Like most middle-aged men, the landlord had allowed himself to deteriorate gradually; leather belt fastened around his swollen gut, floral tie knotted under his shapeless chin.

But he, Billy Riley, knew the advantages of keeping schtum. It mattered not what he thought of the landlord; moral judgements were for those who could afford them. This was business, pure and simple.

'Quiet this afternoon?' he said, making conversation.

The landlord nodded grimly, a sheen of sweat on his forehead. 'We had a coach load of OAPs in earlier. More trouble than some of the youngsters.'

Rotten life for some, he thought. Every day the hole gets a little deeper. Nothing to do except piss and moan about it to the nearest individual.

'Can I get you a drink?' the landlord said.

'You most certainly can, fella. Give us a pint of that Blackmore Special.'

The landlord put his pint down and didn't ask for payment, one more gesture of goodwill to show the fella's gratitude. Now they could move stealthily towards the main event, when the landlord would provide certain details that could be absorbed and utilised later.

'Good health,' he said, raising his glass.

A few of the local lads came in, making more noise than a miner's convention. The landlord muttered under his breath and moved along to serve them.

Watching from his perch at the bar, he felt mildly amused. No one could stop the boys playing up, least of all the fat landlord. They drank their beer without a thought for anyone, revelling in their hard-earned notoriety. Then, when the time was right, they'd move on, and play up elsewhere. Until then, the landlord was stuck with them.

The fella came back and fixed him with a look of appeal. 'It's a thankless task, it really is. They don't seem to respect anything.'

'Sign of the times, fella. They're worse now than they ever were in my day, that's for sure.'

He clocked the gang of lads at the end of the bar. The loudest were rarely the most dangerous, having all the lip and nothing to back it up with. It was the quiet ones you had to watch out for, the ones at the back with the blank expressions.

Leaning on the bar, he sought the landlord's ear.

'Tell us about that yacht of yours, fella?'

The landlord scratched his head. 'Well, as I said, it's not in the water yet. And with everything else that's going on I've not had the time to think about it. Do you have an interest yourself?'

'Not me personally, but a friend of mine does.'

'The landlord opened up a bit, the subject much more to his liking. Talk of shipping lanes and tidal streams made him all glassy-eyed; memories of trips to Cherbourg and Barfleur with his late wife. 'Years ago, we used to race quite a bit – the Fastnet, Round Ireland. Of course, I was younger and fitter back then, didn't have such a paunch.'

Being of a different ilk, he couldn't share the landlord's enthusiasm. For him, the sea was an unknown entity, full of treacherous currents and monsters with sharp teeth. He only had to look at the swell from dryland to feel seasick.

'Does your friend have a yacht?' the landlord said.

'He doesn't, as it happens. But he's looking to charter one for trips up and down the coast – you know, for friends and family and the like.'

Always tight-lipped about the people he was involved with, Gary never gave too much away. But if it came off, this had the makings of a big one, and he, Billy Riley, would be there to oversee the details with his own brand of expertise.

'Give your friend my number, if you like?' the landlord said.

'I certainly will, fella. In the meantime you can make any arrangements through me. Could be a nice little touch in it for you when the bills come in.'

He drank up, eager to get on. The landlord exuded an air of gloom that infected everyone around him. Even the bar staff kept out of his way, slinking off to the kitchen and the alcoves where he couldn't find them. But the lure was there all the same, a future partnership with unlimited potential.

'Right, that's me done.' He put his empty glass on the bar. The young lads had gone, almost by osmosis, carried away to some other part of the metropolis. Without them, the bar seemed unusually quiet.

The landlord shook his hand, limply – not a man's grip but a poor imitation. But now they'd established a bond, a means of communication, and that's all that counted.

About to go, he thought of something else.

'If you're ever in need of female company of an evening, give us a shout. I know a couple of live ones who could sort you out.'

The landlord smiled sadly. 'Thanks, I'll bear that in mind.'

Out on the forecourt, he called Gary. It felt good to be involved in something enterprising again, instead of mooching round at home and chasing bad debts for local companies. A reminder of the old days working for the Big Fella, when life was filled with opportunity. You woke up and leapt out of bed, eager to get on with it.

Carpe diem.

14

Rosalyn

A girl came strolling along pushing a buggy, her face framed in the fur-lined hood of a parka. He thought he recognised her, but couldn't be sure. The last time he'd seen her she was a schoolgirl with freckles and prominent teeth. The lass pushing the buggy was older, seventeen or eighteen at least.

She passed by, tall and gangly, too preoccupied to notice him and the dog. He took a moment to catch-on, stirred by memories of the vibrant past.

'Rosalyn?'

She stopped, and peered back at him, a mixture of suspicion and fear.

'Who are you?'

'I'm the truant officer, sweetheart. Word is you've been jibbing off school.' He grinned good-naturedly, hoping she might appreciate the joke. She rocked the kiddie's buggy back and forth, observing him with a curious but defiant frown. He liked her instinctively for some reason. She had a kind of dignity about her, an inner poise that couldn't be shaken.

'Don't you recognise me?' he said.

'No?'

'I used to knock about with your old fella. Came round your gaff a few years back and watched the World Cup Final. Brazil won 3 − 2 on penalties. Remember that?'

She looked at him as if he were a few bricks short.

'Where you heading?' he said.

'Over the park – see me nan.'

'I'll walk with you, if you like? I'm going your way.'

More images from the distant past. A row of semi-detached council houses on the Parkway, neat little alleyways tucked in between. Jimmy Tibbs's living room with its glazed tiled fireplace and hard-sprung sofa; a bunch of young lads smoking tabs and planning their next juvenile excursion; Jimmy's mum coming in with the lemonade and biscuits. Those days were long gone, but the thoughts conjured up a painful nostalgia.

'How old's the sprog?' he said.

'Coming up two.'

'Don't look too happy, does he?'

'He's alright – aren't you, darlin?' She leaned over the buggy and made a face at the little kiddie who stared vacantly back. Nothing quite like the bond between mother and child, especially when it eased the man out of the picture. Sometimes it seemed that was all they wanted. Leave school, have a kid and go on welfare. They might not even know or care who the father was.

The buggy rolled on towards the cemetery, gravestones pale and speckled in the morning light. One more day on the Parkway, where the resident pond-life rose from its slumber, yawned, stretched and mutated into something else.

They passed the Boys Club on the corner, a shrine to his youth. He'd been good even then. The skinniest kid on the block with the most to prove, dancing round the ring doing his best Muhammad Ali impersonation.

'I grew up in that place,' he said. 'Used to get the crap knocked outta me regular. Toughened me up, though – know what I'm saying?'

She shot him a cautious look. 'Can you lend me a tenner till Friday?'

'Do what?'

'I'll pay you back, honest.'

He walked beside her, the dog straining to get ahead. Rosalyn quickened her pace, jaw set, resolute. He couldn't believe the nerve of the girl, asking him for money.

'Know what I do for a living?' he said.

'What?'

'I chase bad debts. Knock on people's doors, shake 'em up summat rotten.'

'So?'

'I'm just telling you, Rosalyn. You borrow money off me, I'll have to charge interest. Then, when you don't pay it back, I'll have to come looking for you. And you wouldn't want that, would you, sweetheart?'

Rosalyn's fingers gripped the handles of the buggy, her knuckles white. He clocked her face to see if she'd been listening.

'Damage limitation, we used to call it. Every now and then I'd have to give someone a slap to set an example.'

'You touch me I'll call the police.'

He laughed at her front, the way she rolled her lower lip and glared at him. And yet somewhere within that gawky adolescent frame was a streetwise kid, with an awareness of her actions and the likely consequences. She'd grown up on one of the roughest estates around and spent her formative years in the company of crackheads and villains. Not the kind of upbringing Jimmy would have wanted for his daughter.

'When was the last time you saw your old fella?' he said.

She thought about it, the buggy wheels grinding ever onward. 'When I were about twelve, I think. He went to live with some woman in Macclesfield when me mum kicked him out.'

He understood the bitterness and the aggravation, having spent half his life in a similar predicament – only in his case it had been jail cells and long periods of incarceration. Jimmy wasn't the type to maintain close family relations either, always susceptible to the booze and the charms of the ladies. But news of his death had come as a shock, delivered thirdhand on a prison landing.

'Got a boyfriend?' he said.

A flicker of suspicion. 'No, why?'

'Just making conversation, sweetheart.'

She sniffed, her eyes on the babe who stared back beneath layers of swaddling.

'What about the kiddie's father – still see him, do you?'

'He's in prison.'

'What for?'

'Burglary.'

He thought about Jimmy. How they used to skip school and head off down the valley, follow the stream as far as it would go. Neither of them prepared for what lay ahead.

'Maybe you need a change of scenery,' he said.

'What d'you mean?'

'Get away from that fuckin rat-hole you're living in. Go somewhere half decent, just you and the kiddie.'

'Why would you care what I do?'

'Because I'm a caring person, Rosalyn. Can't you tell by looking at me?'

The Boys Club had passed from view, but its spirit stayed with him. His old fella had taken him there when he was a kid, hoping it might instil some discipline in him. The same old fella who came clumping up the stairs in his work boots after a night on the ale, lashing out with his big knuckled fists. They all got it eventually, all six of them – including him, Billy Riley, the youngest and most vulnerable member of the pack. He learned how to soak up punishment without making a fuss. Battered by a fist or a leather belt. Recoiling from the old fella's whiskey breath and promises of retribution.

Sober, the old fella weren't too bad. The drink brought out the worst in him. But he did have principles of a kind. Life was hard. In order to survive you had to get accustomed to it sooner or later. And God help you if you came home crying 'cause you'd taken a beating from some kid at school. You'd get another one from the old fella for being a wuss.

The park had featured in his childhood, too. A layer of frost sparkled on the grass and the climbing frames in the play area, giving it a magical, winter feel. At night the dealers and the gangs moved in, using the various exits as escape routes from the dibble.

They stopped at the shiny black gates at the end, newly added since he'd been away. Rosalyn rocked the buggy, and looked at him awkwardly.

'You're not gonna report me to the Social Services, are you?'

'What – for trying to scam a tenner off me? Do me a favour,

Rosalyn.'

She looked away, unsure.

'I'd better be on me way, me nan'll wonder where I am.'

'Take care of yourself, sweetheart. I'm sure we'll run into each other again some time.'

She nodded, hesitant, not quite ready to go.

He took out his wallet, and palmed off a ten-spot. 'Here … Take it before I change me mind.'

A sudden gleam in her eye at the change in fortune. She took it from him quickly.

'When do I have to pay it back?'

'You don't, it's a freebie. I know your old fella would've done the same for one of mine.'

They parted there and then. Rosalyn took a left towards the Five-Ways. He turned right for Parkway South. It felt good to help out. Satisfied the charitable streak in him. The urge to do something for someone else without demanding payback.

15

Old School

Pullen had the gen: eight hours of surveillance over two days, including video footage, a detailed log of all known movements and a list of any contacts made. According to him, the subject had left home at 9:15 on Tuesday morning, and driven over to Terracotta Road, where she stayed for an hour. After this, she drove into the south side and parked in a multi-storey, taking the lift down into the Sovereign shopping centre. During the course of the two-day surveillance, she met four people – three women, and, on one occasion, an unidentified male, mid-to-late twenties with short, brown hair.

Studying the set of photos Pullen showed him, a sense of dismay set in. He felt stupid, caught out in some grand act of folly.

'You know who it is?' Pullen said.

'Yeah. It's my lad, Connor.'

'Your son?'

'That's right.'

Pullen scratched his head in a similar state of bemusement, his efforts having produced nothing concrete, no clear evidence as such. He was happy to continue the investigation, he said, but it would be costly. Alternatively, he could remain on standby, ready to pick up the trail again should that be necessary. 'Have a think about it,' Pullen said. 'You can always give me a call later.'

'You sure there was nothing else? A chance you could've missed something?'

'You paid for two days' surveillance, Billy, and that's what you got. If there'd been anything else I would have found it, believe me.'

He brooded on it over a full English and a mug of tea in Andy's Café. Working men drifted in from the cold, rubbing their hands and grinning with relief. The boss man took their orders with the same grim expression he wore every day, fat stains on his blue and white stripy apron. Boredom, an unavoidable part of life whatever line of work you were in. Sooner or later you were forced to wrestle with it. The weight of the machine bearing down, making all your plans obsolete.

Consumed by thoughts of Eileen, he found it hard to concentrate on the food. John Pullen's investigation hadn't yielded much, but he was convinced there was more. She'd had years to build a secret existence. Now he was back she'd have to double her efforts to keep it hidden. All he had to do was wait for her to make a mistake, then he'd pounce and confront her with the evidence.

And yet a part of him wanted to be proved wrong. To enjoy the warm, mushy feeling of contentment that came with long-term wedded bliss. A true romantic at heart, he saw himself as the gallant knight, bringing back plunder from distant lands and pledging his all to the grateful fair maiden. The reality was different, not quite the Hollywood version he had in his head, but the sentiment was there all the same.

As he pondered the iniquities of life, an old familiar face wandered in. Seeing him there in the corner, the fella came over. They shook hands firmly, two old veterans reunited after years apart.

The fella took a seat, and stared at him across the table.

'Billy Riley, as I live and breathe. Christ, man – how long's it been?'

'Too long, Dai.'

'Only seems like yesterday we were running all over town like a bunch of lunatics. Remember that coach trip to Blackpool with Pat and Jimmy?'

'I do indeed, fella. I do indeed.'

Here they were, survivors of the old school, knocking on a bit but still there. Dai looked older; his skin had taken on the waxy, industrialised pallor of the city-dweller, constantly exposed to nicotine and periods of drought. His back-combed hair, once dark and lustrous, now showed touches of grey at the roots. A good-looking lad in his youth, here he was, counting the cost of a lifetime's dissolution.

'How's your missus, Dai?'

'Working in Safeway of an evening. I don't see much of her these days.'

'Still dance the tango on a Saturday night, does she?'

Dai looked confused. 'Sorry?'

'Never mind. It's good to see you. We go back a long way, fella.'

Dai's missus had been a real goer back in the day. He recalled a summer's evening on the back seat of his car many moons ago. One of the best blowjobs he'd ever had, administered with an expertise and attention to detail found wanting in the majority of women. Shame it had to have been Dai's missus, but these things happened. Besides, he wasn't the only one. Word on the street was she was at it with half the estate.

'Still selling knock-off meat, are you, Dai?'

'Aye – and there's plenty more where that came from.'

'So I hear. Been serving up most of the women on the Parkway, haven't you?'

'My reputation goes ahead of me, Billy.'

He mentioned the landlord of the Swan, who might well become a future customer. Dai was intrigued, willing to supply as many lamb cutlets as the fella could handle. Perhaps they were on the cusp of something lucrative. With Dai's know-how and his contacts they could start a business.

'Know anything about sailing, Dai?'

'Can't say I do, why?'

'I'm thinking of taking it up as a hobby.'

'Oh, right. Bit of piracy on the high seas to make a bit extra, eh? I can just see you climbing up the rigging with a knife between your teeth. Bit like Errol Flynn but not as good looking.'

Dai laughed at his own wit, his face creasing into a myriad wrinkles. Hard to believe the fella had once been such a name on the circuit, drawing admiring glances from the women and envy from the men. Time did cruel things to people, reducing them to mere caricatures, shadows of their former selves.

Talk of the old days lost its sparkle. He couldn't raise the necessary enthusiasm. Too much regret for the years he'd been missing. And back of his mind, the nagging feeling that in spite of his claims to the contrary, John Pullen might have missed something in his two-day surveillance.

'How long you been with your missus, Dai?'

'Twenty-years this July.'

'Wow – you even remember the date.'

'Aye. Pays me to remember things like that, see?'

'And is she happy?'

'I don't know, I never asked her.'

They shared the joke, while the queue at the counter grew ever longer. Unlike him, Dai had never done a stint upriver, always on hand to keep the spark of his marriage alive. Birthdays, anniversaries; the odd box of chocolates or a bunch of flowers. Women liked these things. And if you really put your mind to it you could make restitution, pull it all back from a hopeless position.

'How about you?' Dai said. 'You must have been with Eileen since God was a boy?'

'And some, fella.'

'So what's the secret of your success?'

'I'm three seconds ahead of her when the crockery starts flying.'

The café was full of working class bods, straight off the buildings or the industrial park, eager for the scran. He couldn't identify with them. Apart from the summer he'd spent hodding bricks up a ladder, that was it. His career path had taken a different course.

Prison was a time capsule. Once inside, your previous existence ceased to be and an alternative version took over. Then, coming back from the frozen gulag you'd been shipped you off to, you found the faces had changed, and the place you'd previously occupied had been filled by somebody else.

Draining his tea, he stood. 'Better make a move, Dai. Good to see you, fella.'

'Aye – good to see you too, Billy. Say hello to Eileen for me, won't you. And if she wants a top prime cut of meat she knows where to come.'

He got a few feet away and stopped.

'What's that?'

'I said, say hello to Eileen for me.'

He tried to process the words, the tone, the look on the fella's face.

'You being funny with me, Dai?'

The fella shifted in the seat. 'No – course not.'

The moment passed. He liked Dai enough to give him the benefit of the doubt. Be a shame to steam-in to him for no real reason, what with them both going back such a long way.

'See you around, Dai.'

'Yeah, sure. Take it easy, Billy.'

Outside in the cold morning air, he turned up his collar and headed for the car. The thought occurred to him that maybe Dai wasn't the friendly face he seemed to be. Those dark eyes that sparkled with merriment could just as easily have been hiding deceit and treachery. How many more were out there, biding their time, waiting for the right moment to get back at him. After all, he'd made a few enemies, kicking in doors and cracking heads, rucking in the streets and the pubs with all and sundry. Maybe it was he, Billy Riley, who ought to watch his back.

Turning the corner, he stopped dead. There it was, perched on a wall, its cold black eye trained in his direction. Desperate to counter the curse it might have put on him, he threw out a mock salute, recalling at the same time the goodly father's warnings about superstition. He couldn't help himself. Something about the shiny black wings and puffed out breast, hopping about on the wall like something from *The Omen*.

The magpie took off. Repeating the old mantra in his head gave him reassurance. One in flight, I'm alright. But the sighting left him shaken. If there was such a thing as fate, maybe this was it. The evil bird was a warning, a harbinger, pointing the way towards some irreversible future.

16
Jesus and the Moneylenders

Perched next to the goodly father, he reflected quietly on life's mystery. The trial and the tribulation, with disappointment aplenty. Each man had to find his own path, learn to live according to his own rules and the dictates of his conscience. The father had a peaceable manner about him, his words carrying softly in the hushed intimacy of the church. The ways of the world troubled the father no longer. He'd found the answer in the Good Book, a message that gave him strength, courage and fortitude in the face of so much upheaval.

'None of us are strangers to calamity,' the father said, in summary. 'It shapes and moulds us. Makes us what we are.'

'Amen to that, Father.'

In the beginning was the word, and the word got mixed up with a whole lot of other things. Not least among them, suspicion, doubt, envy, jealousy and greed. The father lamented upon these human failings with great sadness, as if he were talking about children of his own. Words, he said, were hopelessly ineffectual when describing the torment of the human soul, careering through the firmament on its endless journey. The earthly struggle, as the father called it, an unavoidable burden given each new traveller as he set out. And he, Billy Riley, should know, having suffered more than most, seeing things no man should ever see. Languishing in a prison cell hundreds of miles from home, forced to live on the foul broth served up by heathen jailors who beat and tried to subdue him. No option but to fraternise with men of his own ilk and learn their desperate ways.

The father talked about trouble on the Parkway. You could feel it in the air, he said, a kind of heavily-distilled menace that hung around street corners looking for an outlet. Like an underground movement, the locals were ready to rise up and do battle with the authorities; after putting up with all manner of harassment and provocation without a murmur, they suddenly decided they'd had enough. Out came the half-bricks and the balaclavas. Parkway South's version of the Peasants' Revolt.

'There's tension everywhere,' the father said. 'I've talked to the youth workers and the shop owners. I'm sure it won't end well.'

'Par for the course, Father. It was bound to kick-off sooner or later, if you ask me.'

In his younger days, he would have been in the thick of it, hoisting the flag and leading the cavalry charge. But not now. There was a chance to make some moolar; maybe even cultivate the journalist fella and show him around. Billy Riley, reformed and revitalised, the all new singing and dancing version of his former self.

The father turned to him, a righteous light in his eyes. 'And what of you and Eileen? How's it all working out at home?'

He struggled to find the right answer. And yet the dim surroundings, the candles flickering at the altar and the wooden pews, lent themselves to the moment. They weren't getting on as they should be, he said. Man and wife, divided by petty things. The trials of separation – him being upriver for so long. A hasty reunion without adequate preparation. He wished only to unburden himself of the sadness that lay upon his heart and to make restitution. Put things back to how they were before he'd gone away.

The father nodded, gravely, and smoothed his beard. 'It's been a difficult time for you both, I'm sure.'

'I see her around other men and this, kinda, mist comes over me. I get to thinking bad things.'

'Have you spoken to Eileen about it, Billy?'

'No, Father, I haven't.'

'Perhaps, you should.'

Gazing up at the high, vaulted ceiling, he tried to reflect. The perfect place to contain secrets. Whatever he said would never be repeated outside the church walls – a gift of inestimable value to a lowly sinner like himself. He, who'd never believed in God or the Scriptures, who'd lived his life according to his own rules and done terrible things. The goodly father made no judgement of him, but accepted him as he was, with all his human frailties. And in his long and troubled existence he could count such people on the fingers of one tattooed hand. All the rest – the judges, the police, the psychologists and the social workers – treated him like a number, someone deserving of nothing more than the austere walls of a closed institution.

'Eileen went up to visit Tommy,' he said.

'And how do you feel about that?'

He shrugged. 'We haven't spoken in ages. Last time I saw him the little fucker put the head on me on the front lawn – excuse the language, Father.'

'Do you not think you'll visit the lad yourself?'

'Can't see it. Fella made his bed a long time ago. Nothing I can do to change it.'

Recent events had made it worse. The fracas up the club, where he'd sconced a fella with a beer bottle and scrapped four of his mates. The father might not share his belief in violence as a solution – even if he could claim a certain righteousness on his side. But that was the nature of the business he was in. An eye for an eye, the Good Book said. And didn't Jesus himself dish out punishment to the moneylenders in a rare show of force? In the end, it was a language that cut through all barriers, one that everyone understood.

'I met an old pal of mine's daughter the other day,' he said.

The father looked up, intrigued.

'Proper scally, she is. Lives on the Parkway, just her and a little kiddie.' He didn't know why he was telling the father. Maybe it was guilt surfacing at the lack of interest he'd shown in Gemma and the baby since the birth. So far he'd only seen them once. Eileen was round all the time, taking baby clothes and boxes of nappies.

'Were you close?' the father said.

'What – me and his daughter?'

'No, you and this pal.'

'Oh, aye, very close. We used to do everything together, even played for the same team.'

The statue of the Virgin stood in partial shadow next to the altar. Soon the congregation would file in for morning Mass, the pews filled with sinful parishioners hoping for comfort in this world and leniency in the next. He felt oddly pleased not to be among their number, proud of his righteous stand against penitence in all its forms.

'Tommy had a talent for football, too,' he said. 'Had a trial for Salford when he were nine years old.'

'Perhaps he'll take it up again when he comes out.'

'Not where he's going. His course is already set.'

A couple wandered down the aisle, and eased into the front pew. The woman crossed herself solemnly before sitting.

'Did you see the match last night?' the father said.

'I caught the last ten-minutes.'

'Scholes was brilliant, wasn't he? Passing, making the play.' The father looked at him slyly. 'I might organise another charity match. Pencil you in for right-back. Do you think you could handle that?'

'Have to sort me transfer fee out first. I won't come out the changing room for less than a million.'

The father stood, slowly, hands on hips to ease the transition. 'Well, it's been lovely to see you, Billy. You must drop in and see me again sometime.'

'My pleasure, Father.'

'And remember, things are never as bad as we imagine them to be. Have faith that it'll turn out all right.'

Strolling down towards the Exchange, he turned his collar up against the cold wind. Here were all the roughnecks and the ne'er-do-wells in their heavy coats and winter bonnets, searching for bargains along the market stalls. Nameless, faceless humanity in a world already overcrowded. Sometimes the sheer scale of it overwhelmed him, making the limitations of a prison cell suddenly seem appealing. All God's children, according to the father. Each and every one of them deserving pity or sympathy of some kind;

had the father spent time in the jails and the reformatories like he had, the fella might have formed a different opinion. The landing vultures noticed everything, ready to swoop and steal everything at the first sign of weakness.

Gallows Lane – a hint of the old town in the sights and smells herein. The Turkish delis, their wares displayed outside on green coconut matting and wooden crates. Small coffee shops with gloomy interiors and vacant round tables, like set pieces in a stage play. The narrow section of boutiques and barber shops that doubled as shebeens in the evening, the cobblestones worn smooth from the horses' hooves that had beaten a path along there over a century ago. Still the same as he remembered it from his youth. The real heart of the city, not the steel and glass towers that dominated the south side, reeking of new money. If his Irish heart beat anywhere it was here, where the crack was fierce and fools weren't tolerated.

A jeweller's window caught his eye. Trays of expensive trinkets laid out on beds of black velvet, price tags attached; a thin, diamond-encrusted silver bracelet priced at £750. He'd given Eileen something similar from the proceeds of a robbery once. She'd worn it a few times, then lost it during a drunken tussle outside a night club. Strange how the thought of her face all lit up at some gift he'd bought made him glow inside. The father was right, it was better to give than to receive. Eileen, who'd put up with his waywardness and frequent absences from the family home, but was still there waiting when he came back.

Talking to the father had unravelled part of the knot inside him and given him hope. He was at heart a family man, compelled to help kith and kin, in spite of the grave setbacks that would have defeated most men. Maybe now his luck was about to change. His time had come.

17
Reflections

They supped tea in the comfy bamboo chairs, with a view of the garden. Gary must have forgotten what it was like, having stayed out of jail for so long. He had everything. All the luxuries of a good life on the out. Two cars and a decent pad. A good-looking bird, ten years younger. These were things any man might wish for, and he, Billy Riley, was no exception – apart from the preoccupation and hankering among his peers for the younger woman. Sure, the tender saplings were alright to look at, and even turk on the odd occasion, but they were also immature and prone to sudden bouts of hysteria for which there was no apparent reason.

'Tanya not about?' he said.

'She's at her mum's. Can't you tell how peaceful it is at the moment?'

Eileen reckoned Tanya was with Gary for the money, but he wasn't convinced. They'd been together quite a while and seemed to get on – although he didn't envy Gary the constant spending to keep up his lifestyle. There were some advantages to having a younger model, of course. They looked good and made other fellas jealous when you walked in the alehouse with one on your arm. Plus, most of them hadn't reached the bitter and twisted stage like some of the older ones, always ready with the claws out and the ladling on of insults guaranteed to bring a fella down. When it came to the bedroom department, the older ones knew the score. They had a genuine appreciation of what a fella could do for them – an acquired taste for the covell that made 'em champ at the bit. Lying on his kip up the factory he used to fantasize about a harem, a pick 'n' mix of tits and fanny to get stuck into whenever the mood took him. Sheik Billy Riley, plotted up in a tent like Omar Sharif. In reality, they were all a bag of trouble, young and old. Long spells inside had given him ample time to reflect and draw his own conclusions.

The Parkway was getting worse, Gary said. Six shootings the previous week, all the victims under twenty-one. Hard to relate this to the era they'd grown up in, the likes of Leonard running the show. 'A ten-year old girl got raped the other day,' Gary said. 'Ten, for fuck sake. All it got was a few lines in the paper.'

Back in the day, things had been better all round. Crime bosses like Leonard helped keep order of some kind. You knew where you were with these people, they had a code and stuck to it. The mere mention of Leonard's name was enough to put fear into anyone, without the Big Fella having to show his face. Like the time Social Services re-housed a nonce on the estate and word went round. A few of the lads paid a little visit at Leonard's behest and moved him on – a clear message to everyone that it wouldn't be tolerated. But it wasn't just nonces who qualified for the extradition process. The list could be extended to include grasses, backstabbers, drug dealers, bad debtors, and anyone else who violated the unwritten rules.

'Nice place you've got here,' he said. 'You must be pulling in the moolar.'

Gary shook his head. 'I never stop, mate. It's a constant juggling act, believe me.'

Life wasn't easy whoever you were. The twenty-first century was barely out of the starting gate and already there were untold casualties. He saw himself, like Gary, as being too old for all the hassle of his previous occupation, needing to seek out easier ways of making a living. Working the doors was a young man's game. The late hours, brawling in the street with muppets off their heads on drink and drugs. Who wanted that of an evening? These days he was ready for his kip by eleven o'clock, curled up in bed with a hot water bottle.

'How did you feel when you turned forty?' he said.

Gary pondered. 'Pretty good. Tanya bought me a day out at Silverstone. I got to drive an Aston Martin for a couple of hours. Why?'

Getting old was a joke that finally caught up with you. All those hours in the gym, pumping out the reps – and for what? Even the strongest muscle weakened in time. Hard men went to seed like everyone else, struggling for breath in a nursing home while the nurse wheeled in the oxygen machine – or, like the Big Fella, pegging out in his back garden from heart failure years before his time. Mortality was out there stalking everyone. You had to prepare yourself for it somehow. Like Custer's Last Stand.

Gary tossed him an envelope. 'There you go. Little something for services rendered. Lemme show you the garden.'

Now they could discuss business without some hidden listening device eavesdropping on their conversation. Gary's caution bordered on paranoia sometimes, but given the calibre of the people he was involved with it was understandable.

'Things are starting to move,' Gary said. 'We could be looking at being fully operational in four to six weeks' time.'

They strolled along the border of the neatly-clipped lawn, the profusion of colour appealing even to his untrained eye.

'Did Tanya plant all the flowers?'

'Did she fuck. Gardner comes in once a week, mate.'

At the far end of the garden was a wooden outhouse on a raised decking area. The perfect place for a fella to escape when the heat indoors got too much.

'How soon can the landlord get that yacht in the water?' Gary said.

'No idea.'

'Sound him out. Tell him it's urgent, and remind him of the cash incentive. All we need is a few trial runs up and down the coast, then it's a green light for the big one.'

He couldn't help but feel the excitement, the thought of being in on something major that might yield untold dividends in the future. Gary's secrecy made it all the more enticing. No names, no unnecessary background details. The mysterious contact had insisted everything was organised through him.

Logistics was a problem. Given the size and scale of the operation, storage was crucial. But the locations had to be right, and the set-up handled with discretion.

'What about Shifty?' he said.

'What about him?'

'He's got a lock-up near the waterfront. Could be just what you're looking for.'

18

Steak and Ale Pie

The landlord had his own problems: staffing shortages and brewery policies he didn't like, plus the hiatus hernia that played havoc with his digestive system. 'I should have stayed in Wales,' he said, podgy fingers spread on the bar. 'Taken that nice little country pub I was offered instead of moving back down here.'

Supping ale, the dog at his feet, he, Billy Riley, nodded tactfully. The discourse made him feel benevolent, like a doctor or counsellor come to dispense advice to a sick patient. If it was encouragement they wanted, that's what they'd get. The landlord's heavy face reflected the burden of his many ills; everyone had problems, but his were somehow irreversible.

A pleasant afternoon lull settled over the bar. The dog nosed idly for remnants of pork scratchings on the flagstones. The door creaked every time a new punter walked in, the hint of daylight threatening to spoil the cosy atmosphere. They talked about the youngsters who came in of a weekend, shouting abuse and generally playing up.

The landlord leaned on the bar, and stole a quick glance either side to see if anyone was listening. 'They came in again on Friday and Saturday night. Upsetting the bar staff, causing trouble. Is there anything you can do?'

'Me?'

'Well, yes. That's your line of work, isn't it?'

He sensed a deviousness in the landlord that hadn't surfaced before. But this in itself could only bode well for the future. 'I don't usually deal with minor issues. Someone else sorts it out.'

The landlord looked disappointed. 'So you're saying I just have to put up with it?'

'Well, there is something you could do, but you gotta be prepared for the fallout.' He warmed to his theme, drawing on two decades of experience working on the frontline. 'See, before you make any move at all you need to know the mentality of these people. They're like pack animals, a product of the streets and the alleyways. They'd think nothing of robbing your house, or sticking a knife in you for no reason.'

'Christ, how charming.'

'And that's not all. Some of these cunts have got long memories. You might be out walking your dog a year from now. A car drives by, and sprays you with bullets from a semi-automatic.'

The landlord's face turned the colour of mutton.

'But look on the bright side. They might just go away of their own accord. Pester someone else.'

Another punter stepped in, rubbing his hands from the cold. The landlord went off to serve the fella, leaving him with a bag of pork scratchings and the dog at his feet. He could think of worse places to be – like queuing up to use the phone up the local nick. Here, he had a drop of ale and good company, even if it was just listening to the landlord's prattle.

The fella returned, and took up his position behind the bar. The saga of violent youth continued, with the expectation that he, Billy Riley, could somehow provide a solution.

'I called the police once, but that didn't work,' the landlord said.

'I'm not surprised. Calling the dibble would just aggravate the situation.'

'But why? I pay my rates like everyone else. I'm entitled to some protection.'

He told a sobering tale from the archives. How the Big Fella, Leonard Simms, once ran all the pubs and clubs on the waterfront. In his younger days, Leonard had been a scrapper, willing to have it with pretty much anyone. As time went on and business took over, he preferred to take a back seat from the fisticuffs wherever possible. When he did get involved it was usually spectacular.

'He got a call once afternoon to say there was a bunch of football hooligans playing up in one of his pubs. So he grabbed a few of his lads and drove over there a bit quick. By the time he got there, most of the regulars had left. Now there was just Leonard and his boys, and a bunch of leery out-of-towners all hankering for the tear-up.'

'What happened?' the landlord said.

'Leonard locked the door so no one could leave. The only way out was through the window.'

The landlord absorbed the details, nodding grimly.

'That afternoon was a lesson in psychology. Superior numbers don't always guarantee victory. When it were over, most of the opposition needed hospital treatment. Leonard and his boys were still standing.'

The landlord shook his head, unable to picture such a brutal scene. Clearly not the type to take matters into his own hands, he'd always relied on the authorities to sort things out. Of course, he could always go through the courts to seek redress, an option most straight-goers would take. But that didn't always bring the outcome they desired. In all his run-ins with the Crown Prosecution Service – who chose whether or not to bring certain cases to trial – not once had he, Billy Riley, been disappointed by the system. Wrongfully arrested, fitted-up by the dibble, slandered by arrogant barristers, and weighed-off by sadistic judges, yes – but never really surprised at the end result. All in a day's work for good old British Justice.

The barmaid loitered nearby, a cute little thing with streaky-blonde hair and a smart black top, plastic name tag above her left tittie. Behind her, the colourful chalk board advertising a range of delicious faire. Ten years ago the flagstones rang with the sound of broken glass and the scream of sirens as the dibble raced to get there before the windows were put through. The memorable day a Chief Superintendent had wandered in like the foil in a pantomime, backed by a sizeable force of the local constabulary. The twat made a noble speech in the public bar about law and order, only to bail out quickly five-minutes later, pelted with warm beer and drunken insults from the mob inside. The landlord didn't know the meaning of trouble.

'What's the Chef's Special today, fella?'

'Well, as it happens, I can certainly recommend the steak and ale pie.'

'Sounds good to me.'

When the scran arrived, he tucked in with a real appreciation. A pleasant drowsiness descended, induced by the beer and the hot food. He recalled his childhood days, the dumplings and stew served up by his old ma while the ogre was out. The past, like a photo album where you could choose the things you wanted to see. A freezing bedroom with condensation on the window frames and Bruce Lee posters on the wall. Long hot summer holidays that seemed to last forever. Life was simpler then; get out of the house when the old fella was around, thus avoiding the strap or the toe of his work boot. Mornings spent lugging the old print-soiled paper-bag uphill on the round that earned him the grand sum of £2.40 and a box of cheese and onion crisps. Warm memories, trimmed with nostalgia.

'How is it?' the landlord said.

'Spot-on, fella. Tell the chef he can cook round my place anytime.'

The sense of freedom didn't last. The long hot summers turned into cruel winters that cut through the crappy hand-me-downs he had to wear because his old ma couldn't afford new ones. Truancy and shoplifting led to juvenile court and deferred sentencing, awaiting reports from probation officers and child psychologists who tried unsuccessfully to suss him out. He learned how to build walls early on so no one could get to him. The more vulnerable aspects of his character were covered up. Buried, hidden from sight.

The landlord came back to take his plate. Now seemed the right time to talk business.

'Remember that pal of mine I told you about, who's looking to charter a yacht?'

'Oh, yes. Bit later in the season, perhaps.'

'He was thinking a bit earlier than that.'

'How early?'

'Soon as you can get the boat in the water.'

The landlord went into a spiel about how costly it was to maintain a yacht in dry dock, and how crucial it was that all the work was undertaken before she went back in the water. Then there was the mooring fees and the insurance to consider.

By the time the fella had finished, he felt like he could skipper the vessel himself; his head filled with spars and winches, rub-downs and antifouling. He, who'd never been out on a boat before, and couldn't even swim.

'Think about it,' he said. 'And if you're interested, call me on this number.'

The landlord picked up the slip of paper, looked at it briefly, and put it in his pocket.

Now they had an understanding, a connection of sorts. Intuition told him the landlord would ring, if only out of curiosity. Good old-fashioned greed would do the rest.

19
Shifty

They headed east on the turnpike road. The snow the weatherman had predicted had started to fall, the skies grey and muggy. He drove fast, ignoring Eileen's pleas for him to slow down. Whenever he glanced across she had that look on her face, her mouth set in a firm, disapproving pout.

Easing into the outside lane, he increased the speed from ninety to a hundred, enjoying the feeling of power.

'Are you doing this to wind me up?' she said.

'Doing what?'

'Driving like a fuckin idiot.'

'Take it easy, sweetheart, I'm getting a feel for the road.'

He flashed the driver in front, a grey-haired old man, who moved quickly out of the way. The roads were filled with such people, their reactions too slow – the lack of awareness in itself criminal. You had to know how to drive at high speed and still feel in control. Besides, nothing wrong with a little calculated risk-taking to liven the day. Challenge. Wasn't that what life was all about?

Easing back on the pedal, he cruised at a more sedate eighty-five. The bridge loomed ahead, blue steel cables arcing through the grey mist like a mirage; a feat of engineering that impressed him every time he drove across. Barely visible below lay the channel; a merging of elements manmade and natural.

'Beautiful scenery,' he said. 'Makes you glad to be alive.'

'Concentrate on the road.'

'I am.' He glanced over. 'Fancy a table for two at the Bengal Palace later?'

'I've got too much to do.'

'What – packing babygrows for Pauline? How long's that gonna take you?' He flashed her a mock frown but she ignored it. He put his hand on her thigh; she moved it off without a word.

'What's up?' he said. 'Not speaking to me now?'

'Just watch the friggin road. I'd like to get there in one piece, if you don't mind.'

Love, the great distraction – from bunk-ups in alleyways with garishly painted slags, to extended romps with the woman of your dreams. The whole thing designed to keep the heart beating and the blood pulsing, the continuation of the species at all costs. Someone should have written a manual for men locked away from women. Nights of torment thinking about where she was and who she was with. Some smooth-talking chancer like the Jason fella, grinding one into her in the back of his car. You had to train yourself not to dwell on it too much. Focus on the positive.

'You look great,' he said. 'I might have to pull over and sort you out.'

'Sort you out in a minute you keep on like that.'

They came to a winding country lane, craters and divots like the surface of the Moon. An old farmstead appeared. Rangy-looking dogs wandered on the concrete forecourt; old vehicles were parked beneath corrugated tin awnings. Like something out of *Deliverance*, he thought.

He pulled up outside the house, and turned off the ignition.

'I'm not staying long,' Eileen said.

'I told you, I just want a chat with Shifty, then we'll go.'

An emaciated whippet ambled over, its ribs showing through. It nosed around the car before wandering away. Even the house showed signs of dilapidation, the front garden overgrown and strewn with mechanical parts. Shifty's centre of operations, the place he conducted all his criminal activities with one eye out for the dibble.

Shifty wandered over in his dirty-blue overalls and crusty work boots. He leaned down and peered through the window, reeking of engine oil.

'How's it going, Billy?'

'I'm good, fella. What you been up to while I've been away?'

'Rabbits, mainly. You want a couple, I'll sling 'em in the boot for you?'

'I'm not having dead rabbits in the back of this car!' Eileen said.

Shifty ginned. 'How about a couple of live ones instead?'

Business was good for Shifty. Aside from his rabbit hunting excursions, he'd branched out into the retail sector with Pauline, buying fake football strips from an Asian warehouse on the north side and selling them through classified ads and car boot sales.

'Supply and demand,' Shifty said, by way of explanation. 'We can't get rid of 'em fast enough.'

'Where d'you keep 'em?'

'In me lockup at the waterfront. I've got a few boxes inside if you want to take a look?'

Shifty's garage was crammed with car parts and assorted paraphernalia. Plastic tubs filled with bolts and washers lined the shelves, along with a giant-sized tub of Swarfega. Hanging from the far wall, was a lethal-looking crossbow.

'What's that, to scare off intruders?'

Shifty laughed. 'That's just for show, mate. I keep the real hardware indoors.'

The football strips were at the back, in cardboard boxes. Shifty pulled one out and held it up, reeling off its qualities like a salesman. From a sweatshop in Bangkok to a warehouse on the north side, then out for distribution. And that was just the beginning. Shifty's Asian contact was keen to offload other goods – fake designer labels, handbags, shoes. The list was endless.

'How big's the lockup?'

'Bit bigger than this garage, but without all the junk.'

'Can I take a look?'

'Yeah, sure.' Shifty chuckled. 'Why – thinking of coming in with us, Billy?'

'I just might do that, fella.'

Driving back through Parkway Central, he took a left towards the old town, clocking the rear-view out of habit. Eileen sat beside him, ominously quiet since they'd left Shifty's place.

A few miles later, she broke the silence.

'So now you're all pally with Shifty all of a sudden. A while ago you were gonna kill him for selling me that car.'

'Fella's got a thriving business going. Gotta give him credit for that.'

'Hypocrite, that's what you are.'

The lockup was at the end of a row of garages, sheltered from the road. He parked and got out, getting a feel for the area. A block of flats loomed in the background, tiny balconies breaking up the dull grey façade.

Eileen joined him.

'Are you gonna look inside, or what?'

'I'm thinking.'

'And I'm cold and hungry. Can we get back, please?'

A thickset fella came striding towards them – a barrel-chested town crier with an attitude to go with it. They watched him approach with some trepidation.

'Er – can I ask what you're doing?' the fella said.

Eileen faced him squarely. 'Mind your friggin own!'

The fella stared at her, speechless. Now he, Billy Riley, was forced to intervene.

He turned to Eileen. 'Jump in the car, I'll deal with it.'

'Don't tell me what to do.'

'Just get in the fuckin car.'

She climbed in, and slammed the door, glaring at him through the windscreen.

He turned to the big fella with a friendly smile.

'Sorry about that, pal. No bother, eh?'

'I'm not happy about this.'

'Neither am I, and I've gotta live with her.'

The big fella stayed put, stroking the stubble on his chin and glancing occasionally at Eileen.

'What's your name?'

The fella thought about it.

'Herbie. I'm on the residents' committee.'

'He nodded, getting the measure of the fella. 'Like rabbits, do you, Herb? I could drop you round a couple, show there's no hard feelings.'

The fella scratched his head, disarmed by the civil tone.

'Or, we could sort it out on the tarmac, just me and you?'

The fella took a step back, his indecision compounded by a keen sense of self-preservation. The time to pan him would have been now – the fella's jaw presenting itself as a legitimate target.

Eileen hit the horn, and made a gesture for him to hurry up. The big fella looked distracted, not sure which way to turn.

'What you saying to me then, big fella? We good to go, or what?'

Herbie swallowed hard, and nodded.

'That's the spirit. I'll tell the missus we've sorted it out.'

The fella wandered off, some of the puff taken out of his blarney. But now they'd been compromised, without the lockup even being opened.

He got back in the car, and turned on the ignition.

'Arsehole,' Eileen said.

'He was harmless enough. Anyway, I straightened the fella out.'

'I meant you! Telling me to get back in the car like I was a fuckin teenager.'

'You need to control your temper, doll. Have you thought about that?'

'Just drive.'

'Drive when I'm good and ready.'

Heading back into town, he watched his speed. Cameras everywhere, stationary robots with hooded eyes, programmed to record every detail. The Orwell fella certainly knew what he was talking about. It wasn't just the criminals who were being watched, but the ordinary folk too. All of them under surveillance, waiting to get pulled in.

Parkway South loomed. He felt able to relax. His biggest regret was not taking it out on the big fella's nose when he had the chance, but sometimes diplomacy was the better option.

'Are you going to tell me what's going on?' Eileen said.

'What?'

'All that crap about going into business with Shifty. You expect me to believe that?'

'I'm just keeping me options open, that's all.'

'Don't lie to me. You're up to something, and you know it.'

He watched the road, wrapped in his own thoughts. To succeed in this game you needed to cover your tracks and work out every angle. In logistical terms, today had been a disaster, proving the unpredictable nature of events and people. But he had to give Eileen something, a little taster to keep her off his back.

'I might have summat coming off in the future.'

'Like what?'

'I can't say.'

'Great.'

Since he'd come out of the factory, the balance of power had tipped more and more in her favour. Not good for a man to take a subordinate role in a marriage – went against everything he'd learnt as a kid. But it couldn't go on like that. He was the boss, the wage earner. She was supposed to be there to serve him. To love, honour and obey. Till death us do part.

20
Southside Johnny

He saw Rosalyn out strolling by the Palisade – minus the buggy. Driving by, he lowered the window and called out, 'Hey, sweetheart! What's happening?' Reluctantly, she came over and leant on the window. The kid was with her nan, she told him. She was on her way over to visit her mate who lived on the Warren. He offered her a lift, and without much thought she climbed in, a breeze of cold air and cheap perfume blowing in with her.

'What you been up to?' he said.

'Nothing much.'

'Keeping your nose clean? Not causing no bother?'

She flashed him a coy grin, and settled back in the seat, content to be there, not threatened in any way. He in turn was genuinely pleased to see her, relieved she was all right. Somewhere in the background, the shadow of her old fella hovered – his old mate Jimmy, who would surely have approved.

Turning into the estate he felt the strains of déjà vu. Spray can artwork decorated a gable end – like something out of Belfast in the Seventies. The scallies were out in force already, hanging around on street corners, a mini posse dedicated to trouble and mayhem.

'What you doing for money?' he said.

'Not much.'

'You'll have to go out grafting. Let your nan look after the kiddie.' He glanced across to see her reaction. She had that closed off, quietly rebellious look he knew so well, having perfected it himself on the landings of numerous British prisons.

'Where d'you want dropping?' he said.

'Anywhere round here'll do.'

Turning into Cardinal Way, he pulled over, leaving the engine running. Up ahead, the gasworks, its giant rust-worn frameworks rising from the urban sprawl.

Rosalyn stayed put, in no hurry to get out.

'Still smoking?' he said.

'Only roll-ups.' She stared ahead, clutching her bag. He felt a sense of responsibility towards her, like she were one of his own.

'How much is your rent?'

'Five-hundred a month.'

'Who pays that – the government?'

'I have to pay a fifty-quid top-up out of me benefit money.'

'How much d'you spend on fags?'

'Not much. I get it cheap from someone on the estate.'

'What about drugs?'

'I don't do drugs.'

'Smoke a bit of pot? Drop a couple of E's on a Saturday night?'

'No?' She gave him the same flat, expressionless look intended to convince him; some of the best con-artists he'd ever known had used a similar response for the same reasons. Girls had an added advantage in the fluttered eyelash and aura of innocence so easily perfected for gullible men.

'Where d'you see yourself in five years' time?' he said. 'Still living on the Parkway with no money?'

'What d'you mean?'

'You're either going somewhere in this life, or you're going nowhere – know what I'm saying?'

She fiddled with the strap of her bag, unwilling to speak. He shook his head, quietly amused. Getting her to open up was like trying to prise the lid off a lead coffin.

'You don't talk much, do you?' he said.

'Sometimes.'

'I'm not knocking you, Rosalyn. It pays to keep your mouth shut in certain situations. Most people can't.'

She gazed out, trapped in the same cycle of want and deprivation as most of the kids on the estate, always looking for something to relieve the boredom.

'D'you miss your old fella?'

'Not really. I never saw much of him anyway.'

'Ever meet his other kids?'

'Couple of times.' She stared at her lap, little more than a child, forced to grow up too soon. He wanted to say something meaningful, compensate her for her loss.

'Who knows why these things happen. Sometimes the good die young.'

She looked up, frowning. 'He weren't that young.'

'Well, he weren't exactly old either, was he?'

She took out a meagre-looking tobacco pouch from her bag, and proceeded to wrap one up. He admired her expert manipulations, the countless hours it took to produce a tab of that standard.

'Don't you worry about your poor old lungs when you're breathing in that shit?'

'No?'

'You should be more health conscious, Rosalyn. Young girl of your age.'

'I am health conscious. I eat an apple and a banana every day.'

It felt good, the two of them in his car with a view of the estate through the windscreen. The playground of his youth, where he'd run with a gang called the 'Mad Dogs', stealing cars and drinking cider on the common.

'I'd better go in a minute,' she said.

'Go whenever you like, sweetheart, I'm not stopping you.'

A few of the local scallies came along, mean and sullen-faced, hands in their pockets as if they'd been welded there. He watched them go by, and thought of Tommy.

'Know any of them, do you?' he said.

'Nope.'

'Workshy lazy bastards, look at 'em. When I were that age I were grafting on a building site, keeping three brickies going for eight-hours a day.'

He had the work ethic, true enough. Enjoyed the challenge and the camaraderie. Prison had taken him down a different route, narrowed his options so to speak. But the potential was still there, waiting to be uncovered. The Big Fella had recognized it in him and given him a chance. Opened the doors of opportunity.

Rosalyn just sat there, saying nothing, the cogs in her head going round and round.

'What's up?' he said.

'Nothing.'

'Come on, you can tell your uncle Billy.'

She chewed her lip, cheeks red with the effort of thinking. 'I'm worried Social Services might take littlun off me.'

'What for?'

'I left him with a mate one night and didn't tell no one.'

'Why d'you have to tell 'em in the first place?'

'It's part of me care order.'

He mulled it over, the inevitable complications that came from getting drawn in.

'What about the kiddie's father?'

'He's still in the jail.'

'When's he out?'

'I don't know and I don't care. He's on a restraining order not to come near me.'

Gazing out at the Parkway he saw himself in his previous role. Enforcer for the Big Fella, sorting out everyone else's problems for a modest slice of the pie. Now he was older and softer in the head, allowing himself to be manipulated by a seasoned scally like Rosalyn.

'I'd better go now,' she said, reaching for the door. 'Thanks for the lift.'

'Before you go, give us your number.'

'What for?'

'Be good to keep in touch. I might be able to help you sometime.'

Watching her cut through the alleyway, hood up, hands in the pockets of her coat, he thought how vulnerable she looked. A child growing up in the big bad world. But she did have certain qualities that might come in handy one day.

21

A Basket of Chips

The Grafton Arms, Saturday lunchtime. Punters filed in off the street, faces pinched with the cold and a general mistrust of everything and everyone. A few alcoholic types sat around nursing pint glasses as if they'd been there all night. Abject faces, like the ones in the jail, craving a drink or a puff on the weed, unable to cope with the crap life had thrown at them.

Fresh from another assault on the fruit machine, Gizmo joined him, the look on his face suggesting he'd taken another hiding. A short period of remorse and lamentation followed, during which he, Billy Riley, had to act as friend and counsellor.

'Wouldn't it just be easier to give *me* the money, Giz? I mean, it's fuckin painful to watch – know what I'm saying?'

According to the experts, happiness was achievable for anyone – even the serfs, returning from a hard day's toil in the fields. All they had to do was give thanks for what they had and take no thought for the morrow. And he, Billy Riley, was as up for the song and dance as anyone. As long as the ale flowed and the womenfolk turned out in their summer frocks, who cared what happened?

Just then, a whole new world of opportunity opened up. In wandered the journalist fella with his female assistant. Something irresistible about the combination of education and foolhardiness. A chance to enjoy himself at their expense.

'Round Two,' he said.

Gizmo looked up and clocked the pair of them coming in. 'I

told you he'd be back. Want me to introduce you?'

'I'll introduce me fuckin self, pal. They've got some front coming in here again, that's for sure.'

The pair took a seat in the far corner. They looked like any other couple. Nothing that might identify them as film types or intellectuals.

Supping his pint, he put the empty on the bar and prepared a little speech for the intrepid duo. It wouldn't take much to put them right on a few things, educate them about the way things worked around here.

'Right, I'm off,' he said.

Gizmo looked confused. 'Where you going?'

'See how the land lies. Back in a bit.'

The journalist fella looked up as he made his approach. He put a hand on the back of the fella's chair, and smiled graciously at the bird.

'Mind if I join you?'

'Er – no,' the fella said. 'Please do.'

He grabbed a chair and sat with them, smiling, professional. They looked at him in surprise, their pleasant discourse interrupted.

'Food good, is it?' he said, pointing out the bird's empty basket.

She stared at him. 'Sorry – who are you?'

'I'm the entertainments manager, luv. It's my job to make sure everyone's enjoying themselves and having a good time.'

The journalist fella smiled nervously. 'Haven't we met before?'

'Let's not get ahead of ourselves, fella – know what I'm saying?' He settled back, pleased at the introductions. They sat there gawping at him like a pair of students, just asking to be walked all over.

'So where's Marlon Brando?'

'Sorry?' the bird said.

'I heard you were making a film round here. Thought you might have a few big names lined up.'

She glanced at the journalist fella, who frowned uneasily.

'What was it you wanted?' she said.

'I was gonna ask you the same question.'

The journalist fella flashed the bird an anxious look. She sipped her drink, determined not to be intimidated. But the feisty look contained an element of doubt. They were both on foreign territory and they knew it.

Rocking back on the chair, hands behind his head, he kept them both in his radar. There could be challenges involved in taking them both on. They were an unknown entity, their background and experience radically different from his own.

'Tell us about this movie you're making.'

'We're not making a movie,' the bird said with a touch of arrogance.

'We're doing some research for a documentary,' the fella said. 'That's why we're here.'

'A documentary about what?'

The bird looked at the journalist fella, seeking some mandate. Getting nothing from him, she took the initiative herself. Clearing her throat, she sat up straight to give an impression of authority. 'We're researching crime in the area. Particularly on the big estates like the Parkway and the Warren. Do you know those areas?'

He stopped rocking and leaned forward. 'Let's cut the bullshit, shall we? I heard about your little run in with Sonia Simms the other day. Take it from me, it ain't worth the aggravation.' The bird's thin lips parted in silent protest. He cut her off before she could respond. 'You wanna make a film about folk round here, go right ahead. Just make sure your insurance covers damages.'

The bird intrigued him; small features and a turned-up nose, voice like a newsreader off the BBC. He could have some fun winding her up, but even that would have consequences. Beneath it all, the serious business of protecting territories and deterring strangers. All down to him to set an example.

'Can I ask who sent you?' the bird said.

'Sent me?'

'Well obviously you didn't come over here of your own accord. Someone must have put you up to it.'

He smiled at the folly of her stance. 'I don't think you understand, luv. We do things different round here. There's no customer complaints department you can run to when things go tits-up – know what I'm saying?'

She stared back in defiance. 'I think we're well aware of the risks involved.'

'Really?' … He repositioned himself in the chair, nice and comfortable. 'Tell you a little story, shall I? A few years ago, this fella turned up asking questions about Leonard. Said he worked for a newspaper. Not being one for publicity, Leonard asked him nicely to go away. But he didn't, see? So Leonard made a coupla phone calls and the fella disappeared.'

'Is that a threat?' she said.

'I'm just telling you a story, sweetheart.'

More drinkers filed in off the street. He felt awkward, supping ale with these out-of-towners who'd caused enough trouble already. Someone he knew might clock him and spread the word he'd been seen fraternising with the enemy. Widow Sonia might find out and see it as a mark of betrayal.

'Little word to the wise,' he said, standing. 'Go back to where you came from. Make a film about parking charges or the village fete.'

He strolled back to the bar, dignity intact.

'What's the crack?' Gizmo said

'Pair o' cunts. Had to put 'em straight on a few things.'

'Are you gonna help 'em?'

'Why would I do that?'

'I just thought that's what the deal was. You knowing the Big Fella and all.'

'Listen – the longer they hang around here, the more likely someone's gonna take a pop at 'em. They're in the lion's den, pal, and I for one ain't gonna be in there with 'em when the shit goes down.'

Perhaps he was missing out. A deal with the journalist fella might have been lucrative. They might have been willing to pay for his expertise, his knowledge of the area – of Leonard, in particular.

He saw himself and Eileen strolling along the harbour at Villamora: him in a brightly-coloured Bermudan shirt, sunhat and shades on, a binfull of local denari in his back pocket; her in a lime green bikini, tanned stomach, stretch marks and all. Everything they ever needed right there in the sun.

But there the vision ended, the golden beaches replaced by high brick walls and razor wire. The life of a man was like the spokes of a wheel, turning over the endless ruts and furrows. Nothing much at the end of it save memories and regrets. Wives and kiddies lost to the ale houses and the prisons, fortunes squandered along the way.

He finished his pint. 'I'm away, Giz. Say hello to Pauline for me, won't you. Tell her how much I miss seeing her happy, smiling face.'

He left by the side door, a final warning look at the filmmaking duo on his way out. Maybe they'd take the hint and drop their little project about Leonard. Somehow, he doubted it. Their type had a self-confidence you couldn't easily shake, an attitude that came from being part of the establishment. But he could feel himself being drawn in and becoming involved in some way. The pair of them had turned up for his benefit. Dumped right there in his lap.

22
Going to Work

Sifting through the selection Eileen had left out for him on the bed, he paused and thought about it. All that choice and you could still only wear one thing at a time. He had to give it to Pauline, though. Some of the items she'd sent over were real classy, all laid out in their neat packaging. He couldn't decide what to wear, and settled in the end for a light-blue open neck shirt and jeans. With the gold that conferred status on a man he was all set for the skim and a jaunt into town with his Irish Rose, love of his life and cause of all his insecurities.

Immediate gratification aside, there were warning signs he had to acknowledge. The risk-taking had increased without him being aware of it; the shirts and the dodgy gear had crept back in, in spite of his admonitions to keep the house free of it. Now it was everywhere: a freezer full of knock-off meat from Dai Lewellyn; fake MOTs and tax certificates from Shifty; baby clothes from Eileen's brochure scam that had arrived by the box load – not to mention his own forays into the world of safe houses and lockups for Gary, and the building of a network for major distribution a bit further down the line. All it needed was a knock from McGuinn and he'd be upriver before he could think about it.

Prising open the panel upstairs, he took out the plastic bag; bundles of twenties and tens in neat green binders. Slipping a twenty from a wad, he held it up to the light; the Queen's face on the front, and on the back, the mug of some nineteenth century dignitary who looked like he'd been caught chewing a lemon.

Precision artwork, smooth between thumb and forefinger. Years ago he'd bought two-grand's worth of twenties from the master forger, Stanley Isley. The notes turned out to be so good that the Bank of England had to recall the entire existing circulation from all their branches.

The cash was safe enough, all wrapped up in plastic and hidden away. Even if he was lifted, he couldn't see the dibble finding it. Tommy Blunt, the one-armed bank robber from Wythenshawe, had over a hundred-grand hidden in the party wall of his three-bed semi when he was nicked for a job in Stoke. Settling in to a six-year stint upriver, Blunt was horrified to learn that his soon-to-be ex-wife had sold the house and gone abroad. Being an enterprising fella, he waited until he got parole, then broke into his old pad while the new owners were out and liberated his nest-egg from the upstairs bedroom cavity. Whether or not the story was true, it did have a certain appeal, an inspirational tale for the alehouses and prison landings where the local incumbents soaked up such things with impunity.

Easing a hundred from the pack he put the rest back where Eileen wouldn't find it. Harder to earn than it was to spend. Better to accumulate it for its own sake – a future safeguard and means of securing favours. Soon, he'd have enough money to take the pair of them abroad – if he could persuade her to go with him.

Bathwater roared along the hall. Tapping on the bathroom door, he peered inside. She lay there in a haze of steam and soap suds, her skin all smooth and silky, the globes of her jugs rising through the bubbles.

'Want me to jump in with you?' he said.

'No, I friggin don't!'

'I thought you liked water sports?'

'Out!'

Assailed by thoughts of a devious nature, he lingered. The old adage was true. When the cock goes hard the brain goes soft. Impossible to ignore the flesh in all its forms and provocations. Even Eileen, whose bits he'd seen a thousand times before, and whose bones he'd ridden on countless occasions. She could still give him a sudden tweak when he was least expecting it, a certain suggestive look in her eye that rendered him useless. The goodly father said that lust was one of man's greatest burdens, and he couldn't help but agree. But as a normal, red-blooded fella there wasn't much he could do to change it.

'I'll book the taxi for half an hour,' he said.

'I can't get ready that quick.'

'Sling some clothes on, bit of makeup. What's the matter with you?'

'There'll be summat the matter with you in a minute if you don't leave me alone!'

The letter box rattled as he came downstairs; a flyer pushed through the door advertising a new Indian restaurant. The noise jarred him, alerting his senses to trouble. If the knock came at all it usually came early in the morning, with the door coming off its hinges and size-ten boots tramping up the stairs. But the dibble weren't all that bothered when they came calling. McGuinn would be happy to nick him anytime, morning, noon or night.

While he was waiting for Eileen, he caught the Six o'clock News. A short piece came on about four armed men who'd threatened workers inside the office of a warehouse and got away with an unspecified amount of cash. He smiled at the usual inconsistencies in the reporting, pleased to know that some anonymous firm had got one over on the dibble. Took him back to the days of his youth, and the odd bits of work he was invited in on, always executed with poise and professionalism. Problems like how to deal with bolshy staff, and how to react when alarms went off, were soon dealt with. Once the civilians saw the hardware the rest was easy. Like herding sheep into a pen.

Bitter memories, too, of things that went wrong. Laid up in a police cell, saying nothing, demanding a solicitor be present during interviews. CID coming in to see him, probing and trying to wind him up. 'What were you doing round these parts, Billy? Bit out of your way, isn't it?' Him repeating, 'No comment', over and over until his brief turned up, but even that turned into a fiasco, with the dibble claiming they had fresh evidence and eye-witness statements that had him bang to rights. Hours later, when his brief had gone, came the grand finale, the moment he'd been waiting for. The cell door came flying open and the riot squad stormed in, mob-handed. He tried to get a crack at one, but lost out to superior numbers, bundled head down over the wooden block with a knee in his back and a boot on the back of his head. The cunts tried choking the last resistance out of him, disarming the prisoner according to regulations and thereby not leaving any incriminating marks on his body. Then, cuffed hands and feet, he was hoisted aloft and carried off like an explorer captured by jungle tribesmen. The long ride to Parkway Central nearly finished him off – the metal ribs of the floor digging into his belly, imparting every ridge and every turn in the road – the goons up front laughing and cracking jokes, with him done up like an overstuffed turkey.

Eileen came down to find him at the window, peering through the nets.

'What you doing?' she said.

'Admiring the geraniums … You ready?'

Viewed from the back of a taxi, the lights of the pubs and brasseries along the strip looked inviting. In his jacket pocket, a small roll of tens and twenties, courtesy of his ill-gotten. Now he was on the books for Gary there'd be more opportunity. The chance to work with high-end professionals who didn't fuck about.

'Did you book a table?' Eileen said.

'Don't need to, I know the fella.'

'How?'

'Gizmo arm-wrestled the waiter one night and won. We all got a free meal.'

He recalled such incidents with fondness. The glorious past, infused with richness and colour. But where were they now – those stalwart companions of his, who'd pulled such stunts when they were younger? Hard to reconcile those days with the way things were now. The struggle to make a decent living. The wife who sat beside him in perpetual judgement, wishing she were somewhere else.

'I saw Rosalyn up the Parkway,' he said. 'Gave her a lift home.'

'More fool you.'

'That's nice – where's your Christian charity?'

'You wanna get mixed up with the likes of her that's your lookout.'

'Jimmy was a good pal of mine.'

'Jimmy was an arsehole. He had six kids with three different women and never paid a penny towards any of them.'

'Four, actually. You should get your facts right before you go slagging people off.'

'And you should stop messing with things that don't concern you. Rosalyn's trouble. Always has been.'

Sometimes it paid to compromise for the sake of public relations. The scrap he'd had in the Working Men's Club that night had proved his mettle, and apart from being ejected by the management, no further comebacks had been initiated against him. Eileen had seen him in action. Seen what he could do.

Sometimes fear provoked great acts of courage and vengeance, as history had demonstrated down through the ages. Like the time he'd marched into the Crown and dragged his old fella from his perch at the bar, weighing into him with fists and feet, delivering a long overdue lesson. All the years of abuse and violence meted out to one and all – including him, the youngest, Billy Riley, and his poor beleaguered mother.

Eileen stared at him, trying to gauge his thoughts from the look on his face.

'What's up with you?'

'Nothing.'

He couldn't speak of these things to anyone, not even to her, his wife. They remained buried, locked away inside him like a prisoner in solitary, never to be brought out and examined under the light.

23
Rosalyn revisited

He met her outside Co-op, a merciless wind blowing in – Parkway's version of Antarctica. She seemed oddly pleased to see him, couldn't wait to tell him how she'd walked a couple of miles already that morning and was trying to get fit. He looked her over, remarking on her new haircut, an observation that seemed to please her no end.

'Where's the kiddie?' he said.

'At me nan's.'

'You must be exhausted from all that exercise, want a lift?'

Pulling out into the mean streets of the Parkway felt good. He liked Rosalyn, his protective instinct inspired by her gameness and spirit. She could take the rise out of him, too, and he didn't mind that either. Nothing malicious about it, just a game between them that proved she felt comfortable around him. But eventually all that would have to stop. He couldn't afford to get too involved, even if she was Jimmy's daughter. Any little acts of kindness he showed her would be leapt upon and used to maximum advantage.

'Sorted your arrears out yet?' he said.

'Not yet. But I'm gonna, soon as I get the money.'

'What you gonna do – rob a bank?'

Like most youngsters she was clueless around finances. Perhaps he could help her out, teach her basic economics, but it hardly seemed worth the trouble. They both knew where the money would go, frittered away on junk food and other non-essentials. Small wonder she still had the kid, what with Social Services looking in. She claimed to be taking it all seriously, but somehow he didn't believe her.

'Landlord up the Swan's looking for part-time staff,' he said. 'Want me to put a word in for you?'

'I don't wanna work in a pub.'

'Why not?'

'I can't get a babysitter.'

'What about your nan – can't she help?'

'I can't keep asking her, she's not well.' She looked away, a petulant frown setting in. He tried to get the measure of her, wasn't sure where the truth ended and the lies began.

'How about I drop you over Latimer Road – see if you can pick up a few early morning punters?

She stared at him in horror.

'It was a joke, Rosalyn.'

She slunk further down, outwardly resistant. He pictured the fat landlord, fretting about the bills and the leaking roof, the gang of young tearaways that frequented the place. The sweet moolar driving everything, whether it was yours or someone else's. Even Rosalyn was infected by it – and never a more innocent-looking lass you could hope to find. But she'd marked herself, guilty by association with certain criminal types, a big sign across her forehead for all to see.

Parkway South loomed, with its hi-rise blocks and aura of deprivation. McGuinn's eager taunting came back to him, about the locals torching cars and smashing shop windows. At night, gangs roamed the streets looking to mark their territory, 9mm Glocks shoved into their coat pockets like fashion accessories. Times had changed, and not for the better.

'You like living here?' he said.

'Not really.'

'Why don't you move then?'

'What with – shirt buttons?'

He couldn't help grinning. 'I like you, Rosalyn, you know that?'

'Oh yeah?'

'Not in that way, sweetheart, you're not my type.'

'You're not my type either. I don't go out with old men.'

'Less of the old, luv – eh? I could run half these youngsters off the block, and still have time to finish me cornflakes.'

He admired her commitment to the kid, too. All those sleepless nights and demands on her time, programmed for sacrifice like all child-bearing women. It came naturally to them, gave meaning to their lives. Most men couldn't conceive of such a thing; devoting all hours of day and night to something that puked and shat all over you without warning. Men were better off around other men, fraternising in the pubs or on building sites – even in prison.

His mood changed. The buildings he passed and the people on the streets seemed to reflect back a sense of unease. The skies, too, heavy with the threat of a storm up ahead, an oppressiveness hanging over the hills and valleys. At times like these he was reminded he was on his own.

He pulled in by the swing park. Drab grey high-rises loomed overhead. A young mother pushed a toddler on the roundabout. The kid clung on to the safety bar, enjoying the free ride.

'This where you live?' he said.

Rosalyn nodded.

'Not exactly Carlton Heights, is it?'

'It's alright.'

He turned off the ignition and sat back, taking in the view through the windscreen.

'How'd you like to make some money, Rosalyn?'

'I'm not a prosser.'

'Oh well, that's that career option out the window.'

She pondered, reluctant to answer.

'Depends what I'd have to do.'

The toddler on the roundabout enjoyed the ride, pushed by his devoted mother. Most of the girls on the estate just wanted money, security. Sometimes, all they wanted was a baby, like the little kiddie Rosalyn pushed round in the buggy. Seemed to fulfil a need in them no one else could explain.

'Friend of mine's got a property coming up,' he said. 'You could move in, look after the place.'

'What – and get paid for it?'

'Steady on, luv – one step at a time, eh?'

She faked a more serious look for his benefit, but he wasn't fooled. The young had no respect for their elders. Nature had intended it that way, a process that ran in cycles from one generation to the next. He'd felt the same when he were younger. That sense of invincibility and endless vigour. Then came the court cases and the sentencing. The van journey from Manchester Assizes up the M6 – him and a bunch of lads aged fourteen. Like a film playing he could see it clearly: the snowflakes washed away by ponderous windscreen wipers; the feeling he was being taken far from home. Cracking jokes with the lad next to him to keep up the bravado. The screw in front, turning to him with a sneer, 'You won't be laughing in a minute, son.'

The screw had been right. There hadn't been much to laugh about in that place, or any other HM gulag he frequented from there on. But he got used to it. One thing he could be proud of. No matter what they threw at him, he soaked it up and came back for more. Never let them know they'd got one over on him.

'Crack on then,' he said. 'I got things to do.'

She opened the door, put one foot on the pavement, and stopped. He knew what was coming before she'd opened her mouth.

'Any chance you could – '

'No, Rosalyn, there isn't.'

'You haven't let me finish.'

'I don't need to, sweetheart, it's written all over your face.'

Like a mug, he took out his wallet and peeled off a ten-spot. Anyone watching would have seen a suspect transaction between a forty-year-old male Caucasian and a teenage girl. Not the kind of rumour he wanted floating around the estate.

'Thanks,' she said, with a degree of sincerity. 'I'll pay you back soon as I can.'

'Sure you will. You take it easy out there.'

Watching her stroll off towards the high-rises, he felt again that sense of duty, that somehow he'd been ordained to take on the role of protector. Alone in the world she had no one to look out for her, except her poor old nan who had her own health problems to deal with. But he, Billy Riley, could step in and take charge, raise the girl's standard of living. Jimmy would have been proud of him.

24

The Documentary

He met the fella in Pope's, with its soft lights and long windows overlooking the precinct. They shook hands firmly, on an equal footing now after their little lunchtime chat in the Grafton. Gizmo had set the meeting up, on the understanding that it wouldn't get back to Eileen. No one would find out about it until it was too late. By then he would have found a way to deny it completely.

'Thanks for coming,' the fella said, and motioned two barstools by the window. 'Shall we sit here?'

'Fine by me.'

He savoured the moment, small victory of a kind he'd been unused to so far. Sure, he'd met bods of that ilk before, in the clubs and the bars along the waterfront when he'd been working the doors – minted types flashing Rolexes and designer jewellery, driving cars bought by Mummy and Daddy. The journalist fella was different, more of a serious, academic type without pretension. And if there was such a thing as a free lunch, this was it. Negotiations of some sort would surely follow.

They perched up overlooking the pedestrian precinct. He settled in, enjoying the view and a mild feeling of grandiosity. 'This place was an ice rink years ago,' he said. 'I used to come here when I was a kid. Never was much good at it, mind. Too much like hard work, if you ask me.'

The fella nodded vaguely, taking a sip from his pint. Around them the chatter from office workers and business types taking time out from the routine. All pleasant enough, but he, Billy Riley, wanted to know more, find out exactly what he was getting into.

'So what's it all about? Gizmo said you wanted a word with me.'

The fella scratched his head and took a moment to answer. 'I just wanted to sound you out, really. Ask your advice on a few things.'

'Like what?'

'Well, I know there's been some objection to our filming from some of the locals round here. Do we need permission?'

'You can do what you like, pal, it's a free country.'

'But I thought you said – '

'I said it were dangerous, that's all. Some folk might not like having cameras shoved in their faces.'

'Like Mrs Simms?'

'She's one, yeah. But there are plenty of others.'

The journalist fella stared out at the lead-lined roof speckled with pigeon shit; couldn't have a clue what he was getting himself into. And he, Billy Riley, had to remind himself what the deal was here – some chancer from out of town trying to gain his trust. The fella's easy-going manner and quiet voice was hard to resist, but he wasn't fooled that easily. They were here for different reasons and they both knew it.

To give the fella a sense of background, he told a few war stories from the past. Patrolling the dance floors and the walkways on the North Side with Leonard's security firm back in the 80s. The Palace Vaults and Little Willy's – two of the liveliest venues he'd ever worked in. Standing back to watch the sea of bods on the dance floor, picked out by the strobes and the lasers. Fights breaking out that required his own special brand of expertise.

'You experienced quite a lot of trouble?' the fella said.

'You could say that. Had to be prepared at all times.' He tapped his nut. 'The head's a great weapon when it comes on top. Fella gets too close and bang! You drop the cunt without even thinking.'

The fella recoiled at his graphic demonstration, a natural enough reaction for one who'd never been schooled in the arts.

'How well did you know Leonard?'

'We were pretty close at one point.'

'Was he like they said he was in the papers? You know – bit

of an Al Capone?'

'I wouldn't know, I never met Al Capone.' He waited for a reaction, but got only a mystified smile. 'Actually, he were just a normal fella, far as I was concerned. Did a day's graft and went home to his wife and kids.'

'What about the accusations made against him?'

'The what?'

'Wasn't he supposed to be implicated in several unsolved murders?'

'I don't know nothing about that.'

'Really?' The fella raised an eyebrow. 'It was all over the papers at one point. You must have heard something?'

He shrugged. 'Lotta rumours get spread around these parts. Don't do you no favours to listen to 'em – know what I'm saying?'

The fella tapped his pint glass distractedly, quiet for a moment.

'Someone bent my windscreen-wipers back a couple of days ago. I don't suppose you have any idea who that might have been?'

'Windscreen wipers?' He chuckled at the fella's naivety. 'You were lucky it weren't a concrete block through the windscreen!'

The fella couldn't seem to understand. The kind of bods he was dealing with were mercenary types, well up for the ruck in every way. Someone like Widow Simms only had to say the word and they would all be out roaming the streets looking to carve someone up for the slightest reason.

'So what do you suggest I do?' the fella said.

'About your windscreen wipers?'

'About the documentary.'

'Go back to London. Work on summat else.'

'I don't think I could do that. We've invested too much time in the project already.'

'Your choice.'

The fella peered at him, thoughtfully. 'What if I was to ask you to come on board? In a sort of, advisory capacity?'

'Me?'

'Well – you know the area, the people.'

'I have to live round here, pal. Folks know who I am. I wanna be able to walk out me door in the morning and not get taken out.'

The fella nodded as if he understood, but the look in his eyes implied a certain playful belligerence, like it was a game they were playing.

'What did you think about the riots?' the fella said.

'Not a lot, I was away at the time.'

'Did you know any of the ringleaders?'

'Yeah, sure. What d'you want, their names and addresses?'

The fella smiled lazily, didn't seem to cotton on.

Tired of the subterfuge, he rolled up his sleeve and flexed the muscles of his left arm. 'Here, take a look at this … Sixteen stitches from a machete wound outside a club in Wigan. Fella didn't like it 'cause I'd thrown him out and shown him up in front of his mates. Sly little fucker were waiting for me when I come out. And here's another one …' He bent his head and jabbed his bald nut with a finger. 'See that?... Twenty stitches from an iron bar, trying to stop a ruck outside Pendragon's in Merthyr Tydfil. Only went down there for a weekend to help a mate out!'

The fella looked on in horrified fascination, the war wounds outside anything in his own experience. 'My God. It's a miracle you're still here.'

'That's right, fella. As you can imagine, I'm in the business of self-preservation these days.'

He felt a deep pride at his personal collection, able to remember the time and location of each one. Tracing the scar tissue with his fingers brought back memories good and bad. A sense of awe at the resilience of the human body.

'There you have it,' he said. 'The trials and tribulations of life on the frontline.'

The fella took a drink, a mischievous glint in his eye.

'So … Will you help us?'

'With what exactly?'

'Research. You'd be ideal. Just what we're looking for.'

'Get driven round in one of them fancy limousines, would I?'

'Probably not. But we would guarantee unlimited tea and biscuits.'

A low murmur came from the lunchtime crowd, much more sedate than the raucous prattle from the Grafton mob. The journalist fella must have felt quite comfortable here among the trendy types and the office workers. But it wasn't his kind of place at all. He felt conspicuous, easily identifiable by his tattooed hands and sovvie rings, the taint of prison still upon him.

'What's the crack with you and the bird, Sheila?' he said.

'You mean Angela?'

'That's the one. You married?'

'Oh, no. Angela's a sort of business partner, stroke assistant, if you like. She does a lot of the research, finds the right locations.'

'Chief cook and bottle washer, you mean?'

'Well, I wouldn't say that. She's very good at her job, highly professional.'

'You turking it?'

'Sorry?'

'The two of you. You at it between the sheets?'

'Oh, Christ, no!' The fella frowned, as if the thought had never occurred to him. 'What about you – are you married?'

'I am indeed, fella. Twenty-three years of dodging saucepans and flying cutlery. And she reckons *I'm* the one with the problem.' He could almost hear the church bells – or in their case, the sweet refrain of a registry office all those years ago. The fights they had were legendary, occasionally resulting in the dibble being called out when hostilities got out of hand. Having a wife who could punch above her body weight had its disadvantages – especially when you happened to be on the receiving end. But Eileen was a scrapper and always had been. And in spite of anything else she might have been up to, he had to give her credit for that.

'Women are a strange breed,' he said, in summary. 'Never could work 'em out.'

'Yes, I know what you mean.'

A pigeon strutted on the lead valley outside, jerking its head insanely; pedestrians strolled in the precinct below. He supped his pint and thought about Eileen, what she'd meant to him over the years. How they'd always been a team. Two people who'd always been so close, now enemies under the same roof.

A bunch of students loitered by the bar, laughing and joking. He pictured the journalist fella years ago, starting out on his privileged career – a nice, safe little number in the halls of learning, drinking and carousing with his posh mates. Never making trips upriver for offences against the Crown, forced to mix with degenerates and stone-killers on a daily basis.

So far they'd only skirted around the real issue, a sort of friendly preamble before the main event. He was sure the fella would make some kind of offer to lure him in; the temptation of fame and money to offset the threat of retribution from some disgruntled local. Sonia Simms still had considerable influence among the notables on the South Side, many of whom owed their current status to Leonard's patronage. She alone wouldn't want a documentary made about her recently-departed husband, or any details of his past to arise.

'So let's say I were to take part in this little project of yours – just for argument's sake, of course. What would I have to do?'

'Well, as I said, we need someone who knows the area, the people. Obviously, we're keen to know more about Leonard Simms and his influence. Your involvement would give the project authenticity.'

The fella would never understand what he was up against. The Parkway had a feel of its own. You had to have grown up around the place to truly understand it. Reformers and politicians tried to change things but it never worked. The locals always reverted to type, hiding in a network of cobbled alleyways and red-brick council houses that even the dibble wouldn't enter at night.

Never one to miss an opportunity, he kept the charade going, teasing out areas of weakness for his own benefit.

'I've been doing a bit of community work lately,' he said. 'Helping underprivileged youngsters, that sort of thing.'

'Really?'

'I'm helping this girl at the moment. Daughter of an old pal of mine, she is. I felt it were, like, my duty, so to speak.'

'Well that's very noble of you. Perhaps we could include a link in the documentary – if you felt comfortable with it, of course.'

Tired of the bravado and role-playing, he changed his tone. 'Look – maybe it is a worthwhile cause you're involved in, but I can't help you. You wouldn't be able to afford me anyway.'

'Well at least think about it. There's a huge demand for this sort of thing.'

'What – serving the likes of me up as entertainment?'

'All media is entertainment. But something like this has an educational component too. Take the riots on the Parkway, for instance. That has a huge social significance and could easily happen again. Your insight into why it happened would make people sit up and think.'

'That's how you see yourself, is it – as a social reformer?'

'No, not at all. I just like to make good television.'

He couldn't help liking the fella, the natural, easy-going way he had that put you at your ease. But there were grave implications from anything that might transpire from their conversation. Possible consequences not to be taken lightly.

The fella looked at him intensely. 'What if it was about you instead?'

'Me?'

'Well, yes. What if it was more about you and your background? How would you feel about it then?'

He once shared a cell with an Old Etonian. The fella had just been weighed-off with six-years for fraud and was settling in. Instead of being overawed by the hostile new environment, the fella adapted pretty quick, sussing out the conmen and the scammers on the wing – albeit with a little gentle prompting from his new pad mate, Billy Riley. The journalist fella had a similar refinement, a quiet confidence that couldn't be shaken. And now this – the carrot, expertly dangled.

He finished his drink and prepared to leave.

'Nice meeting you. Good luck with the windscreen wipers.'

'Yes, and thank you. And if you have any questions, give me a call.' The fella slid a business card across the surface. The light in his eyes had changed again. A glint of avarice this time. The look of a prospector who'd just struck gold.

25
A Job for Rosalyn

Her flat was on the fourth floor. From along the hall came the harsh jangle of TV, like the folk inside were hard of hearing and had the volume cranked up. The same stale, airless odour hung around, the kind that seemed to penetrate these places. Standing outside her door, he wondered what he was doing. Billy Riley, morphing into the local neighbourhood support. Next he'd be handing gifts out down the mall dressed up as Santa Claus.

'Oh?' she said when she opened the door, only mildly surprised to see him.

'How are you, sweetheart? Thought I'd pay you a little visit.'

She led him through to a small cluttered kitchen, where he leaned against the worktop while she made tea. He noted the plates stacked in the sink and the general clutter. Some people seemed happy living in shit. Rosalyn was nice enough and clearly took pride in her appearance, but the surroundings weren't exactly pristine. What chance did the kids have, growing up in these places? All the doctors and lawyers came from the other side of town, given a privileged start in life like the journalist fella. The only answer for folk on the estate was to take on a menial job, or go on the rob – a career path most of them took to willingly as soon as they were able.

'Where's the kiddie?' he said.

'Asleep.'

He nodded, wondering if she'd had a fella in and didn't want to tell him. More likely she was on her own and didn't need the aggravation, the extra hassle.

'Go on through,' she said. 'I'll bring your drink in.'

'Got any biscuits?'

'No, I haven't.'

'What kind of a hostess are you, Rosalyn?'

'I got crisps?'

'What flavour?'

'Salt and vinegar?'

'Don't worry about it, luv, the tea'll do fine.'

The narrow hall led onto a small front room. Bleached and wrinkled kiddie's clothes hung from a dryer; against the radiator, a yellow plastic table filled with toys. The window overlooked the city; the tubular struts of the football stadium that drew huge crowds on a Saturday afternoon. The sight took him back to his youth, running with the Red Army – hundreds of them travelling up and down the country causing havoc and mayhem. Life had been simpler then, the pleasures spontaneous and easier to come by: girls, booze and football, but not always in that order. Even the short spell in DC didn't stop him for long. Six weeks and two days locked away from his favourite pastime until his eager return – always watching out for the dibble who were being drafted in in ever-increasing numbers.

Rosalyn came in with the tea. She slumped on the sofa, hugging her mug in both hands like a lost child.

'What did you want to see me about?' she said.

'Progress report. See how you've been getting on.'

She shrugged. 'Alright.'

'Relax, will you? I ain't the dibble.' He sipped his tea and grimaced. 'How many sugars you put in this?'

'Two.'

'I said half a spoonful, didn't I?'

'Sorry …' She made no attempt to move, lost in her thoughts. He settled back, comfortable in the small room, winter sun pooling on the threadbare carpet. His well-being clearly didn't mean much to Rosalyn, but all that would change when she realised how much she needed him.

'Tell us about this boyfriend of yours?' he said. 'What's the crack with him?'

'Nothing much. He kept coming round and hassling me, so I took out a restraining order on him.'

'What about the Social Services?'

'What about 'em?'

'Are they involved?'

'The social worker helped me take out the order on him. Wrote the report and all that.'

On the outside she didn't seem all that bothered, but that was just a front. Maybe she thought it was funny, living in permanent debt and running round with no-hopers, a burden on society.

'Why didn't you tell me you'd been out grafting?' he said.

'What?'

'Don't come the cunt with me. It's common knowledge, sweetheart. Running errands for them scallies off the Parkway. You must've seen what they do to people that fuck 'em about.'

She stared into her mug. 'That were ages ago. I don't do it no more.'

'What – you gave it up to work at Burger King, did you?'

'No?'

Still she wouldn't look at him. He saw her as a statistic, a headline in the paper some way down the line.

'You need to open your eyes, Rosalyn. Look out for yourself and the kiddie – know what I'm saying?'

'Yeah, alright. Don't keep on.'

Gazing at her on the tatty old sofa, it was hard not to feel pity, compassion even. He, who'd stomped fellas to a bloody pulp and enjoyed a pizza five-minutes later. Most of them had deserved it, the kind that took liberties and needed reminding. Rosalyn was different. She brought out the softer, paternal side of him.

Leaning forward, he clasped his hands together, like the goodly father before a lowly sinner. 'Look – I know it's hard for you, sweetheart, but you gotta take some responsibility for yourself.'

'I'm trying, aren't I?'

'Yeah, but you're not trying hard enough. What you need is a bit of guidance. A sort of careers officer like they give school-leavers.'

She slipped back into sullen mode, like a kid in front of the teacher. He glanced over the furnishings, the cheap oddments on the mantelpiece, the glass-fronted unit filled with cheap knick-knacks. Rosalyn's bruised and damaged psyche, like a ward of court that gave him jurisdiction. Her life and the life of the kiddie in his hands, to do with as he saw fit.

'How much do you owe, then, Rosalyn?'

'Dunno.'

'Don't fuck about. How much?'

She shrugged. 'A few grand.'

'To who – the dealers?'

'Credit cards and loans, that sort of thing.'

He finished his drink, and stood. She gazed up at him, a hint of anxiety.

'Are you gonna shop me in to the Social?'

'For what – putting too much sugar in me tea?'

He felt like McGuinn, eyeing a choice suspect. And here he was using the same tactics.

Heading for the door, he took in the threadbare carpet, the kiddie's clothes hanging on the dryer. Rosalyn followed him out.

'I'll be in touch,' he said.

'What d'you want me to do?'

Surprised at the change in tone, he turned to her.

'Huh?'

'The other day you said you knew how I could make some proper money?'

Now they were getting somewhere. She'd dropped the pretence and was meeting him halfway. 'I'll have to think about it,' he said. 'In the meantime, get some decent biscuits in for the next time I come round.'

Two street urchins loitered in the road, proper little Artful Dodgers with torn trousers and grubby faces. Thousands of them all over the city, looking for something or someone to prey upon, the mark of criminality on them like a thumbprint. He saw himself in their cocky demeanour. Billy Riley, already an accomplished housebreaker by the age of eleven; running with a gang of older boys from the South Side, choring bikes from the city centre and stripping them down in Pat Whitmore's shed. The thrill of petty larceny burned into his memory like the sting of Nitromors on his fingers; tiny flakes of paint that stuck to his clothes, his hair. Had he known what was waiting for him up ahead he might have changed course and found a different vocation; become a straight-goer and clocked onto some menial job like the rest of the herd. But it hadn't panned out that way. Life had thrown him a different set of options.

26

Bandit Country

He drove them round the South Side, looking for things of historical and cultural value that might look good on TV. He pointed out landmarks as they appeared. Bird's Hill Rise, where caretaker Brian Read had taken a hostage before being shot dead by the Armed Response. The recently completed skateboard park, sanctioned by the local council – formerly a piece of wasteland littered with condoms and used syringes. A few streets away, the boarded up shop fronts and graffiti-daubed walls of the main drag, where locals shuffled along, shoulders hunched against the cold and ever-present threat of extinction.

'This is where the riots kicked off,' he said. 'Place was crawling with riot vans and dibble. Like a war zone, it were.'

The journalist fella stared out the window. 'Doesn't look too friendly now, either. Not the sort of place you'd want to hang around at night.'

'Ain't much better in the daytime.' He clocked the bird, Angela, in the rear-view. She looked hunched up and severe, as if the frozen wastes outside had penetrated the warm interior. 'You alright in the back there, luv?'

'Yes, I'm fine, thanks.'

They turned into Bendon Terrace, rows of drab, red-brick council houses with metal-frame windows. A pall of neglect hung over the area, visible to any onlooker. But the intrepid duo wanted more, so he duly obliged, doing the commentary like a tour guide, enjoying the sense of authority it gave him, the fact they were taking in his every word.

The Boys Club loomed on the corner – graffiti-splashed walls and broken windows. Like something out of East LA, complete with the deserted basketball court that hadn't been played on in years. Driving past, he felt a touch of sadness; such a memorable piece of his youth left to fall into disrepair.

'See that building over there,' he said. 'That was the place to be when I were growing up.'

'Doesn't look much now,' the journalist fella said.

'It was in its time, believe me. This old boy, Sonny, taught me how to use the jab. Fire off the old ones and twos and keep out of trouble.'

'What's the jab?' Angela said.

'He's talking about the noble art of boxing,' the fella said.

'Nothing noble about it when you're sitting on your ass in front of two thousand people. Done a bit yourself, have you?'

'Briefly, years ago. Can't say I enjoyed being punched in the head repeatedly, but it was certainly an experience.'

His assessment of the fella went up a notch. Anyone who'd gone toe-to-toe in the ring was at least worthy of some respect. Perhaps he'd underestimated him a bit when they'd first met, mistaken the accent and the clothes for weakness.

Turning into Nortoft Road, the Admiral came into view, with its green-tiled façade and obscured windows. 'Rough old haunt that was,' he said. 'Me and a mate used to nick bottles of beer from the yard when we were kids. Sell the empties back to the landlord a few days later.'

'Didn't he find out you'd stolen them?' Angela said.

'If he did he never said.'

Entering Latimer Road from Nortoft, he felt the vibe right away. One long rat-run where any strangers driving in would realise their mistake by the time they were halfway along. The same redbrick council terraces you saw in certain areas of the Parkway, numbers painted on the front, crumbling garden walls and overgrown shrubbery.

'Take a good look,' he said. 'You're now entering the worst road in Great Britain, voted two-years running by The Sun newspaper.'

'Seriously?' Angela said.

'The only time you see the dibble down here is inside a riot van.'

'And Leonard was born here?' the fella said.

'Just round the corner. I'll show you.'

He pulled into the Mews, a confusion of side roads tailing off. The place brought back vivid memories, none of them good.

'There you go,' he said, pointing out a nondescript semi. 'Number Nineteen. Birthplace of a legend.'

'It looks pretty grim,' Angela said. 'Was it always like this?'

'It's had its moments. Drugs moved in in the Eighties and all the decent folk moved out.'

The whole neighbourhood had changed since Leonard's day. Now it was a haven for crack-addicts and prostitutes, making whole areas uninhabitable. And yet, a few streets away the vibe was different – privately-owned council houses with neat front gardens and block-paved driveways. The old folk could walk to the corner shop without fear of being mugged, or run over by a stolen car full of psychotic youngsters.

Pulling in to the parade, he turned off the ignition. A few teenagers loitered by the bus stop, hoods pulled over their heads like shrouds. Visible in the valley below, row upon row of box houses, rooftops glistening in the winter sun.

'That's the guided tour over, folks,' he said. 'Any questions?'

'Can I get out?' the fella said. 'Stretch my legs a bit?'

'You can, but don't go too far. The last tourist that wandered off was never seen again.'

The fella got out and set off across the Arctic tundra, zipping up his jacket as he went. They watched him stroll around the car park, his baggy cords rippling in the wind.

'Have you always lived around here?' the bird said.

'Apart from the odd holiday upriver.'

'Up where?'

'Her Majesty's pleasure … The big house … Stoney lonesome.' He waited for a smile or chuckle to acknowledge the joke, but the bird's expression didn't shift one iota. She sat awkwardly in the back, staring out at the journalist fella. He wondered if he'd get the chance to have a pop at it on the sly, but it seemed unlikely. Weren't his type, really – too thin-faced, not enough meat on the bone. Probably saw him as a bit of rough, the uneducated criminal type she could bamboozle with her big words and superior education.

'What you gonna do now I've shown you round the crib?' he said.

'You'd have to ask Nick. He makes all the decisions.'

'Really? That surprises me.'

'Why?'

'Well, I just presumed you were in charge. You must have that look about you.'

The journalist fella snapped shots of the local architecture on his camera. With his hair blowing in the wind and his crumpled cords he looked distinctly out of place; the mean streets of Parkway South might as well have been the wilds of Borneo. The fella was oblivious, had no idea of the kind of trouble he could get himself into.

'Sizing up the neighbourhood for his next movie, is he?' he said.

'Not quite. Movies are a different medium.'

'How's that?'

'We're making a documentary. You're targeting a different audience for a start.'

'Well tell him the audience round here are fed on raw meat. They don't take kindly to strangers – know what I'm saying?'

She didn't have much of a sense of humour, didn't take part in the banter like the journalist fella did. One of those birds you could wind up without even trying. He didn't like to be ignored, though. Her attitude demanded he respond in kind, try to impress her in some way.

'Me and a pal used to come over here of an evening nicking bikes.'

'Pushbikes?'

'That's right. Had a thriving business going at one point, we did. Used to build 'em to order.' Seeing her frown, he reeled her in a bit further. 'Then we, sorta, branched out into the motor trade. I mean, that were back in the day before everything were computerised. My mate Pat could hotwire anything in under ten-seconds.'

'You stole cars as well?'

'Only the best. We had this RS2000 once. Got chased by the dibble through country lanes out Blackmore way. Couldn't catch our Pat, though. He were like Jackie Stewart in his day – crackin' fuckin driver.'

The passenger door opened and the journalist fella got in, rubbing his hands together. 'God, it's bloody cold out there!'

'Find what you were looking for?'

'There's a real atmosphere, that's for sure. But the backdrop's great. What d'you think, Angela?'

She looked pensive, uncertain. 'I don't know. Possibly.'

A kid on a skateboard went past on the pavement, and joined the gang at the bus stop. The others gathered round him in close conversation, a huddle of sinister monks with their hoodies up, faces hidden.

'The neighbourhood menace,' he said. 'Shoot you as soon as look at you.'

'They're just kids, aren't they?' Angela said.

'Don't be fooled by that. Take one on you take 'em all on, believe me.'

The fella turned to him with a look of sincerity. 'Listen, Billy. We really appreciate you driving us around this morning, it's been fascinating. Could we convince you to join us again tomorrow?'

'I doubt it, pal. I got things to do.'

'Maybe Wednesday, then? I was thinking we could get a few shots of you down by the canal.'

'Then what – bring in the hair stylist and the makeup department?'

'If that's what it takes, why not?'

He saw something in the fella he hadn't seen before; a flicker of real intent, perhaps. Behind the easy-going, slightly absent-minded demeanour was a steeliness of purpose, a determination that wouldn't be put off. The bird, too – she was as committed to the project as the fella. Easy to admire them without taking the danger into consideration. In reality their project was doomed and could only end in disaster. If widow Sonia found out they were going ahead against her wishes she wouldn't be too happy. And for all their bluster and enthusiasm there was one thing they hadn't reckoned on. Cameras could be replaced. People couldn't.

So what d'you want from me?' he said. 'You've had the guided tour of the Parkway and the Big Fella's crib. What else is on the agenda?'

The fella shifted in the seat, uncomfortable. The bird stared out at the scenery.

'We need someone who knows the area,' she said. 'Someone who knows the people who live here and how they would have been affected by the riots, the deprivation.'

'Plenty of folk round here could help you with that.'

'But you knew Leonard, didn't you?'

'So did a lot of other people. Don't make me an expert.'

'Yes, but you said yourself that you grew up with him and played on the same streets. I mean, from our point of view that's a perfect combination. We could do so much with that, we really could.'

Now he knew what the game was. They needed him to deliver the goods on all fronts. Without his involvement they were stuck. All he had to do was play along and convince them he was interested, get what he could from the deal, even if it was just the satisfaction from knowing he'd beaten the system.

'What do I get out of it?'

'Prestige?' the fella said with a grin. 'You never know, this might open up a whole new area of interest for you.'

'Or get me taken out in the process.'

'Well, I'm sure that wouldn't – '

'You ain't got a clue, pal.' He angled himself in the seat, better able to deliver the sermon they so clearly needed to hear. 'Let's be straight on a few things, shall we? It's one thing for me to drive you round the neighbourhood showing you the wildlife. But you start setting cameras up and pointing them in my direction, well that's a different story.'

The fella nodded as if he understood. The bird sat there in the back with a look of sullen indifference. Perhaps they needed something else, a little reminder to further their education.

'Tell you a story, shall I?' he said. 'Might help you understand the kind of people you're dealing with.' He had their attention, their interest. 'Imagine it's early Sunday morning. You're lying in bed – about nine or ten years old. There's a knock at the door, and you're like – who the fuck is that at this time in the morning? You hear your old fella go downstairs cursing and moaning, so you go to the top of the stairs to take a look. The old fella opens the door, and standing there is this big gypsy fella in a vest and an old pair of strides. He looks at the old fella and says, "I've come to fight you on the green."'

'Come to fight your father?'

'That's right, sweetheart. So the old fella slips on his jacket, strolls over the green, and the two of 'em go at it toe-to-toe.'

'Who won?'

'Far as I can recall it was a kind of draw. They beat seven barrels of shit out of each other then called it a day. Point I'm making is, that's the kind of people you're dealing with round here. They don't take prisoners.'

'That's a great story,' the fella said. 'It's got all the elements of drama. You as a child, witnessing something that was – well, so beyond most people's experience. Certainly beyond mine.'

The bird eased herself forward, ready to pounce. 'What would it take to convince you, Billy?'

'Convince me of what?'

'The value you could bring to this project.'

He saw the future, clear as the view from the windscreen. At forty years old, he'd already wandered into that bleak and depressing territory known as middle-age, where nothing much grew except nasal hairs and regular visits to the doctor to find out which illness was gaining first. He needed a change of career, something that required less muscle and wouldn't affect his parole conditions too much. Instinct told him this was it. Throw in his lot with the journalist fella and create a new persona. Billy Riley, star of stage and screen. The potential was limitless.

27
Full English

Rosalyn complained about the cold, her face pinched and livid. The toddler sat propped up in his mean machine, buried under a swathe of blankets, gazing out upon the world with sad eyes. He remarked on the kiddie's mournful look, suggesting he might be cutting a tooth. Rosalyn gazed at the crib with adoring eyes. 'Oh, he always looks like that of a morning. Don't you, darlin'?'

Anyone brave enough to take Rosalyn on would get the kiddie too, a joint package needing constant maintenance. Much as he liked the girl, he couldn't help wondering what she was going to do to sort herself out. The chances of her trapping a fella with money were slim – unless he was a drug dealer, or some other grafter off the estate. Hardly the recipe for long term security, even if she did manage to pull it off. The only thing she did have on her side was youth – that and a reasonably good figure.

'You had breakfast?' he said.

'No?'

'Come on then, I'll treat you.'

They parked up in Andy's Cafe, which boasted the crispiest fried bread in town. The kiddie lay contentedly in his chariot sucking juice from a plastic beaker. Rosalyn tucked into her full English with gusto, happily taking advantage of the free scran. The door chimed regularly, blowing in builders and other strange life forms from the cold outside. Now and then one of them clocked him in the corner with Rosalyn and the kiddie, but no one said anything. If they had he'd have soon put them right.

Besides, he was a married man with responsibility. Rosalyn was like one of his own.

'What's up?' he said. 'Had enough already?'

She burped and rubbed her stomach. 'I'm stuffed.'

'Lightweight.' He stabbed the sausage on her plate, cut it in half and popped one half in his mouth, enjoying the gluttony. 'What you got lined up, then?'

'Not much.'

'No trips up country, holidays abroad?'

'Where am I supposed to get the money for that from?'

'Never stopped you before, sweetheart. And remember, I know all about your background from inquiries I made, so don't be giving me no flannel.'

She made a face and sank back, refusing to look at him. The scene had a certain poignancy for him. Rosalyn was hard work, as all women were in different ways. But she had an innocence about her, a sweetness that brought out his chivalrous side. Getting involved with her was a risk. He knew what Eileen would say – buying the girl breakfast and giving her money – what was the matter with him? All it did was encourage dishonesty and make him a soft touch. The same wherever he went. People always expected something from him – a handout here, an introduction there. The downside of being known as a fixer, a settler of scores. His reputation always went ahead of him.

He wiped his mouth, pleasantly sated. The novelty of all that rich fried food still fresh after so long up the factory.

'I don't make a habit of this, you know,' he said.

'What?'

'The free scran. You gotta keep it quiet. Don't go telling no one.'

'Tell 'em what exactly – that you bought me breakfast up the café because you knew me dad?'

'Less of the lip, sweetheart. I'm trying to help you out, that's all. I don't want people getting the wrong idea.'

He'd read a book up the factory about the psychology of crime. Research showed that most criminals had been exposed to some form of criminality in early childhood. In his own case this was true: growing up on the Parkway and running with various gangs; the gradual progression from approved schools and detention centre, through to borstal and prison. Straight-goers rarely turned to crime unless they were forced into it by a change in circumstance – loss of a job, pressure to pay off debts and loans. In the end it was all about conditioning. Moral values inherited from parents and teachers, the kids you played with in the street. The only way to escape it was to move away and start afresh. The jails didn't help. Wherever you went you were guaranteed to know someone, either bods you'd grafted with on the out, or those you'd done a stretch with previously. One big social club for villains, eager to hit the street and put all they'd learned inside to good use.

Rosalyn was the same. Had she been born somewhere else her life might have been different. But this was her lot. Growing up on the Parkway, with its rundown tenements and underage gangsters looking to blast holes in each other at the slightest provocation. The teeming rabbit-warren she called home, targeted by the dibble every few months as part of its ongoing fight against crime. As a former resident he knew what it was like. Now she could hardly afford to pay the rent, and the council kept hassling her to make up the shortfall. Then there was the Social Services and the threat that they'd come in and take the kiddie away if she didn't buck her ideas up.

Watching her quiet dedication to the kiddie reminded him how different they were as a species. The woman all bound up in the nurturing process for the first sixteen years of the kiddie's life, and never really outgrowing her original commitment. The man's role as nothing more than a sperm-donor, his usefulness over as soon as he'd emptied his sack. But he had to acknowledge the work they put in. If it hadn't been for Eileen, his kids would have ended up starving to death, or shipped off to a succession of foster homes.

'Ever thought about moving?' he said.

'You asked me that before.'

'And I'm asking you again.'

She shrugged. 'I can't go anywhere, can I? I got no money.'

'Apathy and defeatism. That's what I'm hearing from you right now. You need to plan for the future, sweetheart – know what I'm saying?'

She picked at a serviette, stubbornly resistant to anything he said.

'What if I found you a place?' he said.

'Where?'

'Somewhere in town. Nice little two-bed place with a garden. What d'you reckon?'

Now he had her attention, the lure of something she hadn't expected.

'What about all me stuff?'

'Bring it with you.'

'How?'

'Hire a removals van, how d'you think?' He waited for her to crack on, but she stayed all sullen and resentful. 'What I'm saying is, you could end up in a nice little place of your own, away from all these muppets.'

'And what would I have to do for it?'

'I told you. Just maintain the place, that's all. Make sure it's all clean and tidy.'

The kiddie sneezed – a proper little snuffler that reminded them both he was there. Looking down at that puckered face, all soft and innocent, he, Billy Riley, was given to a moment's reflection. His own daughter had presented him with a grandchild whose wellbeing he'd neglected. For some reason he still couldn't stir himself to go round and get involved like a good grandparent should.

'So is that a yes, then?' he said.

She shrugged.

'Might be.'

For a moment, he was struck by a dilemma. His self-appointed role as Rosalyn's guardian and protector – albeit a tenuous one at that – and the conflicting forces that were coming into play. Gary's meeting with his mysterious contact who could open the doors to untold riches. Then the journalist fella and his assistant, promising opportunities of a different kind. Both ventures not without their share of danger.

'Did you ever meet the Big Fella?' he said.

'Who?'

'Bit before your time, eh? Anyway, some London bods are making a documentary about him, and they want me to be in it.'

Rosalyn didn't seem too impressed, but this in itself was no indication of how she might have felt inside.

Engulfed by a wave of optimism, he leaned forward, elbows on the table. 'Stick with me, sweetheart, and I'll see you alright.'

'How?'

'Don't you trust me?'

'I don't trust anyone – except me nan. She'd never hurt me.'

'Well I'm not gonna hurt you, am I?'

'How do I know?'

What a package the ex-boyfriend must have saddled himself with. Rosalyn and the kiddie, draining the fella's resources, taking him away from the work he ought to be doing. And him, Billy Riley, allowing himself to get drawn in like this when she wasn't even family.

'Shame really,' he said. 'I got quite attached to you and the kiddie.'

'What d'you mean?'

'Trying to help you and all that. There's no mileage in it. My missus was right, you're nothing but trouble.'

He dropped Rosalyn and the kiddie off, and drove home, thinking about the general unfairness of it all. You put yourself out for people and they didn't appreciate it. Money was always the rub. You spent your whole life chasing it, and whatever you got was never enough.

When he got back, Eileen was lying on the sofa, dressing gown over her knees. She looked up, vaguely, when he came in, then went back to the TV.

'What's for dinner?' he said.

'If you'd come back two hours ago you would have found out.'

He tossed his gloves on the table, and fussed the dog. Eileen tugged the blanket over her shoulders and shivered.

'Been out?' he said.

'Went to Gemma's earlier.'

'How's the wean?'

'Keeping them up half the night. Gemma's exhausted.'

'She ask about me?'

'I'm tired of making excuses for you. Why don't you go round and ask her? Get off your arse for a change?'

'I will do soon.'

'You've been saying that since the baby was born. What's the matter with you?'

A profound sense of agitation and discomfort stirred in his bones like the changing of seasons. He'd only been back five minutes and already she was putting a downer on him. Coupled with this, the thought that he could be shipped back upriver at any moment. He didn't think he could hack it anymore. Better to go out in style, like a showdown in the Old West. Him and McGuinn in a dusty street, horses tethered outside the local saloon. McGuinn's eyes narrowed in the sun, his hand straying nervously to the six-shooter strapped to his hip. But he would always beat McGuinn in a draw, if only by a split-second.

Slumped in the armchair, he watched the fish zip back and forth across the tank. The novelty had worn off. Now they were just another distraction, like the blurb on the TV, oblivious to him and his troubles.

The news came on. Old footage of damaged shopfronts and overturned vehicles from the riots. Whole communities affected by the aftermath. He thought of Rosalyn and the kiddie alone and vulnerable on the Parkway. The journalist fella, snapping photos on his camera, the bird trying to sell the documentary as if it would enlighten the world.

'I met the journalist fella in town,' he said. 'Drove him round the Parkway. He wants me to be research consultant on the documentary they're making.'

'That's your idea of a career move, is it?'

'Don't knock it, doll. All I gotta do is turn up, tell him what he wants to hear and everyone's happy.'

'What about Sonia? D'you think she'll be happy knowing you're associating with that lot?'

'Who cares what she thinks. It's none of her business what I do. I'm not selling state secrets, am I?'

Eileen turned back to the TV, a permanent scowl on her face. The fish did another lap of the tank, the filter gurgling quietly in the corner. Somewhere beyond the confines of the living room an alternative career beckoned – one with grand hotels and red carpets, book-signings and afternoon teas. Billy Riley, star of the vaudeville circuit, ringmaster supreme. The reservations he'd had earlier had faded, replaced by a sense of his own destiny. He liked the journalist fella enough to put a bit of faith in him. Between them they could create something memorable. A piece of living breathing modern art.

28
Groomed for the Big Time

Tenpins exploded along the twenty-four lanes, a sound that reminded him of his youth. The place had changed since then; no army of teenagers filling the table area, winding up the staff; no jukebox playing by the canteen. Nowadays it was full of stiffs, all practising their swinging-arm technique like Olympic hopefuls.

The journalist fella drank Coke through a straw. Angela answered e-mails on her Blackberry, a cluster of devices on the table in front of her. Every now and then, one of her phones would ring and she'd leap up to answer it, apologising for disrupting the meeting, always eager to continue when she sat back down. Both her and the fella seemed fascinated with the Bowl complex and the stories he told about it. The fact it had featured so prominently in his and Leonard's past.

'You used to come here regularly?' she said.

'Grew up in the place. Used to be an army of us running amok. Mate of mine rode a motorbike through the entrance once for a bet.'

'Seriously?'

'Few of us had the crack, like. We had a gang called the Mad Dogs, and that were one of the initiation ceremonies.' Talking about the old days brought them back with a painful clarity. Time had erased them and many of the people he knew, leaving only memories. But how grand those memories were, and how vivid in his mind, like a film playing on a projector screen.

'What was Leonard like as a child?' the journalist fella said.

He formed an image of a fat kid with health problems,

possessed of a strange self-assurance beyond his years. 'First time I met him, we got chased by the dibble. Leeds fans were all over the town causing havoc and mayhem. Leonard had an asthma attack near the train station. Could hardly breathe, like. Didn't matter to the dibble, though. They just beat the shit out of us anyway and threw us in the back of a van.'

'What for?'

'Running through people's gardens? Having a pop at Leeds fans in the centre of town? Who knows? They didn't need a reason.'

'Why do you call them the dibble?'

'That's what they are. Muppets with silly hats on.'

He started to relax, enjoying the interview and the chance to tell a few tales. With no film crew around and neither of them taking notes, it seemed low-key and casual enough. But the warning signs were there, the knowledge that already he'd given them too much. And like vultures they would expect more, hovering above his still-warm corpse waiting to strike.

Angela watched him closely, the two of them having nothing in common apart from the fact they were at the same table. But she intrigued him nonetheless. One of those women he enjoyed winding up. She had that superior look about her, the tip of her nose turned up like it was all somehow beneath her. But he sensed another element there, too, like he'd seen in the fella. They were two of a kind, dedicated to the project. And he'd somehow allowed himself to be drawn in, seduced by the promise of something previously unattainable.

'And where did you fit in to all this?' she said. 'What sort of role did you play in the building of Leonard's empire?'

'I didn't. I hardly knew him back then.'

She sat back, disappointed, confused by his answer.

'What was the defining moment?' the fella said. 'The catalyst?'

'How d'you mean?'

'Well – did something dramatic happen that set Leonard on that path? Or do you think he was born like it?'

'What path we talking about?'

'The one that led him to prison. The one that ended with him being described as one of the most prolific drug dealers in Britain.'

'That was never proved.'

'Angela scoffed. 'So all that stuff in the papers was made up, was it?'

'Probably.'

He felt awkward, bound by the rules of the playground he'd grown up in. Certain things he couldn't say; limits to the subjects he could discuss without compromising his values – especially knowing his remarks could end up on primetime TV.

'Would you like something to eat, Billy?' the fella said.

'Yeah, sure. Grab us a cheese and pickle sandwich and a bag of crisps.'

'Anything else?'

'Large gin and tonic to steady me nerves?'

They drank coffee and ate sandwiches, the crack and rumble of ten-pins in the background. He lounged around like an actor on a film set, waiting for them to start shooting. If this was the glamorous world of TV he wasn't impressed. Nothing seemed to happen on time, the whole process held up by setbacks and lighting problems, technical hitches and vital members of the crew going missing. But now he'd had a taste of it he wanted more. Something about opening up to total strangers about the complexities of his life, the camera recording all the details, appealed to him. Like leaving a testament for posterity – for his grandkids even.

Angela looked him over. 'How do you feel about being interviewed today?'

'Better call the make-up department in first. I think I need a bit of touching up around the eyes.'

She smiled faintly. 'Just relax and you'll be fine.'

'How long are we gonna be filming for?

'Not long – why?'

'Well – I'd like to get away a bit early, if possible. Me and a couple of lads are robbing a Securicor van this afternoon, and might need some time to plan it.' She reminded him of a teacher at school who always had the suss on him. No matter what he said or did to try and impress her, she always managed to rise above it, leaving him feeling stupid in front of the class. Angela had that same aloofness about her, looking down on him from some higher ground. He felt like a dangerous pet, trained not to misbehave in public.

The Grip and the Soundman turned up with a bag of tricks, including the boom and the furry microphone. After the introductions, they sat around drinking coffee and swapping technicalities. He felt even more out of his depth, but the adrenalin spurred him on. Like being on a job and not knowing what was going to happen, all your senses on high alert. Everyone else looked relaxed and focussed, checking the equipment they were going to use, engaging in friendly banter that didn't include him.

The journalist fella looked at his watch and stood.

'Right, folks. Let's do it, shall we?'

He performed for the camera as required; his first foray into the world of filmmaking. The journalist fella put the questions to him in his dry, monotone voice, but this time, they were of a more personal nature, referring directly to him, Billy Riley, instead of the Big Fella, Leonard Simms. Where had he grown up? What was his earliest experience of crime on the Parkway? He tried to relax, like Angela had said, and to answer naturally. A couple of times he stumbled, not sure how to proceed, but the support was always there to reassure him. At any time he could stop and take a breather. They kept reminding him there was no pressure, but that was easy for them to say. They weren't being dissected under the spotlight.

Lunchtime came. They all sat around a table planning the next stage. The Grip, the Soundman, Angela, the journalist fella and his good self – Billy Riley, reluctant star of the unfolding cabaret.

'How do you feel?' the fella said.

'Great. When do I pick up me Oscar?'

They all laughed, and for a second he felt like he belonged. The moment passed and he was back to being himself again, wondering what he was doing here among the loafers and the corduroy jackets trying to look cool.

'Where did you get all the tattoos done?' Angela said, staring at his hands.

'Must have been an alien abduction. I just woke up one morning and they were there.'

'Do you have them all over?'

'That'd be telling, wouldn't it.'

She stared at him challengingly. 'I've got a tattoo.'

'Yeah?'

'Want me to show you?'

'Go on then.'

'Only if you show me yours first.'

He rolled up his sleeve and flexed his arm – a patchwork of mottled colour and blurred inscriptions, barely an inch of skin showing. She bent to study the strange configurations, mouth open in wonder. 'God, you're absolutely covered.'

Pleased with the effect, he pulled his sleeve down. 'Come on, then. Let's see yours.'

Standing, she hitched up her skirt to reveal a small yin/yang symbol at the top of her thigh. Nick gasped with mock horror. 'Christ, Angela – sit down, you'll get us all arrested!' She dropped her skirt and sat with a mischievous grin. The impromptu act had established a bond between them – Angela and the star performer – revealing a more playful side to her that she'd previously kept hidden.

Filming continued after lunch. The fella wanted a shot of him standing by the entrance, legs apart, hands in his pockets, just as he might have done when he was working the doors. 'Don't smile,' the fella said. 'Just look serious.'

The camera rolled, targeting him with its all-seeing black eye. And still the questions came, drawing him out on his experiences at the frontline. He told them stuff for the shock value. How him and Pat Whitmore had cleared a crackhouse on the north side for a grateful landlord. The tenants had shuttered off the front windows and reinforced the front door with double-bolts and steel girders. The only way in was through the back, using extreme force. In the end, they opted for an SAS style attack, masked up and armed with baseball bats.

'What did you do to them?' the fella said.

'Read 'em their rights then kicked the shit out of 'em.'

'Really?'

'You gotta come down hard on people like that. It's the only thing they understand.'

'How did it make you feel, knowing you had all that power?'

The camera honed in; the boom dangled a few feet above his head. 'Better than being on the receiving end of it, that's for sure.'

'Did you ever come unstuck?'

'Few times, yeah.'

'Can you give us an example?'

'Well, there was this one time. Me and a mate were debt-collecting for a firm on the South Side. We tracked this fella down to a block of flats on the Crescent. We were just about to go in when he started shooting at us from the balcony with an army assault rifle.'

'Was anyone hit?'

'We didn't hang around long enough to find out.'

'What happened?'

'Dibble picked the fella up a couple hours later. Cunt got ten years.'

Angela wanted more answers, off the record. Why had Leonard donated so much money to charities? Was it to divert attention from his criminal activities? He couldn't tell her the truth, that half the kids who came through the Boys Club ended up as runners and enforcers for Leonard's various enterprises. The gym was a magnet for all the up and coming hard nuts from the estate, eager to learn the ways of the world from older, wiser men. The charity donations came from a genuine altruistic streak, even if they were accompanied by the usual publicity. Leonard saw himself as a generous businessman who did what he could to help the underprivileged. Beneath all this was a cynical self-interest and a ruthless determination to build his own empire. Anyone who got in his way was annihilated.

'I hope you're not recording this?' he said, a touch of paranoia creeping in.

The fella smiled and shook his head reassuringly. 'Camera's off, Billy.'

Angela continued her questioning.

'So this gym was a front for criminal activities, is that what you're saying?'

'Not really. More a place for local lads to get together and batter each other senseless. But stuff did go on, I'm not denying it.' Talking about the club evoked fonder memories. He told them about the atmosphere and the camaraderie, not that he expected them to understand. The heavy bag work and the sparring sessions in the ring. Running uphill in the pouring rain at five in the morning to build stamina. He'd done all that and he'd been good, too. Like the movie said, he could've been a contender.

'Was Leonard a boxer?' Angela said.

'You're joking! Leonard was a doughnut-eater, king of the pork pies. You must've seen the photos of him as a kid – he never stopped eating.' Seeing they were having trouble getting the picture, he tried to be more explicit. 'Leonard was always big, see. His old fella were big, too. But he could move quick when he wanted to, believe me.'

'Was he bullied at school?'

'Not that I know of. And if he was he would've sorted it out soon enough.'

'In what way?'

'Well, just sorted it. Bided his time and got even, like.'

'And what about you – were you ever bullied?' Angela had a playful glint in her eye, sitting there waiting for his response.

'I had a few run-ins with older kids on the estate.'

'And did you sort them out the same way?'

'Not me, luv. I'm a pacifist, I don't agree with violence.'

Filming finally wrapped mid-afternoon. The fella seemed more than happy with what they had 'in the can'. Now the star of the show could go home and reward himself with a nice hot bath and a cup of cocoa, knowing he was there in the frame for perpetuity.

Angela looked at her watch. 'Look – I'm going to have to make a move in a minute. Can I drop you anywhere, Billy?'

Why not? he thought. A spin in the motor with a good-looking bird, even if she was a bit on the thin side. Do his ego the power of good.

He shook hands with the fella, who congratulated him once again on a good day's work. They were in league now, committed to finishing the project whatever the cost.

'Are you OK for tomorrow?' the fella said.

'Sure, long as I don't get lynched on the way home.'

Angela drove fast and talked non-stop, firing the occasional question at him with a sideways jerk of her head. He got the feeling she was genuinely interested in him and his life on the Parkway – the two of them so outwardly different they might otherwise never have met.

'I really admire what you're doing,' she said.

'What – making a prat of meself on TV?'

'You don't come across like that at all. Anyway, it's educational. People should know what goes on in these places.'

For the first time, he felt a hint of encouragement from her, that she might even be on his side.

She pulled over by the Pizza Express and left the engine running.

'OK for you here?'

'Fine, thanks.' He made no move to go, comfortable, reluctant to end the conversation.

'Well, I expect I'll see you later in the week,' she said.

'D'you like night clubs?'

She looked at him strangely. 'Sometimes. Why?'

'I could take you to a place Leonard used to own, down on the waterfront.'

'You mean we could film in there?'

'Probably not. More a kind of social visit. Introduce you to some people Leonard knew.'

'Sounds good. I'll tell Nick about it.'

'I was thinking of me and you, actually. Sort of, private arrangement, like.'

She frowned. 'Er – I don't think that would be a good idea, really.'

'Why not?'

'I just don't think it would be. We tend to work as a team. It's better that way.'

He stared ahead, watching the traffic merge at the roundabout. A crossroads in his own life; an uncertainty which route to take and what might be waiting there.

'How can you tell if a woman's having an affair?'

She turned to stare at him.

'Sorry?'

'Mate of mine thinks his wife's seeing someone else. I thought you might have some advice for him. You know – from a woman's point of view.'

She let her hands slip from the wheel and sank back.

'I don't know. I suppose there are signs.'

'Like what?'

'Well … Staying out late, being evasive. That sort of thing.' She forced a smile. 'It's not really my area of expertise, I've never been married.'

'But you're a woman. You know how they think.'

She laughed, and instinctively covered her mouth with her hand. 'Sorry, I wasn't being insensitive, it was just the way you said it.'

Whatever he'd hoped for from Angela hadn't materialised. She wasn't there to listen to his marital problems or offer advice. The look she gave him told him she knew full well that he wasn't referring to someone else. It was, of course, his own conundrum, a pill he had to swallow down and somehow keep from choking on.

'I'd better go,' he said quickly. 'Thanks for the lift.'

'No problem. See you tomorrow, Billy.'

Standing on the corner, he watched her pull out into the traffic. The thought returned that he'd been duped, set-up by the documentary crew who were only interested in one thing. When it was finished they would all go back to their neat suburban homes and not have to worry. He would have to carry on living among his own, a possible target for Sonia, or some deranged resident who didn't like what he was doing. But maybe it was a small price to pay for this kind of exposure. Something he'd dreamed of lying on a prison mattress. The chance to tell the world what it was like to be Billy Riley.

29

Man and a Van

Rosalyn was all set to go. He helped transport her things from the Parkway to the new place in a van he borrowed from Shifty. She didn't have much to speak of in the way of belongings: a microwave and a TV wrapped in old bed sheets, secured with masking tape. The rest was junk, a sorry collection of furniture and oddments that wouldn't matter if it was lost, stolen or incinerated. The baby buggy alone was worth more than all the other stuff combined.

'What's it feel like to be moving?' he said.

'Strange.'

'Looking forward to it?'

'Sort of.'

'You'll be alright. The kiddie'll love it, too. All that space to run round in. You won't know yourself, Rosalyn.'

She perked up when they arrived, walking through the unfurnished rooms with an awed smile on her face. A spacious, unlived-in kind of emptiness pervaded the whole place; a smell of mustiness, too, from the lack of heating. With the kiddie left behind at her mum's, it were the two of them, like a couple surveying their new home. Except Rosalyn would move in with the wean and he'd go back to Eileen – all that unfinished business eating away at him. Rosalyn was like a daughter to him. The more time he spent with her the more protective he felt. But it was all professional and above board – no telling her more than she needed to know. There were serious principles to consider. Serious people involved.

'Shall we start bringing things in?' she said.

'In a mo, sweetheart. I'm just gonna check out the other rooms.'

The kitchen cupboards were bare and lined with yellowing newspaper. At the back of one of the drawers he found an old penny stuck to a resinous blob. Prising it loose with one of the van keys, he held it up admiringly. 'See that?' he said. 'It's a good luck sign. Means we're coming into money.'

'It's just a penny, innit?'

'Don't matter, sweetheart. Look after the pennies and the pounds look after themselves. Didn't your old ma teach you that?'

He washed the coin under the tap, and put it in his pocket. In spite of Rosalyn's scepticism, he believed in the nature of such omens wholeheartedly. There were forces in the world you couldn't necessarily see – invisible strands of energy that governed people's lives, creating and destroying opportunity at will. Some folk could predict these things, like Eileen's grandmother, the old gypsy woman with second sight. She'd even predicted his last stint up the factory, right down to the time and place.

'Right,' he said. 'Let's start moving you in.'

They took a break upstairs in what was to be Rosalyn's new bedroom. The yucca plant she'd brought gave the room a faintly tropical feel, its leaves overhanging the pine dresser. All traces of the previous occupant had been removed, the only reminder being four small imprints in the carpet where a heavy unit had once stood.

Rosalyn sat on the bare mattress and tested the springs, bouncing up and down with childish delight. She stopping rocking and gazed around the room.

'Can I have friends round?'

'Steady on, luv, you've only just moved in.'

'I meant later.'

'Just remember why you're here, Rosalyn. You don't wanna attract attention to yourself – know what I'm saying?'

'What happens if he finds me here?'

'No one's gonna find you here.'

'Yeah, but what if he does?'

'Never mind that, I'll take care of it. You just concentrate on this place.'

Problems would always arise, and this was one of them. The ex-boyfriend, fresh out the jail and hassling her again. The toe-rag obviously hadn't listened to all the warnings he'd been given, the court orders and such like.

'Ever put his hands on you, did he?'

'Couple of times.'

'Ever touch the kiddie?'

'No way, I'd have killed him meself if he'd done that!'

They ate pizza in the kitchen, unpacked boxes lining the worktop. She giggled at the cheese strings that looped from her mouth to her fingers like an excited child. His sense of responsibility towards her increased. This burden he'd taken on from the kindness of his heart – to rescue a poor, defenceless lass from certain disaster. She wasn't aware of it, of course, too wrapped up in herself to notice. All she saw was the house and the garden, the chance of a new life for her and the kiddie.

Opening the patio doors, he stepped outside. A six-foot high fence bordered dense woodland at the back. The neighbours upstairs windows overlooked the garden, but a sense of privacy still remained. Gary had identified the potential, the relative anonymity of the area that suited their purposes. No kids playing in the street. No curtain twitchers waiting by the phone.

'Any good at gardening, Rosalyn?'

'Not really, why?'

'I'll bring you round a pair of marigolds next time and you can start digging. Never know, might have a couple of bodies to get rid of at some point.'

The garage looked promising; a dingy interior with an oil-stained concrete floor. Enough storage space for large consignments of contraband, if needs be. The payoff from months of planning and secrecy. All the loose ends coming together. He could feel a tingle at the back of his neck just thinking about it.

Back inside, he found Rosalyn picking stray mushrooms from the pizza box.

'Fuck me, sweetheart, if I'd known you were that hungry I'd have ordered the extra-large!'

She grinned, and wiped her mouth with the back of her hand.

'Just gonna make a phone call,' he said. 'Back in a bit.'

He sat in the van and called Gary on the cheap mobile. The house was kosher, he said, just what they were looking for. Gary didn't let on, but he could hear the excitement in the fella's voice like an undercurrent. This was it, the reward for months of planning and negotiation, gaining the trust of the anonymous contact from abroad. Soon, they could move on to the next stage, a series of safe houses like the one Rosalyn was in. Then would come the serious task of bringing the product in.

Ringing off, he sat with a view of the quiet neighbourhood. The first and only glimpse the neighbours would see of him. Other than that there would be no trace at all. No link between him and Rosalyn. Nothing to tie him in with events unfolding. He didn't even know the people Gary was involved with, and they didn't know him.

He found Rosalyn slumped in her rocking chair in the front room, staring into space.

'What's up?' he said. 'Finished unpacking already?'

'I was just thinking.'

'What about?'

'How me nan won't be able to get over and see me.'

'Why – jump on a bus, can't she?'

'It's not that easy. She's not all that mobile.'

'Not my problem, Rosalyn.' He stared at her, irritated by her lack of gratitude. 'Get your arse in gear if you wanna lift into town. I've gotta get the van back in half an hour.'

'What about the heating?'

'What about it?'

'It's freezing in here at the moment.'

'I'll get you one of them electric heaters. Now come on, let's go.'

Her minor gripe annoyed him. He'd set her up in a two-bedroom property near the centre of town and she was whinging already. Maybe this was a side to her he hadn't seen. A form of manipulation she'd been waiting to spring on him when he was least expecting it.

'See me as a soft touch, do you?' he said.

'What d'you mean?'

'Someone to bail you out when you're in trouble?'

'I dunno what you're talking about.'

'Sure you don't, sweetheart. Just don't go drawing attention to yourself in the new place. Any bother with the neighbours, call me.'

He dropped her by the co-op, and fished out a ten-pound note as an afterthought.

'What's that for?' she said.

'Milk and teabags for the next time I come round. And get yourself some cleaning stuff. I want the place kept tidy.'

She stared at the money in her hand. He felt himself weaken again.

'Got enough credit on your phone?'

'Yeah.'

'I'll call you in a bit, see how you're doing.'

'Are you coming round later?'

Not tonight, Josephine. I gotta tank full of fish to feed.'

She wandered off in the direction of the underpass, with its graffiti-covered walls and litter blown-in from the road. He couldn't find it within himself to be annoyed with her. She was a kid, barely out of school. The money she'd earned from running errands for drug dealers would have wised her up, a cushion against the deprivation she'd grown up with. But would she be able to keep her mouth shut about the new place and not go blabbing to other people? That was the only major concern and one he'd have to deal with sooner or later.

But first there were other things to attend to that couldn't be put off.

30

Car Insurance

Parking up, he turned off the engine. Beyond the windscreen, red-brick semis with neat front gardens and tiled porches – ex-council houses sold off to tenants, in line with Margaret Thatcher's original manifesto on private ownership. The bow of a small boat covered with a blue tarpaulin poked from a driveway. Elsewhere, signs of accumulated wealth; a sense of pride about the neighbourhood, a step up from the rambling council estates he was used to driving through.

Striding past the houses, a sense of urgency kicked-in. Adrenalin spurred him on. The thing needed to be done quickly and with a minimum of fuss.

Fists clenched in his jacket pocket, sovvie rings heavy on his fingers, he visualised each step. Always the possibility of a reaction, a physical confrontation. But that didn't matter. He had the energy, the motivation.

He rang the doorbell and waited.

The door opened, and a fit-looking bird in sweatshirt and jogging bottoms stared back at him. He guessed she must have been early 40s, faint lines around her eyes and mouth through a pan of makeup.

'Is your man there, luv?' he said pleasantly.

'What's it about?'

'His car insurance. Won't take a minute.'

She frowned, uncertain, and moved off down the hall. Cooking smells drifted along; the faint murmur of a television.

The fella came to the door, mid to late-twenties, the unmistakeable pallid look of the jail still upon him.

'Yeah?' the fella said.

'I'm looking for Ty. That you, is it?'

'Who wants to know?'

He threw a perfect straight left, twisting at the hip to deliver. The fella went down without a murmur, and looked up, dazedly, from the hallway.

Stepping over the threshold, he hit him with two more, and pointed a warning finger at his stunned face. 'Stay away from Rosalyn, you hear me? I have to come back it won't be to swap insurance details!'

The fella nodded stupidly, so he gave the cunt one more.

Striding down the path, head down, he clocked the neighbouring houses for signs of movement. Some way behind him, a hysterical shriek rose upon the evening air – the bird in the jogging bottoms, horrified to find her son stretched out on his own doorstep.

Already the alibis were forming in his head: he wasn't there; he'd been somewhere else when it happened. Plenty of people could vouch for it if the dibble got involved. But that was unlikely. The fella knew he'd done wrong. It was there in his eyes, plain to see.

31
Billy Flint

Filming began down by the canal. Day Four of his contribution, and already he was an old hand. The journalist fella wanted shots of the bars and restaurants on the other side of the water to highlight the old town as it was in Leonard's heyday. Like a muppet, he sat there waiting while they lined up the shot and adjusted the camera. Any locals walking over the bridge would see him and form their own conclusions. Billy Riley – vaudeville star and circus performer, doing a turn for the out-of-towners who'd lured him on board for fame and money.

Angela fussed around him. Since he'd agreed to help, she seemed to take more interest in him, explaining the different aspects of the shoot and making sure he knew what was happening. He'd changed his opinion of her, seen through her earlier frostiness and developed a respect for the way she operated; she honed in on the small detail and wouldn't let it go until she was satisfied it was right. Whatever else you could say about them, both her and the journalist fella were professionals. They got the job done.

'How do you feel today?' she said. 'Nervous?'

'Nah – I do this kinda stuff all the time.'

'Just remember what I told you. Relax and be yourself.'

'Yeah, that's what I'm worried about.'

The journalist fella handed him a coffee in a paper cup and gave his trademark grin. 'You'll be fine, Billy. We'd like to get a few shots of you sitting on the wall with the canal in the background. Are you happy with that?'

'Long as you get me best side. I'm relying on you lot to make me look like Steve McQueen.' He went along with it knowing that in the end it wouldn't work out. All his instincts told him to pull out and disappear, but he couldn't seem to help himself. The lure of the camera was hard to deny. He was its willing subject, being drawn effortlessly in to a strange new world.

The journalist fella asked about the riots, priming the intended audience for what was to come. Angela stayed back, making notes. All the while, the camera's single black eye honed in on him, perched atop the fella's shoulder like an electronic bird of prey. Next to him, the Grip, the fella holding the boom – the long pole that recorded external sound. And in the background, the all-important Soundman, whose genius was spoken of in reverential terms by all who knew him.

He found himself picking up the odd technical word or instruction and filed them away for future use. This was the cutting edge of documentary making, the journalist fella told him proudly. They were making something of great social and cultural significance that might one day be seen by millions. He half believed the fella – in the grip of a profound sense of destiny, like Napoleon, assessing his troops before the march into Moscow.

Inevitably, the questions turned to the Big Fella, a subject they never seemed to tire of.

'When did you first meet Leonard?'

'When I were about fourteen.'

'Did he have a reputation back then?'

'Everyone had heard of Leonard round our way. He were, like, top dog even at that age.'

The camera recorded every word, every detail. He felt exposed and vulnerable, perched on the cold brick wall. Billy Riley, hard man and villain, doing his best not to look like a half-baked shandy-merchant.

'You said you were involved in security and debt collecting for Leonard. Can you tell us a bit more about that?'

'I could, but it were a long time ago.'

'Was there any violence involved?'

'Sometimes.'

'Could you give us an example?'

Maybe they thought he was stupid, a bottom-grader like some of the divvie kids at school. But he had the suss on them alright – a prison psychology test had given him an IQ of 140. Plus, he'd read plenty of books up the factory and pretty much educated himself over the course of a few years. Some of the cons he knew couldn't read or write, a condition that put them at a distinct disadvantage. But you couldn't measure intelligence by how many exams you'd taken, or how many letters you had after your name. It was all about how well you adapted to the real world and pulled in the moolar.

'You can't avoid trouble in this game,' he said. 'It goes with the territory. You gotta think on your feet. Suss out the other fella's move before he knows it himself.'

'Do you ever regret some of the things you've done, the people you've hurt?'

'Why should I? It's biblical, innit? Eye for an eye, tooth for a tooth?'

'Are you religious?'

'Only on Sunday.'

The jail was full of those who never learned, who went out and made the same mistakes again and again. He himself had been a victim of the system, of circumstances beyond his control. Sent upriver when most kids his age were courting girls and playing football. 'Manipulative and self-interested', 'Prone to violent outbursts if provoked.' The nut doctors who made these assessments had known him less than five-minutes, basing their conclusions on a set of Home Office notes. These cunts didn't know him at all. They banged him up, wrote their reports, then went home to the missus and a nice cooked dinner. But they forgot one important thing. For every hour he was languishing in a prison cell he was planning the future, and what he was going to do to get back at the system when he got out.

Still the questions came before the camera's unblinking eye. The journalist fella's insistence on getting at the truth, pushing him to dig deeper. He told them about Leonard's shooting by an unknown assailant. How rival security firms started muscling in from over the water, and how he'd taken a personal role in sorting out the disputes while Leonard was still recovering in hospital. They wanted to know how it had affected him personally and the true extent of his involvement.

'I was running a few doors for Leonard at the time,' he said. 'Pubs and clubs along the waterfront. Some venues further up-town. It just went nuts all of a sudden.'

'How do you mean?'

He thought before answering. 'It were like a war. Running battles in the street. Alarm bells going off everywhere. You'd be working one night and a coach load of fellas would pull up outside the club and you'd have to scrap 'em there and then. They even firebombed the Embassy one night. Took the entrance right out. Lucky we'd all gone home by then or there could've been fatalities.'

Gazing out over the canal he felt a strong connection to the place. His past encapsulated in the grey-brick facades and slate rooftops. On the door of the Winchester at nineteen, knowing the place was under direct threat. Seasoned bods like Big Frank and Geordie Pete on hand to bolster his confidence and cover his back. What a time it had been. A whole squad of them like the reservists in a military campaign.

And as the camera rolled, so his confidence soared. The undeniable feeling that this was his moment, vindication for all the years he'd spent locked away. The journalist fella had never been to the places he'd been – never been manhandled by six rozzers and slung in the back of a police van; never been on the run through streams and valleys, emerging by a moonlit lake. Even the fella's tan marked him out as different from the average pleb. And the gear he wore – the roll-neck pullovers and crumpled cords, the brown loafers. A mama's boy for sure, lazy and conceited, made to feel he should have it given him on a platter, even if he did have a certain charm to go with it.

'Did you know Leonard socially?' Angela said.

'The Big Fella weren't the social kind. That's how he stayed out of trouble for so long. He didn't get involved in the drinking and gallivanting. Preferred to go home to his missus and kids.'

'How did you first become associated with him?'

'Me and a mate did some work on his house, landscaping his garden. He had this mad Doberman, used to prowl up and down snapping at flies. Scared the shit out of us.'

'What were your first impressions of him?'

'Who – Leonard or the Doberman?' The jokes helped him relax and stay focused; the old classroom trick of presenting a cool front, even when you felt intimidated. In a world of such intense speculation image was everything; you were only as good as your last performance. He knew how actors must feel, having to summon up a whole range of emotions on cue no matter what mood they were in.

Later, in a wine bar Angela had found the night before, he felt the same sense of destiny. They talked a different language – people he didn't know and situations he'd never been in, dropping the names of places in London and LA as if they were just around the corner. And yet something strange was happening to him. A catharsis of sorts that he'd never experienced before. Here he was with his shaven head and tattoos, talking the language of the streets – a real outsider in a world he didn't understand, yet thriving on the attention and somehow being energised by it.

'What're you having, Billy?' the journalist fella said. 'I think we can just about stretch the budget to include you.'

'You'd better call in for back-up, pal, I feel a splurge coming on.'

The wine bar was all chrome seats and polished wooden flooring. Affluent-looking customers in suits and expensive casuals stood around vying for attention. The film crew gathered at the bar, where names like 'Kubrick' and 'Bergman' drifted over like code words in a secret conversation. He listened respectfully, the kid at an adult's party, wondering how long it would be before they took him home.

Angela came over, giving him her quizzical gaze.

'How do you think it went earlier?'

'Great. Should give Robert De Niro a run for his money.'

'Oh, I'm sure you'll be a star in your own right, Billy.'

A sense of his own importance grew, and with it the need to bolster the feeling with more drink. But always the shadows in the background to threaten any progress he might have made. Banging out Rosalyn's ex-boyfriend on his doorstep. His performance in the working men's club not long before. Impulsive acts connected to the need to live up to his own code.

'D'you believe in fate?' he said.

'In what context?'

'I keep seeing this magpie, plotted up on a wall. Follows me round like a messenger from the end of time.'

Angela looked at him strangely. 'Sorry – you've lost me?'

'A magpie. You know, one for sorrow, two for joy?'

'Oh, right.'

In a way it was easier talking to her, a relative stranger. At least she tried to understand him, even if it didn't always work out.

'Are you afraid of getting old?' he said.

She gave him a curious frown, as if the thought had never occurred to her.

'Where did that come from?'

He shrugged. 'I turned forty up the factory, and I was like – that's it, me fuckin life's over.'

She rocked gently on her heels, humouring him with a smile. 'I don't really think in terms of time passing, only the unfinished projects I have up ahead.'

'You're not married?'

'To my job, it would seem.'

He enjoyed the conversation in a perverse way, feeding her bits of his philosophy without giving away too much. A part of him wanted to fit in, to be included in their neat little circle with the pastries and the quails eggs, the glasses of white wine. This was how life should be lived, and naturally he wanted a slice of it.

Another part of him felt uneasy. These were the types he'd despised all his life: clever, well-educated bods from wealthy backgrounds, who strove to make a name for themselves by trampling over everyone else. What did he represent to them – the ex-con from a council estate, with his regional dialect and prison tattoos? A kind of perverse entertainment, pure and simple; like the actor in a soap, or the contestant on a game show millions tuned into every week.

'What does your wife think of you helping us?'

He balked at the question. The first mention of Eileen since they'd started filming.

'No idea.'

'You haven't told her?'

'I said I were helping you out with research. Be a shock when she sees me on the telly, won't it?'

The thought of his mug going out on national TV caused him a few minor palpitations. Inevitably, comments would be made around the estate. He wouldn't be able to go anywhere without folk having a sly dig, or making jokes behind his back.

Angela had come up with a stage name for him that ran as a kind of joke between the three of them. 'Billy Flint'. Maybe he'd be up there on the billboards one day. He, who'd come from an impoverished background to achieve success and fame. They'd give him one of those actor's cards, and off he'd go on a world tour, signing autographs and humping actresses in posh hotels. They said fame did strange things to people, but it wouldn't to him. He'd stay grounded, bolstering his income from the proceeds of contraband.

Exhausted from the day's filming, he flaked out on the sofa, the dog licking his face with unbridled devotion. After the movie set he'd been on, home seemed a bit of a comedown.

Eileen observed him from the doorway.

'The wanderer returns,' she said.

'I know how Robert Redford feels. Fuckin hard work in front of a camera.'

'Well I hope you're pleased with yourself.'

'Oh, I am, doll. They're lining me up for an Oscar, apparently.'

'How much are they paying you?'

'It ain't about the money. I'm doing it for Leonard. Laying a few ghosts to rest.'

She glared down at him as if he'd betrayed the family secrets.

'Thanks for running it past me first.'

'Listen, doll – I'm the one out there grafting, so don't start having a pop at me, alright?'

He thought about the effect the day's filming had had on him.

How much of his own character he'd tried to subvert in order to present a certain image to the film crew. And how for one small moment down by the canal, he felt he belonged to something of worth, something that transcended the past and his own troubled existence.

Eileen didn't see it that way and marched out of the room.

'It's just a bit of fun,' he yelled after her. 'What's up wi' you?'

That night, his dreams were filled with rolling black clouds and chariots manned by freakish monsters. In the background, willing their teams on with an unwholesome passion, God and the Devil, their faces spinning ceaselessly either side of a huge gold coin.

32

Omens

The landlord called to say there'd been a holdup. The yacht wouldn't be ready to go back into the water at the specified date, as there was an issue with the electrics. Also, the diesel inboard engines needed a complete overhaul, and the mechanic wasn't available until the following week.

'Can't you find another mechanic?'

'Well, I could, but I don't think it would help. They tend to work as a team down there, and I don't really want to interfere.'

Listening to the landlord, he was reminded of all the excuses he'd heard over the years. Empires were built by generals who lead from the front, not by spineless individuals who preferred to stay at home and let others do the work.

'Tell 'em it's urgent,' he said. 'Offer 'em more money if you have to. Either way, that boat's gotta be in the water by the fifteenth.'

Eileen found him in the kitchen staring out at the grim spectacle.

'What's up?' she said.

'Fuckin magpie's out there again. Been stalking me for days, it has.'

'D'you know how ridiculous that sounds?'

'I don't care how it sounds, it's the fuckin truth.'

Magpies. Cop cars. The leering face of McGuinn popping up in the Crescent to harangue and distress him. Only a fool would dismiss such signs as coincidence. He'd even started to dread leaving the house in the morning for fear the winged-avenger would be perched on a garden wall waiting for him. No matter how much he reasoned with himself, the fear persisted. Even throwing out a quick salute didn't work – a semi-humorous recognition of its power over him and his inability to change it. Still it sat there, mocking him with its cold black eye.

'I'm going upstairs for a lie-down.'

'Why – what's the matter with you now?'

'I'm feeling a bit grim. Must've been them dumplings you fed me last night.'

An idle search through the TV channels confirmed his suspicions. The whole world was obsessed with sex. He'd forgotten how prevalent it was – in magazines and on billboards, streamed in on mobile phones. The porn industry was raking in the moolar, beaming out depravity in every conceivable form. Only the other day he watched a bird dressed up as a nun, getting turked by two fellas dressed as priests. What would the goodly father make of that? he wondered.

Eileen came in, and dumped a pile of clothes on the bed.

'You ever watch porn while I was away?' he said.

'Don't start all that.'

'What? It's a perfectly reasonable question. Did you, or didn't you?'

'I'm not even going there, OK?'

'Going where – round to Pauline's for a quick twos-up on her new boyfriend?'

'Oh, shut up. You're so predictable it does me friggin head in.'

He had a glimpse of their retirement years on the Algarve: alone together in a secluded villa, swimming pool outside and lemon grove nearby. Tanned and wrinkled from the sun, they'd be laid out on the bed in their air-conditioned room, watching the goggle-box in Spanish with English subtitles. In a moment's fitful lust, he'd reach out for her bronzed thigh, only to be rebuffed in the time-honoured manner.

In an instant he saw it wouldn't work. Whatever they had here in England wouldn't translate well in a foreign country. Stuck with each other so far from home, there'd be a whole host of variables to wear them down. They'd have each other to contend with all day. She wouldn't be able to escape to Pauline's, or Gemma's every time they had a row. He wouldn't be able to take off to Gary's, or call in at the Swan for a quick skim. They'd have to work through their problems alone, with the heat and the dust and the dwindling pesetas.

'I was talking to Angela,' he said. 'She was telling me about this fella who thought his wife was having an affair. He even hired a private detective to follow her.'

'Really.'

'The detective didn't find anything, but the fella kept on digging.'

'Dug a big hole for himself and fell right in to it, did he?'

'Are you having an affair?'

'What?'

'Don't fuck about – are you or not?'

'Go take the dog for a walk, you want something useful to do.'

'Don't avoid the question. Look me in the eye and tell me you're not seeing someone.'

'Get away with you.'

'I'm being serious.'

'So am I. Leave me alone.' She made for the door.

He raised himself up on a surge of righteous energy and yelled after her, 'I'll find out if you are, you know!'

She marched back along the hall, and glared at him from the doorway. 'You're sick in the fuckin head, you know that? I'll be taking meself off to live at Pauline's soon, just to get away from you!'

Maybe it was his earlier behaviour – trying it on with her at the cake-making table while her hands were covered in flour. The fact she'd actually let him had been an added bonus, inspiring him to a vigorous and unrestrained performance that was over in less than thirty-seconds. Although she'd given in this time it was quite clearly under duress; no hint of the enthusiasm she'd shown on previous occasions. And why did she have to be in the right mood all the time? Most of their romps were after dinner, or *Coronation Street*, when she'd finished her chores. What was wrong with a bit of spontaneity once in a while?

Lying there on the sofa, he reviewed his position. Like most men, he was ready for action as soon as his eyes opened in the morning, his inner radar tuned to the possibility from there on in. One of the genuine mysteries of life, this one basic difference between the species that gave the female the clear advantage. Man was a dog, unable to control his base instincts. He wanted it all the time, programmed that way since the first prehistoric cave dweller set eyes on a female. The woman knew this and used it against him; she had appetites and desires too, but kept most of them well hidden.

Thinking – the sum total of all man's troubles. But the thoughts were all he had, churning over and over like a mixer-drum full of brick-bats. No way to escape who you were or what you'd done. The unknowable future looming up ahead, waiting to dish out surprises like the clown at a children's party.

Already, the lure of his TV celebrity had faded. Stupid of him to fall for the hype, the encouragement from the intrepid duo telling him how good he was. He was a criminal, pure and simple, a product of the streets with all its coarseness and bravado. If he did get his fifteen minutes of fame it was most likely to be on *Crimewatch*, with the additional warning, 'Please do not approach this man.'

Shrugging on his coat and cap, he checked his reflection in the hall mirror. She came out of the kitchen, saw him and stopped, hand on hip.

'Where you going?'

'Out.'

'Well don't come in late waking me up.'

He stared at her in abject disappointment. 'That's all I get, is it? No tender kiss on the cheek to see me off? I should have stayed in the other place – get more understanding from a fuckin screw!'

Driving fast, he hit the bay road. Beneath the clear, moonlit sky the surface of the water looked almost opaque. The tall outline of the wharf buildings dominated the horizon, the empty dual-carriageway ahead lending an air of desolation. He comforted himself with the certainty of death. His own ending somewhere up ahead. At times like these he was reminded of his own frailty, the small and insignificant speck his presence made on the vastness of all creation. Strange how such a thought could offer comfort, but somehow it did. Looking up at the divination, the supreme majesty of the universe, knowing you were dust, put all your earthly problems into clear perspective. To be gone in an instant and never to return in any comparable shape or form. Beyond pain and pleasure. No light or dark. A uniform nothingness for all eternity.

33
The Confessional

Candles flickered along the recesses, soft white light reflected in the dark wood. Peaceful silence filled the place, a special hush that didn't need the disruption of raised voices. He, Billy Riley, kept his own voice low, so as not to disturb whatever force it was looking over them, while the goodly father listened, gleaning all the information he needed from a cursory look, seeing the anguish so plain in his face.

When it was his turn to speak, the father looked at him with tenderness and compassion. 'What is it that's bothering you, Billy?'

'I'm eaten up with it, Father. Can't help meself.'

'Eaten up with what exactly?'

He found it hard to tell even the father, whose confidence was assured. These torments that visited a man and wouldn't let up. Images he could barely speak of that came to him in the night, or set upon him like devils in the course of his waking moments. Slowly the words came, drawn from the comforting silence and the thought that at last he would be heard without censure or judgement.

'We're not getting on too well at the moment, see, Father. Not living like man and wife should.'

'Go on.'

'I get this, anger come over me. This terrible suspicion.'

'Have you spoken to Eileen about it?'

'I have, but it don't do much good. We just end up rowing.'

The father considered this quietly for a moment. 'It's not an easy thing, the union of man and wife.'

'Amen to that, Father.'

'And you've been through so much together.'

'That's right, we have. But there's things she's not telling me. I can see it in her eyes.' He turned a ring on his finger, absently, thinking of all the good times they'd had together. The nights out on the town in the early days. The holidays abroad. Maybe the father could see the future through some special powers of perception. The wickedness and deceit of a woman, and how skilfully she avoided detection.

'I don't know what advice I can give,' the father said. 'Other than to pray for you both and hope things will get better.'

'I don't think they will. It's gone beyond that now.'

'Well, it can sometimes seem that way. But faith can overcome such things. I've seen if before on many occasions.'

'I couldn't lose her, Father. Couldn't see her with another man.'

'Of course you won't lose her. She's your wife. She loves you very dearly. Look how she's stood by you all these years while you were away upriver.'

He shook his head in frustration, the father's words carrying little weight in the confusion of his mind. The gravity held them both, exposing a truth that couldn't be spoken. And at the back of it all, the realisation that the father had probably known all along. All those damning words and deeds gleaned from Eileen's repeated visits to the confessional to seek absolution. Whatever the father knew, he couldn't say, bound by the oath he'd taken.

'Would you like me to speak with Eileen?' the father said.

'I don't think that would do any good.'

'Well, I could try. I'd be happy to do that for you if you felt it would help.'

He nodded, without conviction, uncomfortable in the spotlight. He'd said his piece, purged himself of some inner conflict, now it was time to move on.

'I got involved with that journalist fella I told you about. He's making a documentary about Leonard and the Parkway.'

The father looked intrigued. 'I see … Is that a paid role?'

'Only expenses and a bit on top.' The thought of the film crew and the omnipresent camera brought a faint thread of hope. Leonard's memory flared briefly in the gloom of the church – the Big Fella, whose exploits had given rise to the legend, still powerful even in death.

'Well, I hope it goes well for you, Billy.'

'So do I, Father. Never know. I might end up moving to the Heights. You'll see me cruising by in an open top Bentley.'

'Ah, well, I hope you'll remember me if it comes to that.'

He thought of something Eileen had said. How sweetly she slept without him – her words when he'd first come back from the factory. Sometimes she tried to explain what it was like, trying to bring up three kids while he was away. Or worse, the dreaded knock at four in the morning when he was home; the sound of the front door being hammered-in and the kids screaming along the hall. Her comfortable world reduced to a nightmare of splinters and glass. All down to him, Billy Riley.

The father stood, bent slightly, his mouth fixed in a grimace of pain. 'I'll walk with you to the door. Be good for me to get some air. Not good being cooped up in here too long.'

At the door, the father laid a hand upon his arm and fixed him with a look of intense sorrow. 'I hope you'll resolve your differences with Eileen, Billy. I'd hate to see anything happen to either of you.'

He nodded without much conviction.

'Why don't you take her somewhere? Talk to her. Tell her how you feel.'

'Aye, I might do that, Father.'

He left with the same confusion. Inside, the growing belief that things were afoot that he couldn't control. And worse of all the thought that everyone else was laughing at him behind his back. Billy Riley, one time enforcer and man of respect, now an object of scorn and derision.

But the father's advice did offer a grain of hope, the chance to rescue that which was almost lost. After all, she was still his wife. And even in this age of selfishness and irresponsibility, that must have counted for something.

34
Natural Selection

They parked up at a red plastic table – vinegar and tommy-sauce bottle between them. There to decide what to do next and in what sequence certain events might transpire. He found her long silences unhelpful – the fact that she wouldn't trust his experience or his intuition. He had the means to make it happen: the contacts, the connections. But he needed certain assurances. Needed to know she'd be right there with him when the going got tough. 'This is us, doll – know what I'm saying? We need to get away for a bit, just the two of us.'

Trailing a chip in a blob of red sauce, she looked morose and irritable. 'You're asking too much of me.'

'How am I?'

'I told you before. I've got Gemma and the baby to think about. I can't just take off and leave her at a time like this, can I?'

'I'm not asking you to leave her. We get sorted abroad somewhere, her and the bab can come out with us.'

'What about Luke and his job? How's he gonna manage?'

People drifted in from the cold, and stood gawping up at the menu. Maybe that was the answer, open a fast food restaurant and reel in the punters that way. Somehow he couldn't see himself standing over a hot fryer serving crispy cod to disgruntled civilians night and day. The good citizen role he'd been avoiding all his life. Working long hours for a meagre pay check, then giving the rest to the tax man.

Eileen's long silences bothered him more and more. This habit she had of withdrawing into her own world, where nobody else could get in.

'Look – all I'm asking you to do is think about it,' he said. 'We fly out for a couple of weeks. You lie on the beach getting a tan, then we fly back again.'

She frowned. 'I can't get me head round it.'

'It's simple enough, doll. We get two passports and take off, just the two of us.'

He had the whole thing planned in his head. The flight to Portugal. The drive down to the coast in a hired car. Gary's mate would set them up in an apartment in Villamora. Once installed there they'd be on their own, opening up a whole new set of opportunities. A dual purpose break, giving him the chance to meet a few criminal contacts and repair the damage to his marriage at the same time.

'I thought you wanted to get away?' he said.

'A weekend in Blackpool, yeah.'

'So what you gonna do here? Run round selling knock-off gear for Pauline for a few quid, always complaining you've got no money? What's the point in that?'

'It's different.'

'How is it?'

'I'm not gonna get put away for fifteen years if I get caught, am I?'

He could understand her reasoning, but to him it didn't make sense. Sooner or later there'd be a foul-up in Pauline's catalogue scam, or the stolen goods she had coming in. One of her contacts would get lifted and open his mouth, then the dibble would start an investigation and everything would go downhill from there on.

'You gotta distance yourself from certain people,' he said, thinking aloud. 'All they do is bring you down.'

'What – like the people you've been mixing with lately?'

'People I mix with are professionals.'

'Yeah, and d'you think they give a shit what happens to you? That journalist fella you've been hanging around with, putting ideas in your head?'

Doubts began to form, fanned by the increasing pressure he

was under. Keeping up a front for the likes of McGuinn, and anyone else sniffing round. Having to make it look as if he was conforming. Much as he hated to admit it, he needed Eileen with him. The thought of drifting around the Algarve on his own wasn't all that inspiring.

He spread his fingers on the table, admiring the sovvie rings and the homemade tattoos. Maybe they'd look good on the cover of a book, propped up in the window of the local Waterstones. *Billy Riley – my life on the frontline*, a no-holds barred account of his rise through the criminal ranks to become an enforcer, and right-hand man to the Big Fella himself. Except the truth wasn't quite like that. He'd wound up disillusioned, feeling used and put upon. The people he trusted had let him down.

Now Eileen. He desperately wanted to salvage his marriage, but she refused to meet him halfway.

'Maybe there's another reason you don't wanna go with me.'

She looked up. 'What's that supposed to mean?'

He thought about his visit to the father, and how they'd discussed the issue in the sanctity of the church. Telling Eileen might have made him feel better in some way, relieved some of the tension between them. But that would have been a lapse in protocol, a compromise of his own moral code.

'Look,' he said. 'I know things haven't been right between us for a while, but I'm willing to forget all that. Make a new beginning – know what I'm saying?'

'That's why you keep making all these comments, is it? Accusing me of things I haven't done?'

'I haven't accused you of anything.'

'Not much, no.' She picked at her food without interest, her resistance at the idea of going away buried deep. But he wanted more than anything to believe she'd be there for him, that underneath it all her love for him was still intact.

'Want anything else?' he said.

'No thanks.'

'Fancy a stroll along the front?'

'It's too cold.'

'I'll warm you up.'

She shrugged, wouldn't look at him.

'Come on,' he said. 'Let's do one. We can take the chips with us.'

Rocked by severe gusts of wind they strolled along the seafront. Further out, the grey seas swelled and dipped, topped by angry white spume. Gulls circled above the flagstones, swooping in low and diving for scraps of food. Somewhere out there, he pictured the landlord's yacht, sailing out to meet the rendezvous. A life changing event for all of them.

But this was home. Hard to imagine being anywhere else. Even lying in the sun in some exotic paradise you might still yearn for it – one of the problems of being British. But when you thought about it, what was there to miss? The rain and the cold, the lack of decent TV. He wouldn't miss the jails, that was for sure: lying around storing up bitterness and resentment at the regime that had taken away half his adult life.

He put an arm around Eileen's shoulder and gave her a hug.

'I'll look after you, doll. Don't you worry about that.'

'I can look after me friggin self, thanks.'

In all the years they'd been together, he'd never pictured himself with anyone else. All through the jail sentences and the times he'd been on the run, he always held a clear mental picture of the two of them, beating the odds. Twenty-five years since they'd smooched in the shadowy recesses of the Town Hall, fights breaking out on the dance floor, and the ageing bouncers wading in to break them up. A quarter of a century battling the authorities, the bills and each other, only to end up here in such a strange and uncertain place.

They sat on a bench overlooking the harbour. The morning sun sparkled on the water, rust-covered jibs and gantries on the far side. Bloated seagulls swooped down and snapped up morsels on the flagstones. He tossed a chip on the ground and watched two huge specimens battle for supremacy, stabbing their beaks and dividing the spoils between them. Darwin was right. The strongest always came out on top. Everything he'd witnessed in his own lifetime had proved the theory again and again.

'So what's this thing you've got going with Gary?' she said.

He had to think before answering. 'It's in the pipeline. I can't say too much right now.'

'And that's why you wanted Shifty's lockup. You had no intention of going into business with him at all, did you?'

Seized by a wave of passion, he grabbed her arm. 'We're not talking about a few knock-off football shirts here, doll. We're talking serious moolar. Enough to pay off all our debts and live in the Bahamas for the rest of our lives.'

She jerked her arm away. 'I've heard it all before. And what happens when it all goes wrong? Who ends up having to visit you in the other place?'

Moored across the water was an oil tanker, its anchor chain thick as a man's arm. He recalled a black and white photo of his old fella in the merchant navy, sunbathing on deck. The old fella was smiling, lean and handsome before the drink took him. Another of nature's cruel tricks. The illusion of invincibility, vitality. You couldn't pinpoint the exact moment it all went wrong, but in his own case it had something to do with turning forty. Eileen's brutal assessment made it worse, a feeling he'd been exposed and found wanting.

She sniffed and gazed out over the water. 'Pauline says the committee met the other day. They've barred you from the club indefinitely.'

'There's a surprise.'

'Don't you care?'

'Why should I? Fuckin beer's terrible anyway.'

More gulls flew in to join the melee. He watched their squawking and dive-bombing with fascination. Nature seemed to have designed all living things with only two main priorities – hunting and procreating. It was only humans who had to complicate the issue with other stuff – arguing over football results, or who'd won poll position in the Grand Prix.

'What else did Pauline say?'

'Nothing.'

'Like fuck.'

'You think we sit around discussing you all day?'

He pictured her in the dusty confessional, beads of light falling through the latticework. Her faltering words gathering momentum. 'Father, I have sinned. I've sought out the company of other men and done terrible things.'

'Why didn't you tell me you met Connor?' he said.

'She stared at him. 'What?'

'Why didn't you just say you were meeting him? Why d'you have to cover it up?'

'I didn't cover anything up. He just came down for the morning and I met him in town. If I'd told you you'd have made a big deal of it.'

He saw himself in isolation. Kept apart – even from his own family.

'That's the trouble with secrets,' he said. 'It all comes out in the end.'

'Oh, so meeting me own son's a crime now, is it?'

'Who else you been meeting on the quiet?'

'What?'

'The Jason fella. Been meeting him, too, have you?'

'Oh, for fuck sake!' She marched off, leaving him on the bench to gaze after her. Stupid of him to blurt out the other fella's name and give the game away, but he couldn't help himself. The need to know had taken over, unleashed a devil inside him.

'Come back!' he said. 'Fuck's the matter with you?'

Maybe the prison psychologists were right. There was something wrong with him. All those stunts he'd pulled when he was a kid: choring cars and being chased by the dibble; getting sent to approved school at the age of ten. His future, mapped out without him even realising it. At least now there was a slim chance he could change the course he was on, prove himself worthy in her eyes.

He caught up with her, and together they walked in silence. Past the fading icons of his youth; the Palace Court Hotel, old and decrepit, nothing like the swinging venue it had been in the Eighties. Working the door had given him an appreciation of the graft that went into running a place like that. Coachloads of holidaymakers, tanked to the gills from an afternoon's drinking. Two doormen covering three floors with hundreds of punters to look out for – before the days of mobile phones and CCTV. Bank holidays were the worst. On one memorable occasion, running battles were fought between doormen from four different venues and a stag party from Newcastle, who'd drawn support from local lads all fired up from being on the ale all day. The dibble took three-quarters of an hour to turn up and by then the worst of it was over. The VIP lounge looked like an exocet had hit, with tables turned over and glass all over the carpet.

The arguments started around that time. Eileen stayed at home looking after the kids, while he worked at the Embassy Club and did odd jobs on Leonard's house to earn some extra money. They had rows about the hours he was keeping and the cash she'd found hidden in the spare room. Then, shortly after Gemma was born, he got twelve months for assaulting the dibble – a case his brief said should have been thrown out long before it came to trial. By then, Eileen had three kids to look after and double the aggravation, always tired and on edge when she came up to visit him. He did what he could to bring the moolar in, but somehow it was never enough.

She must have loved him back then. Why else would she do the things she did on his behalf? Taking the train up to Durham every two weeks when he was ghosted from Strangeways. Making arrangements for him to stay in Dublin when he went on the run. She'd made sacrifices. Proved herself a woman of substance, someone he could rely upon.

She stopped at the level crossing, hands deep in the pockets of her coat. He stood beside her, conscious of the civilians all around, the need to appear normal.

'Fancy one in the Swan?' he said.

'No, I don't.'

The train rumbled by, swept away to another part of the city. He saw himself on it, without a ticket, a destination.

The barrier went up; they crossed with the civilian hordes. This time he stayed beside her.

'Are we alright now, me and you?'

'No, we're not alright. I've had it up to here with your nonsense.'

'I'll make it up to you, doll.'

'What – by dropping dead?'

He thought how lonely he'd be without her, how his life would never be the same. The idea of her being with someone else, the pair of them laughing at him while they strode off into the sunset hand in hand.

He couldn't have it. His entire life had been predicated on the winning of respect. Without it you were nothing, lower than the dirt under someone's feet.

35
Tools of the Trade

They met in the public bar of the Cricketer's in the afternoon, Cyril's preferred time for fraternising. Always a convincing liar, the old fella couldn't resist embellishing his stories, adding colourful new twists to previous tales, changing names and locations to suit. But the stories were always good, delivered with an air of authority no one could dispute.

They shook hands in the time-honoured fashion.

'How goes it, Cyril?'

'Oh, struggling along, Billy. You know how it is.'

With his tweed jacket and narrow tie, Cyril had the look of the city gent, a retired banker or civil servant. But peel away the façade and the real Cyril Stokes was revealed – committed thief and veteran of the prison system, even if he was in semi-retirement. In a previous life he might have been a rodent, a water rat, grazing innocently by the riverbank, or floating casually downstream on a piece of driftwood.

'What you having then, Cyril?'

'Pint o' Chivas Regal, son. Failing that, get us a pint o' bitter.'

A safecracker by trade, Cyril soon learned the intricacies of gelignite and fuse-setting, becoming an authority on the subject in the process. The 'Squirrel's' grandfather had worked for Edward Tann & Sons of London, filling the young lad's head with tales of impregnable safes and minted patrons. The Fifties and Sixties were good years for enterprising boxmen, and Cyril made a fortune relieving certain businesses of their accumulative stock. Times changed and the work dried up. Cyril turned his expertise to other areas, and became a locksmith of some repute, able to replicate the keys to most commercial premises at a reasonable price. But his first love was guns: weaponry of all shapes and sizes.

Taking a corner pew, they reminisced. The old fella talked a lot about the good old days when everything was simpler; you could take a man at his word instead of wondering if he was going to tuck you up the minute your back was turned.

Recalling the local legends, Cyril's eyes took on a distant shine. Leonard's old fella, Big George, was said to be able to lift trucks and bend iron bars with his bare hands. 'Right handful he was. Took on ten squaddies outside the Neptune one night, then came back and finished a game of cards!' Leonard was a different fish altogether. According to Cyril, he were less inclined to socialising like his father, and more geared-up for the moolar. 'Had his eye on the pound note from a young age, did Leonard. But even then there was something different about him. He never indulged in gossip. Always avoided the temptations of drink.'

'Did you go to his funeral?'

'No, lad. Saw it on the telly, though. Some send-off that, weren't it?'

The funeral had been a celebration in many ways. Friends and family taking to the streets en mass to mourn the Big Fella's passing. How dignified Widow Simms had looked, walking behind the coffin in her black-stocking feet, her two grandkids either side.

Cyril looked him over with a shrewd business eye. 'So what's the crack, Billy – you gotta job on?'

'I need a piece. Summat small, not too cumbersome.'

'Cyril pursed his lips in thought. 'I'll see what I can do for you. Anything else while we're at it?'

He mentioned the passports, a brief description of who they were for. At the back of his mind, the vague thought that things might be resolved between him and Eileen. Somehow she might come round to his way of thinking.

'Leave it with me,' Cyril said. 'Shouldn't be too much of problem.'

Business concluded, they could relax and enjoy the surroundings; a few of the old boys played dominoes in the corner, their faces set in grim concentration.

Inevitably, the talk turned to more personal issues, a subject closer to home.

'How's Eileen?'

'Good. We're thinking of moving away.'

'Anywhere in particular?'

'Portugal. Pal of mine's gotta villa out there.'

'Nice. I was out there a few years back with a lady called Joan. Grand lass, she was, but sadly it didn't last. She said I was too set in me ways.'

'With you on that one, Cyril.'

'That's the trouble, see. When you spend so long on your own you get to enjoy your own company. You become more …'

'Independent?'

'Aye, lad. That too.'

'You never been married, Cyril?'

'Engaged once, a while back. Didn't last though. She didn't like the fact I was away so much.'

'Away where – up the jail?'

'No, fishing. Used to spend most weekends down by the canal. Poor lass couldn't hack it.' Cyril's gaze took on a glimmer of mischief. 'Mind you, got meself a nice little cleaner, comes in once a week. Good lass, she is. Polishes the brass up summat wicked.'

He drove home in a trance, brooding over his life and the course it had taken. All the things he knew and was familiar with, the places and the people. Fellas like Cyril, breaking bread with the devil, then going home to an empty room. All the ex-cons and ne'er-do-wells, the wasters and the shandy-merchants, their lives dedicated to leisure and the continued avoidance of employment in any shape or form. The workers, shuffling in from the factories and workhouses on a Friday night to drink their wages and fight among themselves, a demeaning existence he found hard to understand. The work they did was an effrontery to the soul, a form of human bondage dreamt-up by the landowners and paymasters to keep the servile in check. Fighting and drinking was all they had to relieve themselves of the tedium.

Eileen was sprawled in front of the goggle box when he got back. She looked up when he came in, and in that glance he saw a lifetime of duplicity.

'Oh,' she said, 'it's you.'

'Go out and come back in again, shall I?'

Ignoring him, she roused herself to put the kettle on. He sensed her listlessness, the lack of care she'd taken with her appearance.

'What's up with you?' he said.

'Nothing's up with me.'

'Try telling your face.' The old joke didn't work. He tried to assess her from a different angle. Her eyes were unusually heavy, the manifestation of an illness she'd been cooking up just to get back at him in some way.

'What's for dinner?' he said.

'I haven't thought about it.'

'Well I suggest you do. Won't jump in the oven and cook itself, will it?'

She stared at him, unimpressed. 'What *is* your problem?'

'I ain't got a problem, sweetheart. It's you. Face like a boiled fish.' Her slovenly demeanour caused a sudden aversion in him. Alright for her to get all dolled-up for someone else. When he came back of an evening she treated him like the lodger.

He sat at the table and watched her back. The dog came in and nosed at his feet, the only true companion he could count on.

'I met an old pal of mine,' he said. 'Remember Cyril the Squirrel?'

'How could I forget?'

'Fella lives on his own now. Has a cleaner in once a week to give the place a once over.'

'Giving you ideas, is it?'

'Might as well be on me tod, reception I get round here sometimes.' The urge to jump up and thrash her soundly came over him, instigate a row between them so he could storm off to the pub and take it out on the nearest civilian.

Then, out of that place of bitterness and turmoil, came a strange feeling, so powerful it forced him to reassess. That pitiful face, devoid of make-up and reddened around the eyes. Those drooping shoulders that signified a weariness of spirit. Maybe she was suffering for her treatment of him. For all the lies and deceit so intricately woven.

With both hands on her shoulders and a tenderness in his heart, he gazed at her lovingly and softened his tone.

'Look, why don't you put your feet up and I'll bring you a nice cuppa?'

She drew back in mock surprise. 'What's up with you – gotta temperature or summat?'

Gazing deep into the Irish eyes that had mesmerised him for a quarter century, he prepared his forgiveness. And in that moment of compassion and rekindled marital bliss, he doubted himself. Could it be that all his suspicions were unfounded? A simple case of jailhouse paranoia gone adrift.

'Let's make a go of it, doll,' he said.

'A go of what?'

'Us … Me and you.'

Easing herself from his embrace, she started to walk away. He stared after her.

'Where you going?'

'Upstairs.'

He watched her go, his blood pressure rising. 'What is it with you, eh? I try to be nice and you throw it right back at me!'

She climbed the stairs, each heavy footfall an indictment of his love for her, a dagger plunged into his heart.

Bath water surged.

Standing at the bottom of the stairs, he called out to her. She appeared on the landing, a white bath towel wrapped around her.

'What?'

'You need to sort your priorities out, doll, I'm telling you.'

'Anything else – me bath's running?'

'Never mind that. What about me fuckin dinner?'

'Stick a pie in the microwave and stop making such a big deal out of it.'

He laughed good and hard. 'Stick a pie in the microwave? Jesus Christ. Can you imagine your old ma saying that to your old fella? He'd have launched her through the fuckin window!'

She stuck two fingers up at him and lurched off along the hall. The absurdity struck him. The two of them arguing over such pointless trivialities when there was so much else at stake. Their whole union, teetering on the edge of a cliff, about to go over. Could she not see what she was doing to them?

He put a pie in the microwave anyway, reflecting on the nature of compromise. What it meant in terms of an easier life. To prolong that which was comfortable and familiar, trying desperately to hang on to something that had already slipped from your grasp.

By the time she came down, he'd calmed himself, laid up on the recliner with the dog on his lap. She plonked herself down in the armchair by the fire and aimed the remote at the telly. A well-stacked weathergirl pointed out pockets of cloud over the north of England. He gazed at her cleavage, a vague link between the weather and the porn clip he'd watched earlier.

'Tommy might be getting transferred,' Eileen said.

'Do what?'

'I know you don't wanna hear it, but I'm telling you anyway. They're talking about moving him next week.'

'Had a sit-down with the governor, did he? Fella give him a brochure and asked him where he'd like to go?'

'It'll probably mean even further for me to travel.'

'Don't go, then. You think he'd jump on a train to come and see you?'

'He's my son.'

'Yean, and look how he's treated you.'

The weather report finished. He watched the next programme in a trance, isolated from Eileen, from his own family. Inside, a growing conviction that he'd done all he could to make things better. Wasn't his fault Tommy had turned out like he had. The lad had to learn to take some responsibility, instead of whining to his mother every time she went up to visit.

'Have you thought any more about going away?'

'I told you how I felt about that.'

'I'll go on me fuckin own, then.'

'Do what you like, I'm not stopping you.'

Lying there, with the dog on his lap and the TV on, all the

things he was familiar with, he knew it was over. And there in the armchair a few feet away, was the one person who could have changed it. Proved to him she cared enough to meet him halfway.

36
Clipped Wings

Gemma cuddled the babe in the front room. They looked good together, mother and child all wrapped in swaddling. The two of them snuggled up on the sofa with *Jeremy Kyle* and a 2-litre bottle of Diet Coke.

'How is she?' he said.

'Great, she slept right through last night.'

He sat in the armchair and admired the décor. Not a thing out of place.

'You've got it good here,' he said. 'The lad's done a nice job on the decorating.'

'That weren't Luke, that were his dad. He did it as a favour for us before I went into hospital.'

Right away he resented the fella. As if it wasn't bad enough that he, Billy Riley, had missed the wedding – a hundred-and-twenty miles away at the time, being transferred to Sutton Coalfield after a six-month stint in Leeds. Two hours, staring at the back of the driver's head, double-cuffed and flanked by two of the biggest screws he'd ever seen.

Now this. Luke's dad's intervention on the DIY front. The imposition hurt his pride. One more example of his inability to provide for his own family in a time of need.

'Your mum been round?' he said.

'She popped in yesterday with some things.'

'How'd she seem to you, a bit under the weather?'

'What d'you mean?'

'Well, I've been a bit worried about her lately. You know, what with all the running round she does for other people. I thought she might be doing too much.'

Gemma rolled her lower lip. 'She seemed alright to me

He felt a wave of affection for her – his 'Gemsie', always off in a dream world, ever since she was a kid. The weight she'd put on with the baby still showed in her chubby pink cheeks and big hips – not like Eileen, who'd shed all the weight she'd gained soon after giving birth to Tommy. He could still see her, pushing the lad up Bird's Hill, bracing herself against the wind. The whole thing came down to genetics in the end – or, in Eileen's case, a naturally fast metabolism. He'd studied the subject inside, read reams of articles and books on bodybuilding and how to increase muscle mass in the most effective way. On the out, the temptations were manifold, usually in the form of an Indian or KFC – or, in some instances, Eileen's Irish stew and dumplings, the likes of which he could never resist.

'Get up the club much while I were away, did she?' he said.

Gemma made cooing noises to the baby, gazing adoringly at the upturned face.

'Sweetheart?'

'What?'

'I said, did your mum get up the club much while I were away?'

'I don't think so.'

'Come on – did she or didn't she?'

'I don't know – what you asking me for?'

He couldn't get the idea out of his head – a conspiracy of silence among his own to stop him finding out the truth. The trials of having a busy wife who spent most days out of the house attending the needs of other people.

'Remember when you were kids?' he said. 'We took you on a donkey ride up in Whitby? Then we ate egg and cress sandwiches and drank lemonade looking out over Robin Hood Bay?'

'I don't remember that.'

'Well I do, sweetheart. Me and your mum were only looking at the photographs the other day and saying what a joy it were to remember.'

Maybe the good times were an illusion, something he'd dreamed up on his kip to make himself feel better for all the times he wasn't there. The kids' childhood come and gone in an instant. The one chance he had to make a difference in their lives and he'd fucked that up too.

'I did what I could,' he said. 'Made sure you were all kitted-out. Always put food on the table.'

Charlotte Marie gurgled, as if in response. Sitting there staring at the baby's head, he wondered why he felt so detached from it all. And him a granddad. Should have been the happiest days of his life.

'Best be off, I suppose,' he said, standing.

'I thought you were staying for summat to eat?'

'Gotta crack on, sweetheart. Things to do.' He bent to kiss the babe's head, and as an afterthought planted one on the head of his 'favourite' daughter. Still, he hadn't got the answer he was looking for – the thing he dreaded most. The full confession. An admission of guilt to convince the jury.

He stopped at the front door. Gemma stood behind him with the baby.

'You ever come across a lad called Jason?' he said. 'Pauline's cousin?'

Gemma frowned. 'Don't think so. Why – what's he done?'

'I heard his name come up a few times, that's all. Thought you might know him.'

Suspicion grew like a cancer, eating inward, blocking out all means of escape. Up the factory, he'd learned to get on top of it, focussing his mind on other things. Now it had sprouted and grown wings, taking him in a direction he didn't want to go.

'Are you OK, Dad?'

He looked up, snapped back to reality.

'I'm fine, sweetheart. Never felt better.'

37
Intimations

He met Gary by the entrance to the golf course. They walked the dogs on the heath, the usual mixture of gossip and money-making opportunities to be discussed as a matter of course. Gary's meeting with his anonymous contact had moved things up a gear. But there were still considerable logistics involved, organisation on a large scale that would mean dealing with people neither of them had met before. The success of the venture relied on secrecy and speed, a network of runners and distributors at the lower end, who could shift the product without ever coming into direct contact with the major suppliers.

'What's happening with the yacht?' Gary said.

'The landlord had a few problems with the mechanic. Nothing serious.'

'Long as it's in the water by Friday, I've got people coming down who want to take it out.'

He pictured the landlord polishing glasses in the Swan, watching out for rowdy youngsters. The gleam in the fella's eye at the thought of a substantial payday, all for a few sailing trips up and down the coast.

'How's Rosalyn?' Gary said. 'Still buying value packs of burgers from Iceland?'

'She's a nightmare. I tried giving her a crash course in economics but she wouldn't have it.'

'What're the neighbours like?'

'Leave early for work, come back late. Never see 'em.'

'Cameras?'

'Didn't see any.'

Gary frowned. 'You alright, mate – you look a bit down?'

He took a moment to answer, weighing up the pros and cons. Telling Gary would invite more questions, pierce the defences he'd spent so long putting up.

'It's Eileen,' he said. 'I think she's playing around.'

The heath flattened out up ahead, acres of scrubland and trees visible for miles. Years ago, he used to go running up there, getting lost along the dirt tracks and having to double back to get his bearings. The sense of freedom and space called out to him, a strong, primeval voice connecting him to nature, to everything.

'What evidence you got?' Gary said. 'I mean, what exactly did she do?'

'She's been acting funny lately. Going out all the time and not answering her phone.'

'That's it?'

'Then there's this lad, Jason, one of Pauline's cousins. He bought her a drink up the club one night.'

'Bought her a drink?'

'What – you think I'm wrong?'

'Nah, mate. I'm just saying take it easy. Don't go jumping to conclusions till you've got more facts.'

He felt stupid talking to Gary, like he'd admitted some shameful weakness. Relief also, the sharing of a heavy load he'd been carrying ever since he came out of the factory.

Gary ran through the options like a court-appointed brief. There were ways of dealing with these things that didn't involve too much upheaval – always remembering that trouble of any sort was to be avoided.

'Last thing we need is aggravation,' Gary said. 'Once we get moving on this it's gonna be all hands on deck – literally. No room for passengers. We can't afford to draw attention to ourselves in any way.'

Gary's little spiel started to grate. He knew exactly where the fella was coming from and didn't need to be told. But it was all about Gary protecting his interests, no real sympathy at all for his predicament with Eileen.

At the end of the gravel track, they shook hands; the dogs snuffled at the undergrowth nearby.

'I'll make a couple of phone calls if you like,' Gary said. 'Check out this Jason for you.'

He nodded, feeling compromised. Gary looked on uneasily.

'Just don't do anything stupid, mate. When this deal comes off we'll all be minted. You can do whatever the fuck you like.'

The house was quiet when he got back; the dog licked his hand, then shuffled off along the hall, barely a token welcome.

'Doll?'

She must have been out doing her rounds. Soon she'd be back to cook up his scran, one daily ritual he could depend upon. Then they'd eat together at the table like man and wife, and talk about things that were of no real consequence to either of them.

He sat in the armchair and stared at the wall. Outside, the shadows lengthened, the odd flash of headlights across the window. Tomorrow life could change suddenly. He'd be forced into making decisions with no time to think them through.

When he woke two hours later, she still wasn't back. He had the sense that something wasn't right. An intimation.

38
The Big Fella

The narrow path led to a slow rise up ahead, old gravestones pitched at odd angles on either side. Strolling along, he clocked the names of the deceased as he passed, humbled by the brief inscriptions, a reminder of his own mortality.

At the top of the rise the plots were bigger – polished marble and beds of coloured stones. The recently departed, looked after by the folk they'd left behind. A middle-aged couple stood gazing at a headstone, a bunch of fresh flowers laid at the foot. He nodded to them on his way past, wondering who the deceased was: mother or father, son or daughter. The worse thing in the world to have to bury a child.

Stopping by an imposing grave, he made the sign of the cross out of habit. The final resting place of Leonard George Arthur Simms, beloved husband and father, sadly missed by all who knew him.

'Well here I am,' he said under his breath. 'Thought I'd better pay me respects.'

What an occasion it was, captured on mainstream TV and written up in the papers. A real Victorian job, with Top-hat and tails, horses with black plumes on their heads, and the high carriage wheels turning over and over. Paparazzi flashing cameras and risking instant retribution from one of the funeral party. And there at the front – a single red carnation in her black-gloved hands – Sonia, the grieving widow, who somehow managed to look cool and dignified throughout.

Had he not been upriver at the time, serving out his most recent stint at Her Majesty's pleasure, he, Billy Riley, would liked to have been there with them. The pub fighters and the stick-up artists, many of whom he hadn't seen for years. Fellas he'd fought with and drank with, and walked the landings of countless British prisons. Pat Whitmore, the ex-bare knuckle boxer, his face like the side of a granite wall pounded by grapeshot. Barry the Fish, who ran the Bulldog Gym. Old familiar faces like Dai Llewelyn and Malcolm Stockwell, who looked old and gaunt. Sammy 'the hitman' Hart, who'd once been an Olympic Lightweight, until the drink took over and ruined his potential. All good sound men, many of them from his schooldays, growing up around the Parkway and the Warren.

The middle-aged couple had moved on, the winter sun warming their departing backs. Alone among the gravestones, he did what he came to do. Witness to a time gone by, the like of which would never happen again. The Big Fella, paraded through the streets in a horse-drawn carriage with glass sides. Whatever he'd been in life, death had sanctified. The media had given the event a solemn coverage; the funeral cortege in all its glory on the front pages. Snapshots of mourners filing behind the horse-drawn carriage. Men in black suits and ties, women in black hats and veils. A heavy police presence holding back the mob that lined the pavements. Easy to see why the journalist fella had become so obsessed, willing to risk his own safety for the sake of a story. The public's appetite for the details that bore little relation to the truth.

In dying, Leonard had achieved his lifelong goal, making himself truly untouchable. The media had done the rest, turning him into something he wasn't – the sensational version, worthy of a few grainy mugshots and a two-page spread in the Sunday papers.

And now for him, Billy Riley, a similar reckoning. His entire life a kind of charade, where all the things he held as sacred had been exposed as an illusion. There in the sunlit grove, a reminder of death all around him, he felt its grip, a voice mocking him. Looking up at the sky, he wished he could have done things differently. But even as the sentiment formed, so it faded, like a cloud rolling by. His heart had turned to stone, hard as the marble on the Big Fella's grave. Nothing and no one, it seemed, could save him.

With a final nod to the grave, he made his way back up the rise. Outside the chapel, a bunch of mourners were gathered round a hearse. Pall bearers bore the weight of a coffin, and made their way cautiously inside. Winter sunshine lit up the orchard grove and the line of parked cars. A few furtive smokers shuffled their feet in the cold. Easier to respect the dead than the living.

Standing back by the line of parked cars, he called home. Listening to the tones ring he felt the weight of destiny and all that was irreversible.

The answerphone kicked in.

He rang off and stood for a while, vaguely aware of the stragglers outside the chapel. Only one logical direction to take now.

39

Shot in the Dark

A kid on a mountain bike shot across the road in front of him. He slowed and let the kid cross, amazed at his disregard for danger. The old fella used to bleat on about the fact that the young had lost all respect for their elders, and in many ways this was true. He only had to look at his own youth, squandering his football and boxing talents to steal cars and get lifted by the dibble. The truth was, he struggled with the discipline. How many kids wanted to get up at five-in the morning and pull on a pair of running shoes, trudging the cobbles in the pouring rain, firing off the ones and twos like a pro?

Rundown shop fronts, some of them boarded over; a gang of kids on the corner, who watched him drive by with a look of bored aggression. The uniform might have changed but the agenda remained the same – to shock and provoke a reaction from everyone they came into contact with. But he would always be ahead of them, having lived the life they were merely imitating with their swaggering bravado and criminal intent. In all likelihood they'd go the same way, swelling the jails and the institutions, bragging about their crimes to anyone stupid enough to listen.

A beat up Sierra stayed with him all along Latimer Road. He turned right at the next junction without indicating, watching the rear-view. The driver indicated right and followed, cruising sedately some distance behind.

Pulling into a vacant car park, he killed the engine. The Sierra passed slowly by, the driver's gaze fixed ahead. A few more cars went by at intervals, none of the occupants paying him any attention. His heart-rate stayed elevated; a sense of urgency and readiness to take flight.

Minutes went by and nothing happened. The streets looked peaceful, deserted. He fired the engine, the sound explosive in the silence, and pulled out. Now, in place of the fear, a kind of resigned determination. The act he was about to commit was somehow preordained, as unstoppable as an avalanche or tsunami, with consequences for everyone.

Parking a few doors down, he turned off the lights, the ignition.

Nothing stirred in the Crescent.

No movement up ahead. In the rear-view, a glimpse of the traffic lights on the main road.

Locking the car, he walked the hundred or so yards to the front gate. Glancing left and right, he eased the latch and made it to the door, senses primed for the slightest movement.

The house was dark as he slipped inside. The dog came out to meet him, sorrowful black eyes visible in the gloom of the hallway. He bent and ruffled the head, the flanks, gently shooing the old fella back into the front room.

Peering through the net curtain, he looked up and down the road. Nothing moved. He went out to the kitchen and sat in the dark. The bag sat on the table, courtesy of Cyril Stokes, a selection of weaponry he hadn't planned on. In his mind, a calmness he hadn't felt in ages. Even with the knowledge of what he had to do.

40

Exodus

Rosalyn opened the door to find him standing there. Ignoring her semi-dressed state, he pushed past her. 'Get your things together, we need to go.'

She stared at him vacantly. 'What you talking about?'

The sight of her gawping at him made him angry. 'I ain't got time to explain. Grab some clothes for you and the kiddie. We're going.'

'What d'you mean going? Going where?'

'Just throw some gear in a bag and stop arguing!'

She shut the door and marched off along the hall, flashing him a resentful, questioning look on the way. He followed her, checking every room as he passed. Doubt surfaced. The enormity of what he was doing. Involving the two of them in all this.

Rosalyn came back with her coat on and a travelling bag at her feet, a look of sullen acceptance.

'Ready?' he said.

'Can you please tell me where we're going?'

'Just grab the kiddie. Come on, let's go.'

'I can't just – '

'Get in the car, Rosalyn, I ain't got time to fuck about!'

He waited for her in the doorway, glancing round at the neighbouring houses. No obvious movement from anywhere. No prying residents like there were along the Crescent.

Rosalyn swept past him, the kiddie held tightly in her arms, a travelling bag slung over one shoulder. She glanced in the back of the car, and turned to him anxiously. 'There's no seat.'

'What?'

'I can't put him in without a car seat, it ain't legal.'

'Rosalyn – strap the kiddie in the back, and get in the front with me. And hurry up about it.'

He opened the boot and checked the leather bag, covering it over with the tartan blanket. All he had to do now was head for the road and keep driving, put as much distance between him and the Parkway as possible.

Driving north along the motorway he kept within the speed limit. The local radio station played pop songs from the Eighties, mixed with the DJ's mindless chatter. Changing stations, he picked up bits of news, conversations; some old duffer on Radio Four talking about growing cabbages on an allotment. For some reason, the fella's voice was reassuring, an undercurrent of bland normality to offset the tension.

'Please tell me where we're going?' Rosalyn said.

Seeing the anguish on her face he knew there could be problems. And framed in his mind, graphic images of the things he'd done that fuelled a sense of unreality.

'Summat happened back there, Rosalyn. I need you to help me for a bit.'

'What d'you mean?'

'I'm in a bit of trouble. That's all I can say right now. Will you help me or not?'

'Yeah, but where are we going?'

'To the airport.'

'What for?'

'No more questions, Rosalyn.'

'But I – '

'I said no more questions.'

He held out a bag of Werther's. She accepted, begrudgingly, unwrapped a sweet and popped it in her mouth. In the back, the kiddie watched the traffic go by without a murmur. They could have been a family out on a day trip. The three of them. The thought choked him, reopened the wound inside.

Tuning in to another radio station, he caught the news. The final item was an incident in Parkway South. Police were looking for a man in his forties who had carried out two apparently motiveless shootings before fleeing in a stolen car. He quickly switched to a music channel and let the bland rhythm wash over him instead.

Rosalyn stared ahead, lost in her own thoughts. They drove in silence, the vacuum the news had created removing the need for conversation. Mindless pop tunes played in the background, the distance between him and the incident increasing with each passing mile.

'Can we stop somewhere?' she said. 'I need the loo.'

'Why didn't you go back home when you had the chance?'

'I couldn't, could I? You kept saying we had to leave.'

The next stop was fifteen miles away. He worked out how much longer they'd have before he'd need to ditch the car.

'Ok, we'll stop at the next services. But we can't hang about.'

She stared out the window, biting her nails.

'What's up?' he said.

'Nothing.'

'You still pissed off coz I brought you with me?'

She looked over, anxious again. 'I'm worried what you're gonna do.'

'What d'you mean?'

'To me and the kiddie.'

'I ain't gonna do nothing to you and the kiddie. What d'you think I am, a fuckin nut-job?'

She gazed out at the traffic, withdrawn and uncomprehending. He felt again the burden of responsibility, the thought of involving her and the kiddie in such a dangerous undertaking. But they were his cover, his security. Without them he'd be alone and exposed, much more at risk of being apprehended.

'Listen,' he said. 'I'll give you some cash when we get there. Then you can do what you want, alright?'

'I just wanna go home, I'm frightened.'

The pleading note in her voice irritated him. He did his best not to overreact, keeping his tone reasonable, persuasive. 'Look, sweetheart. Soon as we get to the airport you can go. I'll give you the money to get a coach back. You and the kiddie.'

'Why d'you need us in the first place? Why can't you just go on your own?'

'You've gotta stop asking so many questions, OK? I can't have it. I need to concentrate on the road.'

She sat quietly, chewing it all over. A mile or two passed in silence.

'That were you, weren't it?' she said.

'What?'

'That fella on the news. That were you.'

A lorry went past, side straps flapping in the wind; streams of traffic in four lanes, all heading north for some distant rendezvous. Further on, a cop car and a breakdown truck parked up on the hard shoulder; the driver talking to a cop in a fluorescent yellow jacket.

'You'll find out what I done soon enough,' he said quietly. 'And by then I'll be long gone.' It seemed pointless denying it. The thought that Rosalyn might know offered a strange comfort, relieving him of some of the burden.

Pulling in to the services, he found a space in the car park with a clear view of traffic coming in and out. With the engine off and the vehicle stationary, the surroundings closed in. He looked for signs: an unmarked car, a bogus civilian. The makings of a trap for him to walk into.

'Right,' he said. 'Grab the kiddie and we'll go.'

They hurried across the forecourt like any other family – Rosalyn carrying the kiddie, and him beside her holding her arm. If she did try any sudden move, he was confident he could contain it without attracting too much attention.

He stopped her outside the Ladies, and took the kiddie from her arms.

'What you doing?' she said.

'We'll wait out here for you … Go on, hurry up.'

She looked at him, searchingly, before sloping off.

Holding the kiddie felt strange – could have been Connor or Tommy when they were sprogs. Brief moments of normality before he was shipped off to the factory for yet another stint. The kiddie yawned and rubbed his eyes, uncomprehending. 'Everything's gonna be alright, lad,' he said, in a voice intended to reassure.

And in that moment he felt himself weaken, a powerful urge to give himself up and take his chances. Rosalyn came out and the thought faded.

Heading further north, the miles soon clocked up. Rosalyn seemed to lose her nervousness around him, her previous anxiety replaced by boredom. Rather than voice her concern about getting home she became fixated on the money he'd promised her – a streak of avarice he encouraged, knowing it would detract from the reality of the situation and help keep her controlled. For every hour that passed, the greater the risk from being out in the open. Every unmarked car, every van that passed on the motorway was a threat to his liberty, possibly even his life.

Rosalyn opened the glove compartment. He reached out and snapped it shut.

'What you doing?' he said.

'I were just looking.'

'Well don't. If you want summat, ask me.'

She grew silent and obstinate, refusing the Werther's he offered her. Now he had two children to deal with – her *and* the kiddie. Having the two of them along was fast becoming a problem. He hadn't anticipated the emotional strain, the dual pressure of having to keep her subdued and watch out for trouble up ahead. Coupled with this, a constant filter of images from the last few hours that plagued him. Sitting in the house in the dark, with the bag on the table. Eileen's surprise to see him when she walked in, after she'd told him never to come back.

Glancing at Rosalyn, he took a chance. 'It weren't my fault, you know … She kept pushing me. Playing around with another fella.' Her silence goaded him to open up, to justify everything in the absence of a jury. 'I had reasons for what I did. Couldn't put up with being lied to no more.'

The music became an irritant, an unholy blight on his thoughts. He turned it off, relieved at the quiet, the throb of traffic out on the road.

Several more miles passed. Rosalyn looked up.

'I'm hungry.'

'Why didn't you say back there at the services?'

'I wasn't hungry then.'

'You'll have to wait.'

His phone rang. The noise startled him, an unwanted interruption from the world outside.

'Why don't you answer it?' she said.

'I'm driving.'

The ringtones jarred his nerves, becoming unbearable. Watching out for suspicious-looking vehicles, he checked the screen and took the call.

'Yeah – what's up?'

Gizmo sounded frantic, barely able to finish a sentence. He kept going on about it being on the news, that the place was crawling with dibble.

'I can't talk now, Giz. I'll call you later.'

More garbled questions, the same note of disbelief.

'Look – I'm on the road, fella. Talk to you in a bit.' He hung up, and slipped the phone into his pocket.

'Who was that?'

'Pal o' mine, wanted to know how I was' He glanced at her anxious face and made a decision. 'Tell you what we're gonna do. We're gonna stop and get summat to eat, OK?'

'Can I phone me nan when we get there?'

'No, you can't.'

'Why?'

'D'you want summat to eat or not?'

'Yeah, but – '

'Stop whinging, Rosalyn – you're doing my fuckin head in!'

He found a Holiday Inn forty miles from the airport, close enough to hold up while he took stock of the situation. Tired from the driving and the battering his senses had taken over the last twenty-four hours, he turned off the engine, relieved to stop.

The receptionist booked them into Room 113, under Giles, the name on his passport. He took the key fob and headed for the lift with Rosalyn and the kiddie in tow. They were safe here. At least for the time being.

41

The Net Closes

Early next morning, he called the journalist fella. Rosalyn was in the bathroom with the kiddie, taking a shower.

'Nick – it's me, Billy.'

Silence.

'Are you there? … Can you hear me?'

'Billy – where are you?'

'About six miles east of Nova Scotia. There's a big storm coming in.'

'Sorry, I didn't quite – '

'Listen. I want you to pass a message on for me. Can you do that?'

'Billy, for goodness sake, tell me where you are?'

'Never mind that. Ask for DC McGuinn at Parkway South Police Station. Tell him no matter what happens I ain't coming in. You got that?'

'What happened – can you at least tell me that?'

'You know what happened, it's all over the front pages.'

'But why? Was it something we said?'

'Listen, fella, I've been putting up with the same shit for years – in the jail and out. People lying to me, treating me like a muppet. I just had enough.'

'So what're you going to do?'

'I'm getting out. Going somewhere they can't touch me.'

'And you want me to make some sort of statement for you? Is that what you're saying?'

'Just ask for McGuinn at Parkway South. Tell him what I just told you. I'll call you back later.'

'Billy, don't go, we can – '

He hung up, just as Rosalyn came out of the shower, drying her hair with a towel. She looked at him casually, no sign of her previous anxiety.

'Who was that?' she said.

'The journalist fella. He's gonna make a statement to the press, but you ain't gotta worry about that.'

'Are we gonna be on TV?'

'Could be. You'd like that, would you, Rosalyn?'

She slumped on the end of the bed and turned her face to him, all forlorn and weepy. 'When can I go home?'

'Don't start all that again.'

'Can I phone me nan, then? You said I could when we got here.'

'Not now.'

'When, then? She'll be worried sick about me.'

'Enough, Rosalyn.'

She pursed her lips, frowning. 'Why d'you take me phone off me? Don't you trust me or summat?'

'It's not a matter of trust. It's a precaution, that's all. When the time's right I'll give you your phone back and you can call whoever you like.'

She rubbed her hair, listlessly, the towel draped around her shoulders. The kiddie climbed on the bed behind her, and lay back, watching the proceedings with his sad-eyed expression. A ready-made family like any other, suffering the usual trials of boredom and indecision.

'Are you hungry?' he said.

She shook her head.

'Why don't you put the kettle on, make yourself a drink?'

'I don't wanna drink.'

'Don't get leery with me, sweetheart, I'm not in the mood.'

'I'm not getting leery.'

'Just don't give me any nonsense. I've told you I'll see you alright and that's the end of it.'

The priority now was to plan ahead. He knew the journalist

fella would have been on to the dibble. They would then be tracking the calls he'd made and trying to pinpoint his location. He didn't have the time to hang around pandering to Rosalyn's demands and risk a stand-off in a hotel room. Right now, one of the staff could have suspected something and made a phone call. His description and photograph would have been radioed out to all forces, his details brought up on every computer system in the country.

He tried to get the telly working, pressing buttons on the remote control. The technology seemed to be working against him deliberately, a subtle conspiracy to tip him over the edge. He tossed her the handset. 'Rosalyn – sort this fuckin thing out, will you!'

She aimed the remote at the TV, and as if by some miraculous alchemy, the screen came on. Flipping through the channels, he found the 24 hour news. The newsreader talked about nuclear weapons in the Middle East; the stream feed at the bottom gave football results and local weather. Nothing about the shootings at all.

Someone knocked the door.

Muting the TV, he turned to Rosalyn and put a finger to his lips. 'Get the door.'

Resentfully, she went over and opened the door.

'You ordered a newspaper earlier?' the girl said.

Rosalyn took the paper, thanked the girl and closed the door. She tossed the paper on the bed and carried on drying her hair.

Snatching it up, he went over to the window. The headline said 'Manhunt' in big letters across the page. Further down was his picture, a grainy mugshot from a previous incarceration that made him look dangerous. The report went on to say that police were looking for a man in connection with two shootings at Parkway South, and he, Billy Riley, was the chief suspect.

'Get your stuff together,' he said. 'We're going.'

'I ain't put me makeup on yet.'

'You can do that in the car. Come on, let's go.'

Vacating the room, they took the lift down to reception. Rosalyn handed in the key, and joined him and the kiddie outside.

He kept his head down across the car park, feeling especially vulnerable. The cold wind bit through his shirt. Lack of sleep and the immense pressure he was under combined to further darken his mood. Rosalyn and the kiddie were fast becoming a source of frustration, too. Extra baggage he could do without.

While she put the kiddie in the back of the car, he put the leather bag in the boot, taking the revolver with him and secreting it in the glove compartment.

Rosalyn got in beside him and strapped herself in.

'Ready?' he said.

'Where we going?'

'Away from this place.'

'I'm frightened.'

'You got nothing to be frightened of, sweetheart. Nothing at all.'

Pulling into the motorway stream he headed for the airport. By now the plan had changed. The dibble would be looking for him at all major terminals; any attempt to leave the country would be fraught with danger. The most he could hope for was to hole up somewhere and wait for the intensity of the search to die down, but that could be weeks away.

'What you thinking about?' he said.

'Nothing.'

'Still pissed off with me, are you? Blaming me for what's happened?'

'No?'

'You know what I did back there, don't you?' She stared ahead, mute and unresponsive. 'I put two people in the ground, that's what I did. What you got to say about that?'

She wouldn't look at him, her lower lip trembling.

'I can't stand liars, Rosalyn. Snakes going round saying one thing and doing another. What's it coming to in this world when you can't trust your own wife.'

'Are you gonna let us go?'

'What?'

'Me and me baby. Are you gonna let us go?'

He glared at her, incensed by her total lack of understanding.

'See – you're like all the others, aren't you? Thinking about yourself all the fuckin time. Look at all the things I did for you. Getting you a place of your own. Trying to save you from that twat of a boyfriend. Don't that count for nothing?'

She gazed out at the traffic, fingers clasped in her lap. He saw Eileen there instead, consumed with her own life that didn't include him. And now she too was gone. Taken out in an act of vengeance that would impact everyone.

'We were gonna go abroad,' he said. 'Start afresh. But she ruined everything by lying to me. Now she won't ever lie to no one again.' The words came out in a torrent, not in the rational, measured way he'd wanted them to. Rosalyn would never understand, but she was all he had left.

'Have a sweet,' he said, holding out the bag of Werther's.

'I don't want one.'

'Just take one and stop arguing.'

She did as she was told, dropping the unopened sweet in her lap as a measure of defiance.

'Sulking again?' he said.

'No?'

'Yeah, you are. You're sulking coz you've had enough of me and you wanna go home. You're fuckin ungrateful, like all them other scallies off the estate.'

His phone rang. He dragged it from his pocket, and checked the screen, not recognising the number.

'Who's this?' he said.

'Billy – can you talk to me?'

He recognised the distinct nasal voice right away, and was gripped by a burst of wild exuberance. 'You got the message, then?'

'Billy, listen to me. You've got nothing to gain by staying out there. Come in now and we'll talk about it.'

'What – so you can get your name on the charge sheet? You must think I'm fuckin stupid.'

'Where are you, lad?'

'Halfway to Timbuktu.'

'Look, I can arrange for a mediator, a go-between. It doesn't have to end like this.'

He pictured McGuinn at the station, surrounded by eager faces all keen to get a look in. His old adversary, given the job of hunting him down.

'I ain't coming in,' he said, the words like a mantra, a sworn commitment to something hard and unresolvable.

'Listen, Billy. Why don't you tell me where you are and I'll come and meet you somewhere? We can talk about it – just me and you?'

'I don't think so, pal.'

'Let the girl and the kiddie go. They've done nothing, have they?'

So they knew. The revelation changed the parameters. McGuinn had revealed his hand, and in doing so had raised the stakes to another level.

'Nice talking to you, McGuinn. Just like old times, eh?'

'Come on, Billy. You've got nothing to gain by this. Where you gonna go? What you gonna do?'

'That's my business.'

'It's my business too now. And you wouldn't have contacted me unless there was something you wanted to say.'

'Oh, I got summat to say alright. But not here. Not to you. Talk to the journalist fella, he knows all about me.'

'You know Eileen survived, don't you?'

'What?'

'She's critical, but there's a chance she'll pull through. Is that a surprise to you, Billy?'

He couldn't process the information, only the noise in his head that grew louder.

'I got nothing else to say.'

'Come on, lad. It's over. Do yourself a favour and come in.'

He hit the end call button and drove in silence, images of Eileen lying in a hospital bed. In a strange way, McGuinn's voice had been reassuring – a genuine note of concern for his old adversary. They grew up on the same streets, drank in the same ale houses. But McGuinn had joined the other side and made himself an enemy. Life, forcing you to draw a line with a big stick. On one side were folk you could trust – friends, family and people you worked with. On the other side were those out to harm you or tuck you up in some way. Sometimes it weren't clear which side folk were on, so you had to watch them closely, double your efforts and proceed with caution whenever they were around. Worst of all was when a fella couldn't trust himself or any of the decisions he was making. The way ahead became unclear, fraught with impasses and hidden danger.

The miles passed in a blur of traffic and bland countryside. He saw the sign for services and pulled in.

'What you doing?' Rosalyn said.

'You said you wanted to phone your nan. Now's the time.'

He parked up and turned the engine off, glancing at the kiddie in the rear-view. A deep sadness engulfed him at the thought of losing them both, a feeling made worse by the knowledge of where he was going and what he had to do.

'There you go, darlin.' He handed her the envelope and the phone. 'Take care of yourself and the kiddie.'

She stared at the unexpected gift, then at him. 'You're letting us go?'

'That's right, Rosalyn, I'm letting you go.'

'But what will you do?'

'Don't you worry about that. Now go on. Do one before I change me mind.'

She undid her seatbelt and got out. Soon, she had the kiddie, and with a final, sorrowful look, shut the door and hurried off across the car park.

Watching her go, he felt consumed, swallowed up by the overwhelming intensity of being alone; the urgent need to get away as soon as possible.

Up ahead, came the thump-thump of a helicopter passing over the motorway. He tried to gauge its position, wondering how close they were to him. How much longer before someone discovered his position.

The phone rang.

Gary sounded choked, on the edge of hysteria. 'Billy – what's going on? Talk to me …'

'I ain't got much time, fella.'

'Where are you?'

'On the motorway, heading north.'

A woman's voice in the background. Probably Tanya, asking questions, demanding answers. Then Gary, yelling at her to shut up.

'Billy, this is fuckin madness, mate. I can't believe what you've done!'

Easing out of the bay, he kept an eye out for the helicopter, and any suspicious-looking vehicles up ahead. Gary continued to berate him.

'Why did you do it? I mean, what got into your head?'

'Couldn't put up with her lying to me no more. I warned her enough times.'

'Billy – for fuck sake, man. She wasn't seeing anyone!'

'What you talking about?'

'I'm telling you straight, man. I checked it out. You shot the pair of them for no fuckin reason!'

The words didn't register. One more angle to disregard. Maybe Gary had been got at by the dibble and was playing a role they'd set for him.

'Billy? … You still there?'

'I gotta go.'

'Why didn't you come to me first? We coulda talked it through. I could've helped you … '

He turned the phone off, and gazed out at the car park, unable to move. People wandered to and from their vehicles, completely unaware.

The same thought turned over and over. Maybe he'd acted rashly, done the wrong thing. But none of that mattered anymore. It was over, finished.

On the way out, he dumped the phone in a bin. Only one course left for him to take, and one they'd never anticipate.

42
Coming Home

Cruising the flyover brought up strong memories, a sweeping view of the city he'd been born in and intended never coming back. The glass towers of the finance centre dominating the skyline, south-facing panels lit-up by the sun. The estuary weaving snake-like towards the docklands, the place where so much contraband came in from all over the world. A hundred-years ago, in his great-grandfather's time, the dockers were like a rabble army, ready to rise up against the bosses and take back control. Over the bridge, the poverty-stricken north side, a rat-run of cobbled alleyways and overcrowded tenements, where underfed plebs in flat caps and hand-me-downs roamed the streets looking for illicit gain. From the affluent south, an altogether different smell: the taint of money, earned off the backs of the poor. Greed like a virus, respecting no class, but thriving naturally among the well-heeled who looked ceaselessly for ways to increase their fortunes at the expense of everyone else. Money, the one true god. Everyone chasing it in some form or other, willing to betray all values in order to succeed. The rich had a different outlook, seeking more legitimate forms of robbery with no legal comeback; no drawn out court cases and trips up-river in a narrow sweatbox like the rest of the plebs. The bankers and the ruling classes, with their public schooling and family connections; the whole thing thriving on deceit and misinformation, keeping the ignorant plebs down. Government policies fed to the masses by bland-faced politicians who knew exactly what they were doing and didn't give a shit who they fucked over. All the suckers out there, living in ignorance and fear, working their guts out and taking loans they could never hope to pay back, crippled by extortionate interest rates and the threat of bankruptcy. Better to take what you needed, by force if necessary. Crime had a touch of integrity. The way for a man to stand proud among his fellows and throw off the cloak of despair.

Winter sunshine cast a sickly beam across the water. A few thousand years ago, the land belonged to the swamp. Furtive wildlife and marauding bands of tribesmen arrived looking to gain fresh territory, and progress began. A thousand years from now the city might no longer be here, having sunk back into the primordial morass. The noble towers of glass and steel gone forever, the record of all man's achievements ground into dust. And surely that day would come, when mankind had outlived its potential and used up all its resources. The land given back to nature. Nothing but the sun setting low over the river and the birds flying overhead. Peace in the valley at last.

Grim thoughts collected on the periphery; the nagging feeling he might have been wrong that was still with him, however hard he tried to shake it off. Gary's last statement that Eileen was innocent. And according to McGuinn, the shocking revelation that she'd survived the attack. He couldn't be sure of anything anymore.

Lines of traffic headed over the bridge. High-rise tower blocks beyond; splashes of garish colour from billboards advertising perfume and women's lingerie. Everything working in a seamless fashion, the wheels of industry turning without interrupting the flow. The workforce paying into the bureaucrats dream, taking their place on the assembly line day after day, accepting the nature of things without question. And he, Billy Riley, able to both admire and despise them. To be part of such a vast undertaking and set apart from it at the same time, you came to view the whole as an observer. By rejecting society's laws and living by your own you somehow rose above it. Yet there it was, tireless and immovable, the huge machine that churned out orders and directives with a sweep of its mechanical arm.

A siren cut through the traffic grind, a chill, far-off wail somewhere up ahead. Then a second, from a different sector, its distinctive cry merging with the first.

The lights up ahead turned green.

Taking the left-hand lane, he increased his speed. The car had become a target, an identifiable burden with him trapped inside. Next to him, the revolver covered with the tartan blanket. Beads of sweat ran down his forehead; senses heightened like the adrenalin before a robbery or a tear-up.

Out on the dual-carriageway he opened up, passing traffic swiftly, careful not to lose control. Past the Rubicon Theatre with its white-fronted hoardings, the White Horse, where his old fella used to drink. Familiar landmarks that looked alien, as if he were seeing them for the first time.

A white transit van shot across the front from a side road, blocking the right-hand lane. He braked and slewed into the left, narrowly avoiding the car in front. From behind came the scream of another siren. Flashing blue lights.

Unable to stay in the lane, he lost control, mounted the pavement and smashed into a metal barrier. The world outside ceased to be. Everything happened in slow motion. Then the survival instinct took over, a ringside voice from his boxing days yelling, 'Get out! Get out!'

Exiting at once, he leapt over the bonnet of a parked car, and ran down an alley. Behind him, frantic shouts to stop. Male voices charged with tension, authority. Anticipating shots behind him, he kept running.

A shopping centre – civilians idling along the terrazzo floor. Strange looks from a gawping women and a young girl as he tore past. Then a strident male voice barking out an order for him to stop. A second voice, yelling at shoppers to stay back.

Turning the corner, he ran into a charity shop, knocking over clothes racks and dummies in a panic to get away. An open doorway led to a storeroom, where two women were sorting boxes. They looked up in mute surprise as he blundered in.

'Where's the back door!'

Stricken with fear, they stared at him blankly.

Tearing along a short corridor, he came to a locked door. The window beside it wouldn't open, corroded into place. He picked up a metal bucket in the corner and smashed it into the frame repeatedly.

The window opened onto a small back yard. Sweeping jagged pieces of glass aside, he swung his leg through. Urgent voices barked questions from the front of the shop, demanding to know where he was.

His shirt caught on the window frame. For a moment he hung suspended, halfway out. With a desperate wrench he pulled himself free and dropped onto the pavers outside, jarring his knee. Up ahead, a wooden gate and high wall. Beyond that, freedom.

'Armed police! Stop where you are!'

He got to the gate and yanked it open.

'Stop where you are!'

He ran blindly on through and into an alleyway.

Up above, a helicopter circled. Police radios squawked.

If he could just make it to the end of the alley.

Get his bearings.

Flag a motorist down.

FICTION

<u>The Butterfly Collector</u>

What happens when everything you have is not enough?

Restless property developer, Peter Calliet meets a sullen young woman at a party and an obsession begins that links past and present in a deepening tragedy.

Peter has everything in terms of material success and security. The obligatory fast car, lucrative contracts with his powerfully connected father's property empire and a plush renovated flat. Devoted fiancée, Claudia, expects to move in and marriage is imminent. But Peter has a dark past that taints his movements. Meeting Natalie, a volatile artist with an equally disturbed background, can only lead to more heartache. If Claudia discovers that Peter has been seeing Natalie, her dream world will be destroyed, adding to his burden of guilt. But even that can't stop him. The secure and rewarding life he has worked so hard to achieve begins to unravel.

'Peter Calliet is very believable, with that mix of liberal thinking and callousness that's essentially human.'
Nikki Copleston

'Dickson has a talent for expressing emotional anguish perfectly in prose and it makes the characters feel even more believable.'
The Kindle Book Review

Castra publishing

FICTION

<u>Drowning by Numbers</u>

It's 1994. Blur and Oasis are in the charts. New Labour are on the horizon. Ladbroke Grove is the place, a thriving hub of art, music and cultural diversity.

Emerging from the wreckage of another lost weekend, Indie Guitarist of the Year, Joe E Byron, hurries home on the Tube to face the consequences of his actions. Ten years on the road has taken its toll. He should be spending more time with Justine and the kids. Instead, he's restless, angry, and in conflict with his manager and the rest of the band. Dark habits threaten his marriage and his career. The curse of addiction which will rob him of everything. And at the heart of it all, a yearning to be free, to take off and never come back.

But that can't happen.
There's too much at stake.
Besides,
He's a god.
He's a legend.
And the only thing worse than dying
is the prospect of fading away.

'If you're looking for a happy ever after ending, this book is probably not for you, but if you're looking for an excellent read with a hopeful ending, you will love Drowning by Numbers.'
Pamela Fudge

Castra publishing

NON-FICTION

Surfing The Edge
A Survivor's Guide To Bipolar Disorder

The TV's on
The computer's on
The stereo's on
Sleep is a waste of time

Welcome to the world of Bipolar Disorder, a journey to the outer edges of the mind. A series of conversations told with humour, honesty and insight by Adam, Faye and Alastair, three survivors who have experienced the illness first hand. With contributions from Mental Health professional, Chris Kelly.

'Couldn't put this down, it rang so many bells for me. I recommend this to sufferers and recoverers or even just the nosey parkers.'
Angela Warren

Castra publishing